There, gleaming softly under the harsh overhead light, sat a silver convertible.

"It came three days ago." Randy ran his hand lovingly over the sleek curve of one fender. "Isn't it beautiful?"

"That it is." I began to circle the car. I didn't want to prick Randy's balloon, but all I could think of was how inappropriate this expensive car was for a novice driver. The potential for a serious accident was incredible!

If Randy met a sycamore in this marvelous car, he would be in big trouble.

I bent down to peer inside. I might as well study the upholstery before it was drenched with Randy's blood.

Someone had beaten Randy to it.

Blood stained the passenger seat and floor.

I knew there had to be very little, if any, left in the very dead man who slumped against the gray leather interior....

"Did you meet Tom in Newark or here? Or somewhere else?"

Books by Gayle Roper

Love Inspired Suspense

See No Evil #39
Caught in the Middle #50
Caught in the Act #54
Caught in a Bind #58

GAYLE ROPER

has always loved stories, and she's authored more than forty books. Gayle has won a Romance Writers of America's RITA® Award for Best Inspirational Romance and finaled repeatedly for both RITA® and Christy® awards, won three Holt Medallions, a Reviewers' Choice Award, the Inspirational Readers Choice Contest and a Lifetime Achievement Award as well as the Award of Excellence. Several writers' conferences have cited her for her contributions to the training of writers. Her articles have appeared in numerous periodicals including *Discipleship Journal* and *Moody Magazine,* and she has contributed chapters and short stories to several anthologies. She enjoys speaking at writers' conferences and women's events, reading and eating out. She adores her kids and grandkids, and loves her own personal patron of the arts, her husband, Chuck.

GAYLE ROPER

CAUGHT IN A BIND

REVISED BY AUTHOR

Steeple
Hill®

Published by Steeple Hill Books™

STEEPLE HILL BOOKS

Steeple
Hill®

ISBN-13: 978-0-373-44248-5
ISBN-10:   0-373-44248-3

CAUGHT IN A BIND

This is the revised text of the work which was first published by
Zondervan in 2000.

Copyright: © 2000 by Gayle G. Roper

Revised text copyright: © 2007 by Gayle G. Roper

Printed in U.S.A.

When I am afraid, I will trust in you.
—*Psalms* 56:3

For Christine Tangvald with love.

You are a woman of God who knows how to live godly in Christ Jesus. And you are fun! I wouldn't have missed all those writers' conferences and Disney World visits for anything.

ONE

This time I got myself into trouble without Jolene's help. Not that she didn't contribute, but at least she wasn't the cause. Edie was. Or rather, Edie's husband.

Edie Whatley is my coworker at *The News: The Voice of Amhearst and Chester County,* where she is editor of the family page and a features writer. I'm a general reporter and features writer.

"Edie," I called across the aisle that separated our desks. "Can I do the ironmonger's mansion at Hibernia Park for the Great Homes of Chester County series?" I thought it would be fun to write about that the big pale orange home set on the knoll above the gently sloping lawn.

There was no response from Edie.

"Edie!"

Still nothing.

I frowned. It wasn't like her not to answer, especially since she was doing nothing but staring at her CRT screen.

Then spoke Jolene, Queen of Tact. "Edie, what in the world's the matter with you, woman? You've been a mess all day."

"Jolene!" I was appalled, but I had to admit that she got Edie's attention. Edie blinked, skewered by Jolene's accusing gaze.

"Spill it," Jolene demanded. "Is it Randy?" Randy was

Edie's fifteen-year-old son whose life journey kept all of us glued for the next painful installment.

"Randy's fine," Edie said.

Jolene and I looked at each other, then back at Edie.

"He is?" I blurted with more disbelief than was probably good for our friendship.

"Well, probably fine is too strong a word, but he's not bad."

"He's not?" Jolene's surprise was equally obvious.

Edie's face scrunched momentarily as she understood what we had inadvertently revealed about our opinions of her son. Then she got huffy, Edie-style. "I said he's fine."

"Well, if it's not Randy," Jolene continued, unabashed at having hurt Edie, "then what? Is it Tom?"

Edie smiled too brightly. "Tom? What could possibly be wrong with him?"

A good question. He and Edie doted on each other and didn't care who knew. Being around them was instant tooth decay due to the sweetness of their relationship. I don't mean just lovey, which I happen to think is good, or considerate, which I happen to think is necessary. It was the touching, the patting, the unconscious back rubbing and collar adjusting.

Tom was Edie's second husband, and therein lay part of Randy's problems. He didn't like his stepfather.

Not that Tom should take that lack of appreciation personally. Randy didn't appear to like any adults. He also didn't like many kids, and I strongly suspected he didn't care much for himself either.

But Tom took the brunt of all the boy's angst and anger. More than once, Edie had come to work teary-eyed, only to tell Jolene and me about Randy's latest verbal abuse and disobedience.

Randy's father was a giant of a man, all muscles, charm, and good looks, a certified financial planner who over the years had made a mint in the stock market both for himself and his clients. Randy resembled him in size and coloring, a fact that gave the boy immense pride.

Tom on the other hand was a slight man, five feet eight inches in his hiking boots, gentle, pleasant and balding.

"He's a car salesman!" Randy would mock, as if automotive retail was on a par with prostitution.

"Is Tom sick?" I asked.

Edie shook her head. "Not that I know of."

Not yes or no. Not that I know of.

"Did he lose his job?"

Edie actually smiled at the thought of Tom losing his job. "Hamblin Motors would fall apart without him."

I nodded. Even I, a relative newcomer to Amhearst, knew that Tom was Hamblin's mainstay. Of course, my major source for this information was Edie, and I recognized that she was a wee bit biased.

"He just won a trip for two to Hawaii because of his winter doldrums sales. Only ten prizes were awarded in the whole country, and he won one."

"Hawaii?" Jolene looked impressed. "When do you go?"

"In three weeks." Edie looked uncertain, then nodded. "In three weeks."

"Then what are you so upset about?" Jolene wouldn't let well enough alone. "I mean, Hawaii!"

"I'm not upset."

"And I'm not Eloise and Alvin Meister's little girl." Poor Edie. She was about to be slaughtered on the altar of Jolene's curiosity and need to know.

"Jo," I said quickly, "I think your plants need watering." If anything would distract Jo from Edie, it would be her plants.

Jolene glanced around the newsroom at the lush greenery that made the place resemble a nursery. A giant grape ivy that had once tried to eat me alive sat on the soda machine. A huge jade plant graced the filing cabinet, and spectacularly healthy African violets sat in perpetually blooming splendor on the sill of the big picture window by the editor's desk

She shook her head as she checked the soil of the spider plant on her desk. Baby spider plants erupted from the stems like little green and white explosions. "They're all fine. I watered them yesterday." She checked my philodendron and Edie's croton, then returned to her grilling undeterred.

"Come on, Edie. I know something's wrong. Of all the people who work here, you're the most stable."

"What?" I turned to Jolene, irritated. I was unstable?

Jolene grinned at me. "We all know I'm an emotional wreck, though you've got to admit I've been getting better in recent weeks."

She paused a minute, looking expectantly at Edie and me. After a short pause, we realized what she expected.

"Right," Edie said hastily. "You're getting better."

I nodded. "It's church. You're listening to Pastor Hal."

Jolene shrugged. "Maybe. Maybe not." Church was new to her and still made her uncomfortable. She returned to her commentary on office personnel. "We all know our noble editor Mac is so on edge over the buyout of the paper that he can't think straight."

Edie and I nodded. Mac was certainly acting strangely though I thought maybe Dawn Trauber, director of His House, had as much to do with his foul mood as the paper.

"And you, Merry," Jolene continued, "are so bemused over Curt that you're always on some far mental planet."

"I beg your pardon," I said, miffed. "I am very much in control, aware and on top of things."

She gave her patented snort, the unfeminine sound always a surprise coming from someone as lovely as Jolene. "That control and awareness are why Mac has been waving at you for the past five minutes, I guess?"

"What?" I looked quickly over my shoulder toward the editor's desk. Sure enough, Mac was scowling at me so intensely that his eyebrows were one long line from temple to temple.

"You could have told me." I rose and made my way toward Mac. "And Edie, ignore her. You don't have to answer any of her questions."

Jolene agreed. "We'll wait for Merry. She wants to hear what's got you in such a tizzy too."

Edie smiled weakly at me as I walked past her desk. "I'm okay," she said with all the spunk of a groveling puppy.

Suddenly Mac's bellow tore through the newsroom. "Edie, for goodness' sake. Get over here!"

I stopped and pivoted to return to my seat.

"Where are you going, Kramer?" Mac snarled.

"But you said Edie."

"I want you both."

I turned back and walked to his desk. Mac had been acting editor for the past several months while the *News* was for sale. Recently the paper had been purchased by a man named Jonathan Delaney Montgomery. As I saw it, the greatest danger in waiting for Mr. Montgomery to decide whether Mac still had a job wasn't Mac's career. It was the incipient development of ulcers in everyone in the newsroom.

I spoke softly across his cluttered desk. "Please be easy with Edie. She's upset about something, and if you yell at her, it won't be good."

"You mean she'll cry?" he asked in disgust.

"Could be."

Mac looked at me with barely concealed contempt, whether directed at me for offering unwanted advice, or Edie for being a possible crier, I couldn't tell. "I am always considerate of my people," he barked.

I bit my tongue and said nothing.

He turned from me to Edie. "Now, Whatley, I've got a great assignment for you. I want you to do an article on spousal abuse."

Edie shuddered and actually swayed. She put out a hand to steady herself, gripping Mac's desk hard enough to whiten her knuckles.

"Edie." I grabbed her elbow. "Are you all right?"

"And you, Kramer." Mac plowed on as if he hadn't noticed Edie's distress, and he probably hadn't. "You are to do a profile of Stephanie Bauer, director of that organization that helps abused wives. You know the one. It's down a couple of blocks on Main Street."

I kept hold of Edie. "You mean Freedom House?"

"Yeah, that's it. Find out how the place works and see if you can interview some of the abused women. You know, tear-jerker stuff like you did with those pregnant girls at Christmas."

I nodded. Not a bad assignment.

"You two are to work together on this thing." Mac looked from Edie to me and back. "Got that?"

I nodded. Edie just turned away, removing herself from my support.

"Edie!" Mac's voice was abrupt.

She turned a white face to him, but he didn't see. He was looking at something on his desk.

"Do you understand what I want?"

"Yes. But I hate it." The last was under her breath.

"What?" Mac demanded.

"Nothing. Nothing at all."

I blinked as I followed Edie back to our desks. She hated this most interesting assignment?

"What's wrong, Edie? And don't tell me nothing," I said as she opened her mouth to say just that. She even got the *noth* out.

Edie was a genuinely nice lady whose fine, light brown hair was cut shoulder length and hung straight, swaying when she turned her head. Her blue eyes were often sad though never more so than today. She wore all her clothes a size too small, not because she wanted to be sexy or provocative but because she kept hoping she'd lose that ten to fifteen pounds.

"Let it go, Merry. Please." She turned abruptly and almost ran to the women's room, a one-person operation where she could find privacy.

I watched her go, and as I turned back to my desk, I saw Jolene watching too.

"No more questions, Jo," I said. "When she wants to tell us about it, she will."

"You're no fun." But when Edie finally returned red-eyed to her desk, Jo kept quiet.

I spent the balance of the day reading about Freedom House in either our paper files or e-files or online. I learned it was established five years ago and that Stephanie Bauer had been its only director. I learned that in addition to providing counseling and comfort to abused wives, Freedom House sponsored training workshops for churches who wanted to know how to help abused women in their congregations.

I studied the pictures of Ms. Bauer and saw a woman of about forty, very slim and attractive with great dark eyes and dark curly hair.

"I was an abused wife," she was quoted as saying in one article. "I know the fear and desperation of these women. I know their feelings of being powerless. I also know God can help them deal with the overwhelming helplessness. I know they can live again."

How did she learn to live again? What specifics marked her flight from her husband to her position at Freedom House? Or had he reformed and she was still married to him?

I called Freedom House and got Stephanie Bauer on the line. "May I come interview you some day soon?"

"How about tomorrow?" she asked. "I know it's Saturday, but my schedule is crazy what with the ministry, the Easter holidays and my kids."

I had rehearsal with the bell choir tomorrow morning for the upcoming Easter service, and in the evening Curt was taking me to the reception that Mr. Montgomery was throwing for the *News* staff and his invited guests. But I was free Saturday afternoon.

"Is two o'clock all right?" I asked Stephanie.

"Will we be finished by three? I have an appointment with my daughter at three. We're going shopping. She 'needs' some spring clothes."

"We'll be finished by then," I promised. Then thinking it might fit into the article, I asked, "How old is your daughter?"

"Fifteen."

Just like Randy, I thought. Poor Stephanie.

"A teenager at the mall," I said, sarcasm dripping a bit too freely. "It ought to be an interesting afternoon for you."

"It will be interesting," Stephanie said, ignoring my tone. "I enjoy anything I get to do with Sherrie. We're both so busy! And Rob is no better."

"Rob's your—?"

"My son," Stephanie said. "He's eighteen. We've been filling out financial information for colleges all year, and the hardest part is finding a night when we're both home!"

When I hung up from my conversation with Stephanie, I glanced at Edie. Stephanie's relationship with her children seemed the polar opposite of Edie's with Randy. Both women had had marital hard times, but one had fun with her kids and the other cried. Interesting.

It was almost five o'clock when Jolene said, "Hey, Merry, Edie, let's go get dinner together."

"What a good idea." I hadn't been looking forward to a lonely Friday night. Curt was away overnight on a men's retreat, and he'd talked Jo's husband into going along. Apparently she wasn't any more anxious to fritter the night away alone than I was.

"Thanks, but I can't," Edie said. "I need to get home."

"But Tom works on Friday nights, doesn't he?" Jolene asked.

"Well, yes."

"And Randy's certainly big enough to feed himself."

Jolene had obviously been thinking about this dinner for some time and had figured out all the angles, something for which she was justly famous.

"He won't be home for dinner," Edie said, then realized she had thrown away her best excuse to decline. With a sigh she shrugged. "Let me call and leave a message telling him where I'm going."

Jolene was delighted. She'd now have Edie in close quarters for an hour. More than enough time to turn the screws.

"Now you be good," I managed to whisper to Jolene while Edie was talking to Astrid, the hostess at Ferretti's, Amhearst's one and only decent restaurant. "Edie doesn't need you badgering her."

"Me? Badger?" Jolene looked aghast.

This time I was the one who snorted.

Within five minutes we followed Astrid to our booth.

"Eggplant parmigiana," Jo told Sally, our waitress. "Raspberry vinaigrette dressing on the salad. And lots of garlic bread."

"Spaghetti and meatballs," I said. "Parmesan peppercorn

dressing and lots of garlic bread too." I looked at Jolene and grinned. "There's something to be said for not seeing the guys tonight."

"A cup of chicken noodle soup," Edie said. "And a roll, no garlic."

"A salad?" Sally asked.

Edie shook her head. "Just the soup."

"You're on a diet! How wonderful!" Jolene said with her usual diplomacy.

"I'm just not hungry," Edie said, tugging self-consciously at the gaping front on her shirt.

"You can tell Tom's coming home tonight," I said, winking at Jo. "No garlic bread."

And just like that, Edie began to cry.

TWO

"I'm sorry." Edie grabbed her napkin and blew her nose. "I'm all right. I am." The tears rolled down her face.

"Oh, Edie." I put my arm around her shoulder. She began to cry harder.

Jolene grabbed my arm, looked at me over Edie's bent head and mouthed very clearly, "Fix it."

"How?" I mouthed back.

Jolene made a desperate face and gave a great shrug.

I shoved my napkin into Edie's hands. "Here. Blow again." I patted her shoulder some more. When in doubt, pat.

"I'm sorry," Edie said again. "I'm such a baby."

"No, you're not. And we don't mind the tears, do we, Jolene?"

She mumbled something that sounded like, "Mmmphmm."

I rolled my eyes and said softly to Edie, "We just mind whatever is making them fall."

She smiled weakly at that.

Jolene took one look at that travesty of a smile and decided Edie was well on the way to recovery. She awkwardly patted Edie's hand. "Okay, girlfriend, that's enough. It's time to straighten that spine."

Once again I was appalled and once again Edie responded positively.

"You're right." She stuffed the napkins into her purse and sat up straight. "No more."

Jolene nodded as if she expected nothing less. "It's Randy, isn't it? Has he gotten arrested? Failed a big test? Gotten kicked out of school?"

Edie shook her head. "It's not Randy, believe it or not." Her eyes were full of pain.

I frowned. "Then it's Tom?"

Edie looked at her clenched hands and nodded.

I always hated it when a husband and a wife had trouble, but I especially hated it now because Curt and I were so happy. Not that we were husband and wife, but I knew it was just a matter of time. I wanted everyone to be as happy as we were.

"What's he done, Edie?" Jolene leaned in, fire in her eyes. She was ready to hate Tom for Edie's sake.

"I don't know," Edie whispered.

"What do you mean, you don't know?"

I shot Jolene a look. "Easy, girl."

She scowled at me but lowered the intensity level considerably.

"I don't know," Edie repeated, her voice again full of tears.

I stuffed Jolene's napkin in Edie's hand just to be prepared. "Then how do you know there's a problem?"

She forced herself to look at us. "Tom didn't come home last night." Then she looked away, embarrassed.

Jolene slapped the table, making Edie and me jump. "Another woman! It's got to be. The rat!"

"Jolene!" I was appalled at the suggestion.

Edie paled. "No! Please, God, no." It was an anguished prayer.

"That can't be the problem," I said, ever eager to comfort. "I've seen you and Tom together. If ever two people loved each other, Edie, it's you guys."

"I always thought so too." She looked at us with haunted eyes. "But what if I'm wrong? What if Jolene's right?"

Just then our waitress brought Jolene and me our salads. I stabbed a cucumber, but it might as well have been Styrofoam for all the taste it had.

"He wasn't in an accident or anything, was he?" I asked. "Maybe he was injured and couldn't contact you."

"Merry the Merciful." Acid etched Jolene's comment. "Always looking for the Pollyanna way out."

"It's better than always assuming the worst." I stabbed a poor, innocent cherry tomato since I couldn't stab Jo, and it shot through the air and landed on the table of an elderly couple across the aisle. When they looked up in surprise at the incoming missile, I made believe it wasn't mine.

"I spoke to the hospital and the police," Edie said. "The hospital says he's not there, and the police say there was no accident involving bodily injury last night anywhere in the county."

"That's good." I gently skewered another tomato. It shot a stream of red juice and seeds straight at my heart. I stared at the red stain on my new pink blouse and sighed. That's what I got for not being brave enough to own up to the first cherry bomb.

Edie smiled weakly. "I can't decide whether it's good news or bad news."

I remembered the old line: If I have to choose between another woman's arms and mangled in the street, I'll take mangled in the street anytime.

"Well, it's only one night." Jo took a huge bite of garlic bread.

I think she was trying to be encouraging after her initial outrage, but Edie shook her head. "We vowed when we got married that we'd never be separated for the night unless it was unavoidable. And then we'd always call."

"So he couldn't find a phone." Even without Edie and Jolene's stares, I knew that was a foolish line in this day and age.

"Did he show up at work this morning?" Jolene asked.

Edie shook her head. "They haven't seen him at the dealership since nine last night. It's like he's disappeared."

"Aliens," said a snide voice behind me. "Though why they'd want him is beyond me."

"Randy!" With a mixture of surprise and hurt Edie looked at her son looming behind her. "What are you doing here?"

"I got your message about going to dinner with the girls." Somehow he made those few words sound like Edie was participating in a Roman orgy. "I came to get some money."

"How did you get here?" Edie asked.

"I rode my bike." He glanced out the window where we could see it chained to a parking meter. "Only four more months until I get my car. Then I'm never riding a bicycle again in my life!"

He was getting a car for his sixteenth birthday? He bad-mouthed Tom and still expected a car? What gall!

He extended his hand to Edie, palm up. "Money." It was a command.

"But I gave you your allowance the other night." Edie scrambled to sound forceful but failed. "You wanted it early because you and the guys were going out somewhere."

"Well, it's gone. I need more." He stared down at her, tall, handsome and hostile.

I wanted to poke him hard, inflict a little pain. Edie just sighed and began rummaging in her purse.

"By the way, Mom." I could hear the nasty glee in Randy's voice and knew he was going to say something that would hurt Edie. "The police were at the house."

"What?" Edie grabbed his arm. "Did they say anything about Tom? Is he hurt? Where is he?"

"Don't get all overheated, Mom." Randy pulled free. "They

don't know where Tom-boy is. In fact, they're looking for him, just like you."

Edie blinked. "But why?"

I studied the blond man-child with the wicked glint in his eyes. "Exactly what did the police say, Randy?"

"They said—" and he paused for effect. "They said that they needed to talk with Tom."

"That was it?" Edie asked.

He looked at his mother with a smirk. "Isn't that enough, Mom? I mean, the cops are after him!"

Jolene opened her mouth to retort when a sweet young voice called, "Hey, Randy."

Randy jerked like he had been hit with a taser. He spun to look at the lovely girl passing us on her way to a table on the other side of the restaurant. Gone was the smart-mouthed kid who delighted in causing his mother distress and in his place was a self-conscious, thoroughly smitten young man who stared at the little ebony-haired beauty, his heart in his eyes.

"Sherrie," Randy managed to say. "Hey, yourself." He wandered after her as if he couldn't do anything else.

"His tongue's hanging out so far he's going to step on it any moment," Jolene muttered, but she was laughing.

The girl was with a woman who had to be her mother, their hair and eyes showing that relationship clearly. A young man was with them, probably a brother by the casual way he treated Sherrie. When Randy, all charm, took the last seat at the table without waiting for an invitation, the young man looked at his mother and just shook his head.

Edie stared at her son in wonder. "Look at him. He's being polite."

"You've done a good job as a mom, Edie," I said. "Maybe a better job than you realized."

She grunted, unconvinced, and we finished our meal.

When the bill came, we gathered our belongings and went to the cash register. Edie glanced toward Randy, but he was studiously avoiding us as he listened attentively to Sherrie's mother talk.

Edie giggled as we left the restaurant. "He never did get the money he wanted. He'll ruin any good impression he might be making when he pulls out an empty wallet and that poor girl's mother has to pay for his food."

"Serve him right," Jolene said succinctly.

We walked in the spring dusk to the parking lot behind the *News* and dispersed to our separate cars. I was just about to put the key in my ignition when a thought struck me. I climbed out of the car and walked to Edie, who sat staring out the windshield of her little red Focus.

"Edie, Tom will be at work for two to three more hours." Assuming he was at work and not missing. "Let's stop for a video and watch it together until he gets home."

I watched Edie's shoulder sag in relief and knew she'd been afraid to go home. I resisted the urge to pat her, got in my car and followed her to the video store. We argued gently over our choices of films and ended up with a comedy and an action/adventure, both nicely escapist.

I followed Edie to the outskirts of town where she pulled into the driveway of a white and brick split-level with maroon shutters and lots of uninspiring yew bushes. Clumps of daffodils nodded their heads among the yews, warm splashes of sunshine in the glow from the light beside the slightly buckling walk.

Edie unlocked the front door, painted maroon to match the shutters, and we stepped into an entry hall. The first thing I saw was a beautiful cherry pedestal occasional table with a delftware bowl and a pair of matching candlesticks on it. Above it hung what could only be an original Curtis Carlyle.

"Hey, great painting." I shrugged out of my coat. "Great artist."

Edie actually smiled. "You're prejudiced."

I looked at Curt's lovely portrayal of a creek running beside a stone farmhouse. The roses and golds of early morning turned the water into a shimmering mirror reflecting the lush greens of the towering evergreens beside the house. I felt restful and serene just looking at the scene. I reached out and ran my fingers over the signature.

"You're smiling," Edie observed.

I smiled more broadly. "I'm not surprised."

"You love him."

"Very much."

Edie studied the picture. "I prize this painting. Tom gave it to me for our fifth anniversary last October." She blinked rapidly, turned and led the way into the living room. She indicated a couch with a wave of her hand and kept on walking. "I'll just be a minute. I want to check the answering machine."

"Of course you do. Go right ahead."

I turned and looked at the living room, really looked at it, and I felt my mouth drop open.

The living room was full of the softest robin's egg-blue leather furniture I'd ever felt. It sat on the plushest of pastel floral carpets and was lit by Stiffel lamps in glowing brass. The end tables were cherry with a satin sheen, and the coffee table was a great glass and cherry rectangle that took up half the room. The drapes—no, they weren't drapes; they were window treatments—repeated the blue of the furniture and all the pastels of the rug. The walls were covered with more original watercolors including a Scullthorpe, a Gordinier, a Bollinger and another Carlyle, this one with a dark and stormy sky of deepest purples and blues. As I looked at it, I could feel the heaviness of the storm, hear the crackle of lightning, smell the ozone.

Edie came into the room. "Nothing. Not a single message, let alone one from Tom."

I turned to tell Edie how sorry I was and my eyes fell on the adjoining dining room. Again the furniture was magnificent. Too overwhelming for the size of the room, but magnificent. Cherry sideboard, table and breakfront gleamed above an oriental rug of luminous crimsons and blues laced with cream. The drapes echoed the colors of the rug, as did the matching seats on the heavy chairs crowded about the table.

I thought of my apartment with its well-used furnishings, most taken from either my bedroom or my parents' attic when I left Pittsburgh and moved to Amhearst. I had started to slowly buy better pieces, but it'd be years if not forever before I could afford the quality Edie had. Tom must really be doing well at the dealership.

When we slouched on the blue leather sofa to watch the videos, I felt I'd slide right off the cushy piece onto the floor. I pushed myself upright time after time, only to feel myself slip south, a victim of the smooth grain, featherbed softness and gravity.

It was almost eleven when we finished watching both films, and Tom wasn't yet home.

"Would you like me to stay the night?" I asked. I hated to leave her alone.

She looked momentarily tempted, then shook her head. "No, thanks. Tom'll be home soon."

Neither of us added, "I hope, I hope, I hope."

No sooner had we fought our way out of the sofa's warm embrace—no easy feat, let me tell you—than the doorbell rang.

Edie looked frightened, and I didn't blame her. Who rang your doorbell at eleven at night? Only people bringing bad news. The question was: Was the bad news about Tom or Randy?

She straightened her shoulders and walked into the entry.

I trailed behind and watched as she looked through the little peephole in the door.

"It's the police." Her voice shook. "William."

Somehow that made me feel better. We both knew Sergeant William Poole fairly well from our work at the paper. We were always in contact with the police about one story or another, and William was frequently our contact man, but as soon as I saw his face, I knew he wasn't here for PR now. Officer Natalie Schumann was with him.

William looked distinctly unhappy as we all stood in the entry, his deeply furrowed face pulled into a great frown. William was the human equivalent of a shar-pei, those Chinese dogs that are all wrinkles. Tonight he appeared to have acquired a few more.

"Is it Randy?" Edie's voice was tight with fear.

William shook his head. "I'm not here about Randy."

Edie exhaled in momentary relief. One fear defanged. One to go. She closed her eyes as if gathering herself. "If it's not Randy, then it's Tom?"

William nodded. "I need to speak with him."

"What about?"

William shook his head. "I need to speak with him, Edie."

Edie's shoulders sagged. "I need to talk with him too."

"I know you spoke to dispatch about him last night." William's brow creased more deeply. "He's still not here?"

"No." It was obvious that confessing to his absence pained her deeply.

William reached into a shirt pocket and pulled out a tablet and pen. "When did you last see him?"

"Yesterday morning about 7 a.m. when I left for work."

I watched William scribble Th 7 a.m. "Did he act in any unusual way? Say anything that in retrospect seems significant?"

"No. It was a morning like every other. He leaves for work later than I do, so he walks me to the car and sees me off. He—" She broke off and looked embarrassed.

"What?" William asked. "Tell me, Edie."

"It's just a little ritual we have. He presses me against the car and gives me a big hug and kiss. We started it when we were first married because Randy didn't like to see me kiss Tom. The garage is private."

I thought of having to go to the garage to kiss your husband. Another blot against good old Randy.

"Randy told me you were here earlier looking for Tom," Edie said. "Now you're back. Something serious is going on here."

William returned Edie's direct look. "Charges have been filed against him, and I need to question him."

Edie paled. "Charges? What do you mean, charges?"

William watched Edie carefully. Watching for a guilty reaction? "Eighteen thousand, five hundred dollars is missing at Hamblin Motors."

Edie stared at William. "And they think Tom took it?"

"It's missing, and so is he."

Edie looked wild. "But William, that's circumstantial! No one saw him take it, did they? Of course they didn't. This is Tom we're talking about. He'd never take anything!"

"Then where is he, Edie?"

"Believe me, I wish I knew." Edie ran a shaking hand through her hair. "Then you'd know." She turned desperate eyes on me. "Tell him, Merry. Tell him Tom would never do such a thing."

Oh, Lord! It was a plea shot straight from my heart to God's ear. *What do I say?*

And an answer came.

"William, how did over eighteen thousand dollars go missing?" I asked. "It's not like Tom walked up to a cash register and grabbed it, is it? Or held up the dealership like a bank robber does bank tellers? When people buy cars, papers get signed, down payment checks get written, but cash doesn't get exchanged."

William just looked at me.

Suddenly I was overcome with doubts. "It doesn't, does it?"

"It seems that Tom sold a car to an elderly couple Thursday night," William said. "The deal was concluded about 8:50 p.m. This couple paid cash and drove the car off the lot at 9:05."

"Cash?" I was surprised. "They walked into the dealership with eighteen thousand, five hundred dollars on them?"

"In her purse. In fact, they had about five thousand dollars more because they weren't certain how much the car they finally decided on would cost."

"And you think Tom just kept this money?" Edie's voice shook with outrage.

William's craggy face was impassive. "The register was closed for the evening by the time the deal was concluded. Policy in situations like this is to seal the money in an envelope, have it initialed by the salesman and the manager and lock it in the cashier's drawer until morning when it can be entered into the record appropriately."

"And Tom didn't follow procedure?" I asked.

"He did," William said. "That's how we know about the money."

"You mean that if he hadn't had the manager initial the money, no one would have known?" I was intrigued. "He would have been able to walk off with the money?"

William nodded. "At least no one would have known until the monthly inventory of cars on the lot, and one was found to be missing. Or until the couple brought the car in for servicing, and there was no record of the sale or the service warranty."

"But surely if Tom wanted to steal the money, he wouldn't have gone to the manager," I said. "He'd have pocketed the money and walked out the door."

William flipped his notebook shut. "The manager says Tom didn't get the chance to just walk out because he was passing by as Tom took possession of the money. Together they prepared the envelope as soon as the couple left."

"So it's Bill Bond's word against Tom's." Edie eyed William. He nodded.

"Now there's a tough call." Edie was derisive. "Bill Bond is not the most stable of men."

"Why do you say that?" William asked.

"Tom's told me lots of Bill Bond stories. One day he's fine, the next he's not. One day he's your friend, the next he's out for your hide. He's difficult to work under, very egocentric. Not that he does anything illegal. He just likes to ride awfully close to the line. Obviously he has finally crossed it."

William said nothing.

"What?" Edie asked. "Don't you believe me?"

"Edie," William said gently. "Bill Bond is here to talk to. Tom isn't."

THREE

Tears sprang to Edie's eyes as William made his pronouncement, and next thing I knew, I was patting her shoulder.

When in doubt, pat.

"I'm sorry, Edie." William looked sad but stoic. "I have to consider the facts, not feelings or instincts. Bill Bond may not be the world's most charming man, but he hasn't disappeared."

Edie looked resigned. "I know. It's just that Tom is such a good man! He'd never take eighteen thousand, five hundred dollars. It isn't even logical. Eighteen thousand, five hundred dollars isn't worth ruining your life over."

"What if he wanted to disappear? Eighteen thousand, five hundred dollars would be a good starting point."

"But why should he want to disappear?" Edie obviously found the idea incomprehensible.

"People disappear all the time. They want to get out of dead-end jobs, dead-end towns." He looked at her carefully. "Dead-end relationships and marriages."

Edie's head jerked like William had slapped her. "Never! We have a wonderful marriage. And believe me, because of past experience, I know good when I see it."

William nodded noncommittally.

"It's true, William. It's true! Tell him, Merry."

"It sure looks like a good marriage to me," I said, glad that this time I could answer the question.

William listened politely to me, then turned back to Edie. "Tell me about Tom, please."

Edie took a deep breath. "He's wonderful, caring, encouraging. He's gentle—"

"Not character traits," William said. "His history, family background, things like that."

Edie became engrossed in studying her fingernails. I thought for a moment that she wasn't going to answer William. Of course, she didn't have to if she didn't want to, at least not without a lawyer present. I wondered briefly what old Mr. Grassley of Grassley, Jordan and McGilpin would think about being called out in the middle of the night.

Then Edie spoke, and Mr. Grassley was allowed to sleep.

"I really can't help you, William." She glanced up from her nails, her face grim. "All I know is that Tom didn't like to talk about his past. He said it was too painful."

Too painful? Or was Tom harboring secrets? As soon as the thought crossed my mind, I felt like a traitor.

Edie studied her nails again, picking at a piece of frayed cuticle. "I know about painful pasts, so I've never pushed him."

"You don't even know where he was born? Where he lived before he came to Amhearst?"

"He was born in Philadelphia and lived in Camden, New Jersey, before he moved here."

William smiled, the furrows of his face going through a seismic shift in the process. "See? You know things about him. When was he born?"

"He just celebrated his fortieth birthday on February 15."

I waited to see if William would ask for his Social Security number and his mother's maiden name. With that information,

Tom's name, birthplace and birth date, he could find out anything he wanted to know about Tom.

Then it occurred to me that Bill Bond could supply the Social Security number from the dealership's financial records and that he'd probably do so with great enthusiasm. He wanted that money back.

Again I felt guilty because I was assuming Tom had the money. I was forgetting innocent until proven guilty. I determined to remember that a reporter is supposed to be unbiased and a friend is supposed to believe.

"Has he always been a car salesman?" William asked.

"I don't know."

"When did he move to Amhearst?"

"I don't know."

"Where does his family live?"

"I don't know."

"Who are his friends?"

Edie's head came up and her shoulders straightened. "Me."

William looked at her for several ticks of the antique mantel clock. Edie held his stare. Then he gave a little smile. "Thanks for talking with me, Edie. If Tom comes home, please have him contact me immediately." He handed her a card.

"*When* Tom comes home, he'll call you immediately."

After William was gone, Edie curled up in the corner of the blue sofa, hugging herself like she was trying to warm the chill inside.

"Where is he?" The tears she had controlled when William was here flowed down her cheeks unchecked. "Doesn't he know how scared I am?"

I watched Edie and struggled with what to do with the information we had just received from Sergeant Poole. The missing money definitely made the missing man a news story. In fact, it made Tom a major story in a small town like Amhearst.

But Edie was my friend. How could I lay her pain before the whole county? But how could I not? I knew Mac would go with the story as soon as he became aware of it, and the fact that Edie was an employee of the *News* wouldn't make any difference. In fact, it couldn't be allowed to make a difference.

And wasn't it better that I write the story than—than who? There was Edie or me. Or Mac. Obviously this story wasn't one Edie could write. And it was definitely better that I write it than Mac. Given his major grouchiness these days, anyone was better than Mac.

"You know this is going to make the *News*," I said.

Edie nodded in resignation. "I know. You'll write it, won't you?"

"Probably."

"Please. I want it to be you. I know you'll be fair. You'll make it clear that just because Tom is gone and the money is gone, they don't have to be together."

I nodded and sighed. "I'm sorry."

"Me too. I thought my days in the paper were over."

I looked at her, intrigued.

She shook her head, obviously regretting her slip of the tongue. We sat in silence for a while. Then suddenly Edie started crying again. "Oh, Merry, where is he?"

I had no answer, just useless sympathy. "Edie, why don't you go to bed? You need some rest."

"Like I could sleep." She looked at me through puffy eyes. "But you go on home, Merry. There's no reason one of us can't have a good night's sleep."

I sat in the blue leather chair, my feet tucked beneath me so I wouldn't slide onto the floor. "I can't leave you like this."

"Pish-posh. I'll be fine."

"Pish-posh? Now where did that come from?" If you aren't patting, distracting is good.

Edie gave a weak smile. "My father always said that."

"What was he like?" I asked, pleased that distracting was working. Maybe I should ask Mac about doing an advice column.

"He was a professor at the University of Delaware, a charmer, a marvelous guy—when he wasn't drunk." She became very interested in the needlepoint pillow in her lap, picking at nonexistent loose threads. "He was a nasty drunk."

I made a distressed noise. So much for the efficacy of distraction.

"Don't let it worry you," she said. "He's dead now. And Mom and I survived."

I wondered what was involved in *survived*. "Where does your mother live now?"

"Still in Newark." She said it with the *ark* in Newark getting just as much emphasis as the *New*, unlike Newark, New Jersey, where the accent was definitely on the first syllable. "That's where I lived until I divorced Randolph."

"That's about an hour away. Randy must get to see him frequently. Wait. I'm assuming Randolph is still in Newark."

"He's still there, but Randy doesn't see him much. Randolph's lack of interest is probably the main reason Randy fights with Tom and me all the time. A kid always wants what he can't have. Greener grass, I guess. It's an ego thing or a control thing or something. Or maybe it's just as simple as a broken heart. He can't do anything to make Randolph pay attention, so he takes out the pain on us because we're handy and won't turn him out."

"You guys are very good to him."

"Of course we are." Edie looked surprised that I'd find that fact worth commenting on. "I'm his mother."

And that said it all.

I watched Edie trace the pattern on the pillow she held. "Did you meet Tom in Newark or here? Or somewhere else?"

"Here. When I moved here, I lived in a tiny two-bedroom apartment and drove the oldest, most endangered car you've ever seen. Finally the car died, and I had no choice but to buy another even if I couldn't afford it. I went to Hamblin Motors and the rest, as they say, is history." She smiled softly to herself.

"Love at first sight?"

"At least serious like," she said. "He asked me out as soon as I signed the sales papers. I found out later that the price was so good because he didn't take his commission."

"Wow! That is indeed serious like."

"We were married in two months, and I've never regretted a day of it."

At least until last night, I thought, but I didn't say it.

The front door flew open, crashing into the hall wall.

Edie sat straight up. "Tom?" The hope in her voice broke my heart.

Randy stalked by the living room without so much as a glance in our direction. He continued down the hall to the back of the house. In a moment I heard him opening the refrigerator.

Edie checked her watch. "It's 1:05. No kid his age should be out this late, but tonight I'm just not up to the confrontation. All I can think about is Tom."

I nodded, thinking that Randy had been counting on just that and was taking advantage of her preoccupation. The kid was clever, a master strategist and champion manipulator. Usually that meant a keen intelligence. What a waste, I thought, to use your mind to wound and distress.

"I just hope he hasn't been with that adorable little Sherrie all this time. Too cute. Too many hormones." Edie shivered.

Randy appeared in the doorway, a can of Mountain Dew in one hand and a bag of Chips Ahoy in the other. He had enough caffeine and sugar there to keep a small town awake for hours. He'd probably wolf it all down and fall immediately into a deep slumber.

"No word from Tom-boy?" he asked his mother.

She shook her head.

He smirked. "Aliens, Mom. Or else he's deserted you."

"Randy!" I couldn't help it. He was being so unkind.

He ignored me. "Just like you did Dad." His smirk deepened. "I guess you're finally getting what you deserve."

Edie sighed. "I'm not going to discuss why I left your father, Randy. You know that. He's your father, and I won't talk against him."

I watched Randy absorb his mother's comments without any perceptible change of expression or posture. I concluded that Edie's comments on this subject were as familiar and frequent as were his barbs. He turned to me without a blink.

"That your car in the drive?" he asked.

I nodded.

"I'm getting a car in a couple of months." He looked back at his mother and said, "My father is giving it to me."

Obviously he meant Randolph, not Tom.

He laughed. "It's a good thing because Tom wouldn't get me a car if I was the last person on earth."

"And neither would I." Edie's eyes were unflinching as she looked at her son. "Things like cars and the trust to let you have one have to be earned."

Randy shrugged. "I guess I'm lucky that Dad doesn't agree." He turned to me. "Want to see my car?"

I glanced at Edie, who raised her hand in a be-my-guest motion. I turned to Randy. "Okay."

He put his Mountain Dew on the glorious occasional table in the hall, and I could see Edie bite her lip to keep from reprimanding him about it.

Randy opened the blue bag of cookies. He pulled out a handful to fortify himself while he showed me his dream car.

I expected him to pull out a picture, but he didn't.

"Come on," he said. "It's in the garage."

I glanced again at Edie.

"Randolph can never remember Randy's birth date," she said. "He thought it was sometime in the spring, so he sent the car ahead so he wouldn't be late."

Randy turned on his mother. "He knows my birthday! He wants me to have the fun of anticipation."

Edie shrugged. "If you say so."

"When is your birthday?" I asked.

"July 13." Randy scowled at me, daring me to make something of the midsummer date.

I merely nodded. "Well, show me."

Still scowling, Randy led me down a level, through the family room, to the connecting door to the garage. He went through first and flicked on the lights. I followed and blinked at what I saw. I knew then that Edie and Tom didn't have a chance.

There, gleaming softly under the harsh overhead light, sat a silver, ragtop Porsche convertible.

"It came three days ago." Randy ran his hand lovingly over the sleek curve of one fender. "Isn't it beautiful?"

"That it is." I began to circle the car. All I could think of was how inappropriate this expensive, classy, powerful car was for a novice driver. The potential for tragedy was incredible!

I bent down to peer inside. I might as well study the upholstery before it was drenched with Randy's blood.

Someone had beaten Randy to it.

Blood stained the passenger seat and floor, great quantities of blood, overwhelming quantities of blood. I knew there had to be very little if any left in the very dead man who slumped against the gray leather interior.

FOUR

I made a noise halfway between a scream and a burp at the sight of the body. My first thought was that Tom had finally come home.

"What's the matter with you?" Randy demanded, ever sympathetic to a woman in distress.

I couldn't find my voice, so I pointed. He bent and peered in. Next thing I knew he was retching in the corner. So much for perpetual cool.

I made myself look in the car again. I had to know if the corpse was indeed Tom.

It wasn't. First, the body looked too tall, even slumped. Tom was slight all over, and this man had wide shoulders and a paunch. Also, Tom wore his hair closely cropped, and this man had straggly hair that should have been cut weeks ago. And of course, this man had the wrong face, with strong, broad features instead of the narrow, almost delicate ones that typified Tom.

I straightened from my quick second glance with a deep sigh of relief and turned to Randy, who by now was leaning weakly against the side of the car.

"Get off the car! It's a crime scene!"

Randy, green around the gills, jumped and obeyed.

"We don't want to touch it and contaminate any evidence."

Randy nodded as he swayed.

I gave him a push. "Back into the house. We need to call 911."

Edie took one look at Randy as we stumbled inside and surged to her feet. "What's wrong?"

"There's a dead guy in my car!" Disbelief was Randy's dominant emotion now that he was away from the scene. Feelings of outrage and violation would follow shortly. "And there's blood all over!"

Edie looked wide-eyed at me, seeking confirmation—or denial—of Randy's comments.

I nodded. "Where's the phone?"

They both pointed to the kitchen.

I called 911 and returned to the family room just as Edie and Randy walked back in from the garage.

Edie was white-faced as she looked back toward the garage. "I never saw him before in my life."

The police didn't recognize the corpse either.

"How'd he get here?" Randy demanded of anyone who'd listen, and that was usually me. "And why in my car?"

Like I knew.

"How long's he been dead?" he demanded of the police. "How did he die? And why in my car?"

"Speaking of your car, son," William Poole said quietly, "when was the last time you looked into it?"

"Ah." Randy looked very wise. "You want to know when the body got there."

William nodded. "That's the idea."

"Well, I sat in it just before I left for dinner. I met Mom at Ferretti's, not that she invited me."

"And there was nothing unusual about the car or the garage when you last saw it at what? About 5:30?"

Randy thought for a minute. "Yeah, about 5:30. And if by

unusual you mean there was a dead body lying around bleeding all over the place, no, there was nothing at all unusual. I just sat behind the wheel making believe I was driving." Randy's hands were in front of him, steering.

William adjusted his gun on his hip. "One piece of advice, son. Don't even think about taking that car onto the road before you have your license."

Randy blinked and flushed. "I'd never do something like that."

I could almost hear William's mental *Right*.

"Besides," Randy continued, "Mom has the keys."

William nodded. "Good. Make certain you leave them in her care. If you break the law here, we can make it twenty-one before you get a license."

Randy stared. "Twenty-one?"

"Twenty-one," William repeated. "But since you're not going to take her out early, there's no problem. Right?"

Randy nodded reluctantly. Busted by the cops before he even committed the crime!

"And when you do get your license," William continued, "don't see how fast she can go."

Randy held up his hand. "That's two pieces of advice. You said one. Two's one too many."

William ignored the disrespect, and Randy resumed pacing, cursing and muttering under his breath. I suspected that beneath the distress and excitement of being part of an official murder investigation, he was livid about the blood spilled all over his new upholstery.

This suspicion was confirmed when he leaned close and whispered out of the side of his mouth like a gangster in a B movie, "How do you get blood out of things?"

I was tempted to say, "Wash it thoroughly in cold water," and offer him the hose, but he was just being fifteen and Randy.

For Edie a dead man in the garage upped the ante considerably on the scariness of Tom's disappearance. The fact that the police no longer seemed to see Tom as a husband jumping his matrimonial ship added to her tension. The big question became whether they now saw him as another potential victim like their John Doe, or whether they saw him as a thief and a murderer. Neither option was comforting.

Edie lay on her sofa under a blanket that I'd brought from upstairs, and still she shivered as with a terrible chill.

"I know this is hard, Edie," William said. "But you know the drill."

She nodded. "I've never seen him. I don't know who he is."

William was unfailingly polite, but I thought I detected a subtle skepticism. Not a happy observation.

After the police, the coroner and the body left, Randy disappeared in the general direction of upstairs and, I presumed, his bed. I knew he would have preferred to begin clean-up operations on his car, but it was off-limits as part of a crime scene. With any luck, the police would impound it until his twenty-first birthday, saving themselves a few years of dealing with him behind the wheel of that speed machine.

Edie and I stayed in the living room where she slept restlessly on the sofa, muttering occasionally in her sleep, at other times sighing as though in despair. I took catnaps in my cushy leather chair.

I pulled myself awake at seven and took my burning eyes and sour mouth into the guest bath where I did my best to transform myself. It was about as hopeless as turning coffee dregs into fresh brew. Still, when I pulled up to the window at McDonald's and ordered an Egg McMuffin, the sleepy teen who took my order and money understood what I said.

I wrote the story on Edie's mysterious body, still a John Doe when we went to press. He had carried no wallet, no driver's license, no credit cards. His clothes were from Penney's, his jeans were Levis, available countless places, and his sneakers Reeboks, same thing.

With Mac's approval I had chosen not to mention the missing money in my story. There was, after all, no definitive connection between the murder and the money. As soon as I finished writing, I turned the article in to Mac and left the *News* before he thought of anything else I should do. I made it to bell choir practice with one minute to spare.

The good thing about bell choir is that it takes every ounce of my concentration not to mess things up, so every other worry gets put aside for the duration. It's the only real benefit I have found to being a marginal musician. Smiling to myself, I lined my bells up, C-sharp, C, B and B-flat, glad to put Edie, Tom, Randy and the corpse aside for a while.

When we played the first piece for the third time and I actually got it right, I was euphoric.

"Maddie, did you hear that?" I turned to my best church friend who stood next to me and played the D and E bells. "I got it right!"

"You're wonderful," she said. "Talented and beautiful and. . ." She peered at me. "And you've got dark circles under your eyes that rival mine. I know it wasn't a late night with Curt because he's on the retreat with my Doug and the rest of the men. And you can't blame it on a baby like I can. What gives?"

"Covering a story," I said. "Read about it in the *News*." I didn't want to shatter the respite of bell choir by reviewing the crime. To divert her, I asked, "How's Holly?"

Maddie's face lit up. "Even after a sleepless night like last night, I wouldn't trade her for anything." She turned toward her pocketbook resting on the floor behind her. "I've got pictures of her getting her bath."

In the few months of Holly's life, her every move had been recorded and lovingly shared with anyone breathing. I was tempted to ask how this week's pictures of Holly bathing differed from last week's pictures of Holly in the tub, but I was afraid Maddie would tell me. "See? She's got a bigger smile. And that's a boat floating there, not the rubber ducky. And her hair is a sixteenth of an inch longer!"

"All right, people," said Ned, our director, arresting Maddie mid-search.

"Later," she whispered.

"Later," I agreed.

"You may remember," Ned said, "that we will be accompanying the youth choir on Easter morning. We won't actually practice with all the kids until next weekend, but today we're going to practice with the soloist, Sherrie Bauer."

As he spoke, a familiar raven-haired beauty walked in. She had music in one hand and dangled a backpack from the other. I half expected to see Randy trailing after her, tongue lolling.

Sherrie Bauer had a wonderful voice, very full and controlled for someone as young as she. For her solo, we traded our bells for chimes which made a much softer sound and didn't drown out her voice. They also didn't amplify my mistakes as clearly as the bells.

As I listened to Sherrie and concentrated on my notes, I thought that Ned might have inadvertently given me the perfect combination of things to get Edie and Randy and hopefully Tom (fully restored to his family from wherever he was) to church. Easter and Sherrie sounded like an unbeatable combination to me.

When rehearsal finally ended, I managed to escape before Maddie remembered Holly's pix. I felt like a lousy friend, but I was just too exhausted to wax enthusiastic over chubby little knees and shampoo Mohawks. All I wanted to do was collapse and sleep for hours, but I couldn't. I had an interview ahead with just enough time for lunch and a shower first.

Whiskers met me at the apartment door with several gruff meows. For a time he stalked around the living room, tail held high, mad at me for being away so long. Then he forgave me and butted my shins until I picked him up. He purred like a formula car awaiting the green flag at Indy.

I fed him, and while he ate I listened to my answering machine.

Jolene: "So what happened when you went home with Edie last night? Terminal boring, I'll bet. Sort of like my night without Reilly."

Wait until she read the paper. That'd teach her to shirk doing good deeds.

Curt: "Where are you, darlin'? Out carousing with the girls, I bet. Sigh. I miss your sweet voice, Merry. I remember when a weekend with the boys was at the top of my fun-things list. Not anymore. I'll see you tomorrow evening at 7:30—if I last that long."

I smiled, delighted that I had replaced the boys in his life. He'd certainly replaced everyone else in mine.

I glanced at the clock. 1 p.m. An hour before I had to meet Stephanie Bauer at Freedom House. Six and a half before I saw Curt. I smothered a yawn and hoped a shower would do something to stimulate my brain cells.

Forty-five minutes later I drove to Freedom House. I loved interviewing people, learning about them, looking for what made them tick, finding out what mattered to them. I parked in front of a large Victorian in what used to be the elite section of Amhearst. In fact the whole street was full of once-great homes that were now medical and dental suites, photography studios and offices for financial planners, psychologists and ministries. Some of the homes still had their pride intact with their well-tended lawns, fresh paint and gilt signs. Some were showing their age, all wrinkles and creaky joints, peeling paint and sagging shutters.

Freedom House was in the latter category, a dull gray with white-and-rose trim. It desperately needed painting before the rose became grayer than the gray. The wooden steps were soft underfoot, and the wraparound porch rippled like a lake under a strong breeze. Two spindles were missing from the porch railing, and the shutters looked like they had a bad case of psoriasis.

No financial resources to speak of, I guessed. The perennial problem of ministries.

Stephanie Bauer met me in the front hall. "Welcome!"

Her smile was so warm I smiled back automatically. "Hi. I think I saw you last night at Ferretti's."

Stephanie nodded. "I was there with my son and daughter."

"I was there with the mother of the tall kid who crashed your family party."

"Randy." Stephanie laughed. "What a delightful, funny guy."

Randy? Delightful? Funny? Wow! Wouldn't Edie love to hear that.

"I'm also in the bell choir, and I heard Sherrie sing this morning. She's wonderful."

Stephanie beamed, a proud mama. "She is, but I'm proudest of her for her commitment to the Lord."

What a refreshing thing to hear a mother say about her child. "It's probably from watching you and Freedom House."

Stephanie grimaced. "I haven't always been the best example of a healthy Christian woman." She turned toward the back of the house. "My office is in the old dining room. Follow me."

On the way we had to step around considerable clutter in the entry hall.

"We're getting ready to open a secondhand clothing shop," Stephanie explained. "We're collecting both clothes and supplies in preparation." She waved her hand at a couple of clothing racks, a slightly dirty, well-used store counter and several bags of clothing shoved into a corner. "We want to use the store as a training facility so that the women we counsel can become financially independent if they need to. Too many women stay in abusive situations because of lack of money."

"When will the store open?"

"In a couple of months. We're going to call it Like New. That's what the women are when they find Christ and learn that with His help, they can control their lives." She grinned. "We just signed the lease for a store in the center of town, and I have no idea where the monthly rent is going to come from. As you undoubtedly noticed, we can't even afford to paint this place. If the store succeeds, it'll be all because of God."

She spoke as if trusting God this way were commonplace, and I thought that for her, it probably was.

I peered into the living room as we walked past. It was filled with chairs of all sizes, colors and fabrics.

"A motley mess, isn't it?" Stephanie said cheerfully. "But we don't have the luxury of being choosy. If someone offers us a chair, we take it. As long as it'll hold a woman up safely, we don't complain about the looks."

We settled on a dirty, well-used sofa and chair in a corner of Stephanie's office. I checked my little tape recorder to make certain it was working properly. Satisfied, I leaned back.

Stephanie patted her chair, and thousands of dust motes burst free, sailing through the air like seeds from an exploding pod. "A mission in Allentown was going out of business and they offered us first dibs on their furniture. Isn't it comfortable?" She was clearly delighted.

"It is," I agreed, though I had just been thinking that I

wouldn't give the ratty stuff house room. I swallowed, feeling shallow and materialistic.

"How did you get involved in Freedom House?" I asked. I knew the short answer to this question from my research, but it was still a good place to begin.

Stephanie looked away from me for a minute, staring out the window.

"It always amazes me when I have to admit that I was an abused wife. Not that I'm ashamed or feel guilty. I'm just amazed. How did I let myself get trapped like that?"

"How did you?" I marveled that someone as strong and assured as the Stephanie sitting in front of me had once been a victim.

"I got trapped for two reasons. I wanted to please. And no one had ever taught me the power of choice. And I was only eighteen when I married."

"Is marrying at a young age typical of abusive situations?"

She nodded. "Often, though not always. In our case it was too many stresses before we had the ability to handle them. When I married Wes, I was in a romantic fantasy. I saw him as strong and knowing, my knight to protect me from the world. I would be the best wife a man could ever have, and he wouldn't lose his temper at me anymore because I'd make him so happy."

She looked into space, I suspected seeing herself at eighteen, twenty, twenty-five. "I bent over backwards to please him. When he got angry, I knew it was my fault because I hadn't tried hard enough. When he hit me, I knew I deserved it. When he heaped verbal abuse on me, I knew I was all those terrible things he called me. After all, he'd never say them if they weren't true."

"But you're an intelligent woman," I protested.

She nodded. "But he was incredibly clever, a master manipulator. And he always begged for forgiveness with tears in his eyes. 'I'm sorry! I didn't mean to hurt you. You just made me so mad. Let's agree that you'll never do that again. Then I won't have to hurt you again.'"

"That's no apology at all."

Stephanie nodded. "I know that now, but then I only heard the I'm-sorry part, not the it-was-Stephanie's-fault part."

"How long were you married?"

"Nine years. Nine long years."

"Why did you finally leave?"

"Deep inside I knew it was wrong to hit people, even stupid wives. I just couldn't admit it out loud. But I started reading things about abuse after a nurse talked to me the time Wes gave me a concussion and broke my arm."

"How did he break your arm?" I cut in.

"He threw me down the stairs for not making the bed with the sheets he wanted."

I blinked. "You're kidding."

She shrugged. "At least that's what he said. In reality he was about to lose another job and was taking it out on me. You see, if it was my fault he hit me, then he was still the good guy. I was the evil woman."

She smiled grimly. "When you're in an abusive marriage, it's like you're addicted. There's this intimacy and these soul ties from the sex, often violent or demeaning. You think you can't live without him even as he's killing you. You think it's normal to live with this tension, this pain. And you know everything will be all right if you can just love him enough.

"Which of course you can never do because for him the issue isn't love but absolute authority. Total control. That's the goal of every abuser."

"The puppeteer pulling the strings," I said.

"That's too kind an image, but it definitely gives the idea."

"How were the kids during this time?"

Stephanie smiled. "They were the one bright spot in my life. But they misbehaved, as all kids do, and I began to fear that Wes would beat them too."

I thought of vivacious Sherrie and felt sick at the thought of someone hitting her. "Did he?"

She shook her head. "Wes never laid a hand on them, but they learned what they saw modeled. One day I was outside in the garden when I heard Sherrie begin to cry. She was about five years old. I rushed inside and found her and Rob in the living room. Rob was yelling at her like Wes yelled at me. He was calling her the same names that Wes called me. And on her cheek was a red handprint from where Rob had hit her."

My blood chilled as I thought of the handsome kid in the booth last night at Ferretti's.

"'She didn't do what I asked,' Rob said. 'I told her to get me something to drink and she didn't.' 'I didn't, Mom,' Sherrie said, hanging her head. 'I'm sorry.'"

Stephanie swallowed hard, the memory obviously still painful. "'You can't hit her like that, Rob,' I told him. 'It's not right.' 'Why not?' he asked. 'Daddy hits you.'" Stephanie looked at me. "That's when I knew I had to leave. I couldn't let my children become Wes and me. I called that nurse and she sent me to a safe house. We lived there for two months. I couldn't go to my regular job because Wes could find me there, but I found another one in another town nearby. And for some reason I began to go to church."

She turned and pointed to the photo of a little white building that looked more like a VFW hall than a church. It hung on the wall beside this year's school pictures of Sherrie and Rob.

"The safe house gave me protection when I needed it and helped restore order to our lives, but it was at church that I met

Jesus. There I learned the power of choosing God's way. That's when I determined to offer women everything the safe house had offered me plus the power of God to redeem broken lives."

"And Freedom House is the result?"

Stephanie nodded. "We only make a small dent in a very large problem, but we can do that."

"Did you ever see your husband after you left?"

"I saw him in court when I fought for sole custody of the kids." Stephanie smiled. "I won. After all, I had all those medical records of my various injuries. And a judge who understood the issues at stake."

The phone rang.

"Excuse me." Stephanie went to her desk. "I'm on a twenty-four-hour page because of the nature of Freedom House."

I thought of my father, who was an absolutely wonderful husband and father. I thought of Curt, so kind and loving, and I was suddenly ashamed for all I'd taken for granted.

"Tina!" The command in Stephanie's voice drew me. "Tina! Now listen to me. A bad morning at work doesn't give him the right to unload on you."

Tina murmured something.

"We've talked about this before, Tina. You're panicking, doing what comes naturally to you. Don't let yourself do that. You've got to choose to do the right thing, not the known thing. It's your choice. To stay or to go—it's your choice." She listened for a minute. "I know it's scary. Oh, Lord, please give Tina Your strength and Your courage. Help her make wise choices for her children's sakes. And protect all of them, Father. Protect all of them."

I listened to Stephanie's prayer and wondered how many women she'd prayed with through the years, either over the phone or in person. How many women now lived without fear because of Freedom House?

Stephanie hung up and sat quietly for a minute or two with her eyes closed. Then she looked at me.

"One of the things we do for women who want to escape and are willing to take that risk is plan what to take and where to go. Some, like Tina, have been under their husbands' thumbs so long that we have to begin with things as elementary as getting their purse and the kids. And some like Tina need time to save the taxi fare."

"Do they live here if they bolt?"

She shook her head. "Once in a while someone stays here if there's no other option. But I don't take people in often for two reasons. My family and I live here, and I don't want to endanger my kids. Also, we're too public to be a safe house. A true safe house is a closely guarded location."

"If this isn't a residential facility, what do you do besides plan escape routes?"

Stephanie stood and walked back to the easy chair across from me. "We're basically a training ministry. We teach women all about the power and freedom of choice. We teach them they can make good choices or bad choices. It sounds so obvious, this choosing well, when we say it to each other, but it's a new truth to many women. And of course we teach the women that the greatest power and freedom of all come from choosing to believe in Christ."

"So how do you teach this? What specific programs do you have?"

"I have a staff, mostly volunteers, who work with me. We teach Bible studies. We have support groups. We counsel. These programs might not sound like much, but they represent hours and hours of work each week."

I didn't doubt that for a minute. "May I come to one of the Bible studies?"

She looked at me carefully. "I need to know that you'll

respect the privacy of these women. It's crucial to protect them. Their lives are literally at risk."

"Believe me," I said, hastening to reassure her, "I understand that. I promise to protect them."

She nodded. "Okay then."

A knock sounded on the door of the office, and there was Sherrie grinning at us.

"Hey, honey," Stephanie said. "Is it three already?"

"Just about." Sherrie came in and sat on the sofa beside me. Her eyes sparkled with life and good humor.

"This is Merry Kramer," Stephanie said. "She's a reporter at the *News*. She's going to write an article about Freedom House."

Sherrie looked at me. "Hey, that's great. Somebody needs to write about Mom and all the good stuff she does."

The phone rang again, and Stephanie went back to her desk to take the call.

Sherrie leaned toward me. "Can I be in the Freedom House article? I've got stuff I want to say, stuff I think kids need to hear."

"What do you mean?"

"Well, I've lived here for a long time now, and I watch the women." Her young face was serious, her brow furrowed. "I listen to Mom when she talks to them. I even go to some of the Bible studies. I've reached some conclusions that might keep girls from getting into marriages with the wrong guy. Sort of preventative stuff."

I smiled broadly. "I think I'd like to talk with you. Monday after school at the *News*?"

"I'll be there." She grinned happily.

A high-pitched, desperate voice wept through the phone loudly enough to attract both Sherrie and me.

"Easy, Tina," Stephanie said calmly. "Tell me the place you've chosen to go in times of trouble."

"Poor Tina." Sherrie shook her head. "She's a nice person, but she's a waffler."

"A waffler?"

"She can't decide whether to get out or not. One minute she's leaving him, the next she's going back because he loves her." Sherrie snorted. "He doesn't love her. He likes to control her."

Tina's terrified voice cut across the room again, her apprehension clear even if her words were not.

"How will you get to your parents?" Stephanie said into the phone.

I was now openly listening and thinking like mad. I had Stephanie's personal story. I had the facts about Freedom House and the services provided. I might even have a sidebar article from Sherrie aimed at kids. But an interview with an abused wife! And right in the middle of a crisis! Wow.

I leaned toward Stephanie. "Can I help Tina? Drive her somewhere?"

Stephanie looked at me thoughtfully. "Just a minute, Tina. I need to check something."

"I mean it. I'll be glad to help."

"She's not just fodder for an article," Stephanie said bluntly.

I flushed, caught. "I know that."

"Promise you won't write about her without her permission, and promise you'll flatten her story so she can't be identified."

That wasn't a hard promise to make. I certainly didn't want Tina to suffer any more harm or hurt. "I promise."

Stephanie nodded, satisfied. "She needs a ride to Phoenixville. Public transportation isn't a possibility. And for financial reasons neither's a cab."

"Phoenixville's not that far," I said. "About a half hour up Route 113."

"It'll be very messy emotionally," Stephanie warned. "And that's the best possible scenario."

"That doesn't bother me." Anything for story color. "Has her husband come home? Is that why the sudden panic?"

"He called from work and is full of fury. Apparently things have gone badly today, and she and the kids are about to bear the brunt of his frustration if we don't get her out."

"Where does she live?"

Stephanie returned to the phone. "Tina, I have someone here who can take you to your mother's. I want you to tell her how to get to your house."

I took the phone. "Hi, Tina. I'm Merry. I'll be glad to drive you where you need to go."

"I'm scared," she said, her voice a mere whisper.

"I know. Now tell me how to get to your house."

She gave me directions hesitantly, pausing several times to yell at a crying child who responded by wailing louder.

"I'll be there in about ten minutes," I assured her.

She sniffed. "The kids and I will be waiting. And please, please hurry!"

FIVE

Tina's cozy, tree-lined street looked like a Norman Rockwell setting made for raising happy, well-adjusted children. I wondered what secrets lived in the other houses.

A new red sports car sat in the driveway of Tina's home, its sticker still on the window. I glanced at the price as I walked past and flinched. He might be having trouble at work, but obviously he made a good income. Too bad Tom Whatley hadn't been at Hamblin's to make the sale. There had to have been a very nice commission on this one.

As I stood on the front step, I could hear raised voices inside, first deep and masculine, then shrill and feminine. Then I distinctly heard a slap and a cry of pain.

Suddenly getting a good bite for my story seemed unimportant, even selfish. A woman's very life might well be at stake, and journalism faded to insignificance. I put my shaking finger firmly on the bell.

All noise within ceased. Then the woman inside this house began to cry.

I rang again.

The door opened and a floridly handsome man glowered at me from the other side of the storm door. He wore a dress shirt with the sleeves rolled to the elbows, revealing strong arms and wrists. Did he develop those muscles with exercises other than beating on Tina?

"Hi." I smiled brightly, ignoring the turmoil in my stomach. Not only did I have the long tradition of Nellie Bly and Brenda Starr to uphold; I had right on my side.

"We don't want any," he snarled. "I gave at the office. Go away."

I grabbed the storm door and pulled, praying it wasn't locked. It wasn't. The door opened wide. He blinked in surprise at my audacity.

"You must be Tina's husband. I'm Merry." I held out my hand and stepped into the house. He was forced to either collide with me or step back. He stepped back. He did not shake my hand.

"Hey, Tina, I'm here," I called gaily.

She appeared behind her husband, a red handprint clearly visible on her cheek. Her eyes were full of fear, her face wet with tears, but her chin was held at a determined angle.

"Ready to go?" I asked.

"Go?" He sputtered like an outboard motor misfiring. "Go where?" He glared at Tina, then at me.

Tina and I ignored him. She turned and disappeared.

I'd lost her! "Tina?"

She reappeared with two small children, a boy about six and a girl about four, each carrying a little backpack. They looked more frightened than children should ever have to look. The girl had obviously been crying, her face mottled, her nose running.

Tina's husband turned to her with a roar and grabbed her by the upper arm. She winced, and I knew she'd find a bruise there in a short time.

"Go," she whispered to the kids. "Out to the car."

"Mommy?" The girl looked at Tina with huge eyes dripping tears.

"Aren't you coming, Mom?" the boy asked, trying not to cry.

"I'm coming," Tina said. With her free hand she shooed the children. "Go."

"Don't you dare!" At their father's voice, both children froze halfway down the steps.

I turned to them and smiled, hoping my lips weren't quivering too much for my smile to be reassuring. "Why don't you two climb in the backseat and buckle yourselves in?" I suggested quietly. "Your mom and I will be right there."

The boy looked at his father, at his mother, at me. Then he grabbed his sister's hand. "Come on, Lacey."

Together they ran to the car. He pulled the rear door open, and I almost smiled as he helped her in and tried to buckle the seat belt around her.

"You can leave if you want," Tina's husband told her in a steely voice, "but I'll find you, you know. You're mine. You can't escape. Ever."

Could she possibly stand up to such focused intensity from someone who absolutely vibrated with the necessity to bend her to his will?

For a long minute she said nothing, just stared at him like a trapped rabbit.

"Tina," I said. "Look at me. Look at me!"

"You stay out of this," he hissed, his eyes never leaving Tina. "This is between my wife and me."

"Tina!"

She pulled her gaze from her husband's.

"It's your choice." I tried to remember what Stephanie had said. "Remember—the power of choice."

When she responded, her voice was only a whisper and she talked to the floor, but she'd made her choice. "Let go of me, Bill. I'm going with Merry."

He was startled at her unprecedented audacity, and

taking advantage of his shock she wrenched her arm from his grasp.

He grabbed for her. "That's what you think."

I stepped quickly out the door onto the porch, though I kept the storm door open. I looked at the empty yard next door and called, "Hi, how are you doing today?" I even gave a little wave.

The idea that there was someone watching what was happening caused Tina's husband to check for a minute. She saw her chance and darted past him, ducking as he slapped at her. She and I hurried toward the car.

I stopped halfway down the walk and turned back to the house. He stood on the front steps, his face red with fury, his hands clenched in fists.

"There's something you should know before you lay a hand on your wife again." I was so angry my voice shook. "I write for the *News,* and I'd be delighted to write about you by name. I'm sure they'd like to know at work just what kind of a man you are."

He stared, clearly surprised. Then he shouted, "You wouldn't dare! I'd sue you for all you're worth! You have no proof." He looked at his wife who was climbing into my car. "And who in their right mind would ever believe her?" The contempt in his voice gave me the chills.

"How about me? I believe her." And I turned my back.

When we arrived at Tina's parents', they welcomed her and the children with obvious relief.

"Finally," her father said with tears in his eyes. "And this time you're staying."

Tina burrowed into his arms as he patted her awkwardly on the shoulder.

"Come on, Lacey, Jess." Tina's mother took a small hand in each of hers. "I bet I can find some ice cream in the freezer."

"Don't let them eat all mine," their grandfather said in an attempt to lighten the moment.

"It's okay, Grandpop." Lacey stopped in the doorway, trying to swallow her disappointment. "We don't have to have any."

With a sad smile, Grandpop said, "Honey, I was teasing. You eat as much as you want."

Lacey looked at him hesitantly.

"I mean it," he said. "It's all yours."

"It's okay, Lacey," Jess said. "Isn't it, Mommy? It's okay here."

"It's okay here," Tina repeated and began to weep.

Tonight's black-tie reception was important for my career as I'd be meeting my new superboss for the first time, and I wanted to impress him. I was going to wear one of those rare, it's-exactly-right dresses that made me feel like a million dollars but which I bought for thirty bucks in a secondhand clothes store. It had a fitted sapphire blue silk top covered with so many sequins that I shimmered like the Caribbean Sea awash in sun jewels. Its soft silk skirt fell in a graceful column.

But it was Curt I really wanted to impress. I wanted to knock his socks off, make him drool, froth at the mouth and go weak at the knees. I grinned at the absurd thoughts. I'd be happy if I could make him whistle.

I was standing in front of the bathroom mirror in my underwear, one eye made up, my hair in hot rollers, when I realized that my dress, fresh from the cleaners, was still hanging in the car. I shuddered when I thought of its condition after sharing a backseat with Lacey and Jess, but it was the only truly fancy dress I owned—unless you counted four frou-frou bridesmaid dresses, including one from Jolene and Reilly's wedding. Of course I wouldn't be caught dead in any of them outside a church.

I glanced at the clock. Ten minutes before Curt arrived. I grabbed my new red coat and threw it on over my undies. I ran out the front door. I was halfway across the porch when I heard the door not only slam closed but snap in the way that meant only one thing: locked. And the key was in my purse on the sofa.

I stared at my front door. A couple of months ago someone had broken into my apartment by shattering one of the small panes of glass in the door. After that I'd lobbied my landlord for a new, all-wooden door. He hadn't been happy with the idea, but when I offered to share the cost with him, he'd agreed. My new, solid door with the peephole was impregnable, unless you happened to be carrying an axe in your coat pocket.

I had ten minutes—no, probably about eight by now—to get back inside before Curt arrived and found me in my rollers, underwear, half-made-up face and slippers with the Winnie the Pooh heads on them. I began a frantic search for a secret way into the apartment.

I was behind the yew hedge by the front window, trying in vain to open it, when I heard a deep voice say, "It's a cinch that no one at the reception will hold a candle to you tonight."

For once the voice didn't thrill me to my toes.

I turned to face him. He looked absolutely gorgeous with his black curly hair and dark eyes behind his new brown wire-rimmed glasses. He was wearing a tux. A tux! And I was wearing a coat and underwear!

He studied me closely, looking from one eye to the other. He was trying rather unsuccessfully not to laugh.

I stalked out from behind the bushes, clutching my coat to me. "I'm locked out."

"Ah." Then he saw my feet. "Hey! Maybe I can get a pair of Tiggers!"

"Very funny. Go away. Come back in twenty minutes."

Instead he leaned over and kissed my cheek, getting poked in the temple with a roller in the process.

"Sorry." I rubbed the little red marks left by the roller's teeth.

He looked at the front door. "You're sure it's locked?"

I just looked at him.

"All right then." He retraced the route I had just taken, trying all the windows I had just tried. Whiskers followed his progress from window to window, meowing encouragement from inside. I was perversely pleased to see that he had no more luck than I.

"So you really are out in the cold," he said.

"And it's getting colder. It's breezy under here."

"What?"

"Nothing," I said quickly. "Just break a window and get me in!"

"I guess there's no alternative. But let's make certain it's absolutely necessary first." And so saying, he pulled open the storm door of my apartment and tried the front door.

It opened obediently.

I stared at the open door, feeling betrayed. "But it clicked!"

"Yeah. That was probably the storm door."

I wanted to gnash my teeth.

I had finished my second eye when I realized that my dress was still in the car. I grabbed my red coat out from under Whiskers, who had decided that if it was dumped on my bed, it could be his bed. He glared at me and I glared back. I went once again to my traitorous front door.

"Well, your eyes match," Curt said as he looked up from the magazine he was reading. *Today's Christian Woman*. I bet he was enjoying that. "But something tells me you're not quite ready yet."

"My dress is still in the car."

"I'll get it. At least I'm decent." And he grinned.

I looked down and saw that while I clutched my coat closed above the waist, below the waist the left side had caught behind me when I swung it on. The only thing I can say is that it wasn't quite as bad as if I'd caught my skirt in my panty hose.

When I finally got myself together and emerged from the bedroom in one piece, Curt let out a low wolf whistle.

Suddenly the evening looked enchanted.

I chatted happily as we drove across town, telling Curt all about Edie's troubles. "And Tom's still missing," I concluded.

Curt raised an eyebrow. "Missing?"

I nodded, grinning at him.

"I can tell by your smile that you're very concerned."

I blinked. "Of course I'm concerned." I leaned toward him and smiled again, full wattage. "I'm smiling because I'm with you," I all but purred.

This time he blinked.

City Hall was a beautiful old stone mansion. I loved the grounds with the gracious beech whose branches swept the ground like the skirts of a great lady, the towering oak that stood like a sentinel watching over the lady and the glorious magnolias whose waxen, white petals even now promised spring as they dared a frost to wither their beauty.

Curt and I stepped into the Brennan Room, tonight alive with the strange combination of anticipation and concern. Jonathan Delaney Montgomery had done a masterful job of keeping his plans for his new newspaper a secret. The *News* was but one of his papers, now numbering twenty-five, all small dailies, making him a mini Rupert Murdoch. Our concern was that he had, in fact, bought many more than twenty-five. The others had ceased to exist shortly after Montgomery's purchase.

We waited with trepidation to see which side of the ledger the *News* ended up on.

"Well, it's about time you showed up!" A thoroughly disgruntled Mac Carnuccio bulled his way through the crowd to us. His tux almost fit him, and if he'd smiled, he'd have looked quite handsome.

"And a pleasant good evening to you, too, Mac." I smiled sweetly.

Mac looked at me for a long minute, then turned to Curt. "How do you stand her? She's so stinking saccharine she gives toothaches on sight."

Curt looked at me. "I don't know, Mac. I think her smile's kind of cute." He put his arm around my shoulders and gave a gentle squeeze.

I rested my head on his shoulder for a brief moment, reveling in the fact that this marvelous, talented man loved me.

"Relax, Mac. Enjoy the evening." I smiled again, knowing it would drive him crazy. It did.

"Ditch her, Curt. Save yourself while there's still time."

"I'm afraid it's already too late."

I glowed while Mac glowered.

"No date tonight?" I asked Mac innocently. If he could jab at me, I could jab at him.

Mac snarled. "Now that woman is a case of terminal sweet if I ever saw one." He scowled at his own reflection in a window made a mirror by the dark night outside and the bright light inside. Mac astonished me with the depth of his affection for Dawn Trauber.

"You're right. She's a sweetie," I agreed.

"I got stood up for some girl who's having a baby. Can you believe that? One of the most crucial nights of my life, and she's at the hospital going, 'Breathe deeply. Now pant, two, three, four.'"

Dawn Trauber, the object of Mac's frustration, was the director of His House, a home for girls in trouble, most of whom were having babies without the benefit of marriage. Frequently Dawn was the birth coach for one of the girls, and apparently tonight was a command performance.

I laid a gentle hand on Mac's arm. "You know she'd be here if she could."

Mac looked unconvinced.

"She's crediting you with the courage and class to get through tonight on your own. She knew the girl having the baby couldn't make it, given her age and situation, but she knew you could."

"You're saying I should feel honored that I've been stood up for a baby?"

I nodded. "And I'm sure it won't be the last time." I smiled sweetly again.

Mac rolled his eyes at Curt. "It's your life, but I'm telling you, tooth decay and mind rot. Before you know it, you won't have a decent gripe to your name. She'll Pollyanna them all away."

"You're just jealous because my girl's here and yours isn't." Curt snagged a canapé from the tray going by.

Mac grabbed a couple and passed one to me. "I'm so nervous I can barely stand it."

Poor Mac. "Have you been through the receiving line yet?" I asked.

He shook his head. "I haven't had the nerve."

"Then come with us." I slipped a hand through both Curt's and Mac's arms and led the way to where Jonathan Montgomery was standing, royalty giving his beneficent nod to his adoring public.

We fell in line behind the mayor and her husband and two of the local councilmen. The politicians were delighted to meet Amhearst's newest minimogul, and everyone had a great time glad-handing. While we waited, I looked at Mac.

"Do you want this man to retain you?" I asked.

He looked at me as if I was daft.

"Then smile, for goodness' sake. Be pleasant. You may hate that he's kept you on a string ever since he purchased the paper, but it is his right."

"Yeah, yeah. I know. Dawn's been telling me the same thing for days. And she's praying." He looked confounded by the idea. "She's praying!"

"Of course she is," I said. "I've been praying too."

Mac rolled his eyes.

Curt leaned toward him. "I've been praying too."

"Aaugh! I don't know if I can stand this." Mac ran a distracted hand through his already rumpled hair. "I'm not used to religion that's every day."

"That's one reason we're praying," Curt said.

Mac just stared.

"Hello. I'm Jonathan Delaney Montgomery." A hand reached for Mac, who blinked, then rubbed his right hand quickly against his trousers. With his best smile pasted into place, he shook hands with the man who would decide his future.

"Mac Carnuccio, acting editor of the *News*. It's a pleasure to meet you, sir."

"Oh, yes, Mr. Carnuccio. I've been reading your editorials as well as studying your paper."

We all waited but the man offered no opinion, positive or negative, about Mac's work. While Mac sputtered something about loving his job, I studied Mr. Montgomery. A control freak, I decided. He wanted to keep Mac squirming as long as he could.

And then Mac was dismissed and it was my turn. I held out my hand, prepared to introduce myself.

"Mr. Montgomery." Curt reached around me. "Good to see you again, sir."

"Well, Curt, my boy. You're looking well."

While I was assimilating the fact that the love of my life knew my new boss and had neglected to mention that little fact, Curt said, "I'd like you to meet a special friend of mine, Merrileigh Kramer."

Mr. Montgomery beamed at me. "Miss Kramer, I'm pleased to meet you. Any friend of Curt's is more than welcome at this reception." He took my hand and patted it benevolently. Then he proceeded to ignore me.

"So tell me, Curt. How's the artist doing?"

"Fine, thank you."

"Delia's been telling me the same thing. You took a risk giving up your teaching, son, but it seems to be paying off."

"I do not regret my decision one bit."

"And does your little lady approve?"

With a jolt I realized he was talking about me. Little lady? What century was he born in?

Curt smiled at me. "She does."

"Has she met Delia yet?"

"Not yet. There's been no occasion."

"You'd better warn her, boy."

"When I think there's something to warn her about, Mr. Montgomery, I will."

"Don't be a fool, Curt."

Curt looked at me while I stared wide-eyed, trying to decipher the conversation. "I think I'm already a fool, sir, for beautiful eyes, mismatched or not." His smile melted my bones.

Mr. Montgomery glanced at me again to see if he'd missed something. Apparently he decided he hadn't because he looked at Curt without understanding. Then his gaze slid over Curt's shoulder, and he broke into a wide grin.

"Ah. Here she comes."

Curt's head swung in the direction of Mr. Montgomery's

look. In fact, the head of every man in the room swung in that direction, and a few of the women's heads too.

I turned and my blood chilled.

A blonde with the most perfect features I'd ever seen glided up to us, her eyes fixed on Curt. I'd seen lionesses look less predatory as they circled a wildebeest in a nature film on Animal Planet. She was dressed in black from the tiny straps of her slip dress to the toes of her four-inch stilettos. She looked sleek and sophisticated and perfect.

Suddenly I felt every one of the thirty dollars I'd paid for my dress.

"Dad," she said in a husky warm voice. She stood on tiptoe as Jonathan Montgomery leaned down to receive her kiss on the cheek. "Quite a crowd. A success, aren't we?"

Then her eyes were on Curt in a proprietary way that made me most annoyed. I was the only one allowed to look at him like that.

"And Curt." She leaned up and gave him a kiss on the cheek, leaving a perfect petal-pink imprint on his skin. She tucked her arm in his, her perfectly manicured, utterly synthetic nails resting lightly on his jacket sleeve. "How wonderful to see you again," she all but purred. "I've missed you since yesterday."

Curt smiled fatuously into her big blue eyes. After an eternity, he blinked and recalled who he'd come to the dance with.

"Delia, I'd like you to meet—"

"Curt," Delia interrupted. "I need something to drink. It was a long drive from Philadelphia, and I even closed the gallery early to make it for Dad's special night. It's all made me quite thirsty." She smiled up at him. "To say nothing of hungry. Help me out here?"

Before he knew what hit him, he was halfway across the room. He looked back over his shoulder at me and made a helpless face that was supposed to convey what-was-I-to-do? I felt like making a return face that said drop dead. The trouble was that I wanted to make it at Delia, and she was too busy fawning over Curt to deign to glance my way.

"Well, if it isn't Delia Big Deal-ia Montgomery," said an acid voice in my ear.

"Jolene!" I spun around, nearly poking Reilly in the stomach with my elbow as I did. "You know her?"

"Sure," Jolene said. "Everyone knows Delia."

Reilly nodded. "Can't say they all like her." He smiled indulgently at his wife, who looked gorgeous in a vivid red sequin-and-chiffon number. "That homecoming-queen crown was a prized treasure, you know."

"She cheated, Reilly! You know she did!" Jolene's eyes flashed and her cheeks flushed. "She got people to vote three and four times. I mean, nobody liked her. She had to buy her votes!"

"I suspect she did, Jo, my sweet. But it was a long time ago and I think it's probably time to let go of the anger, don't you?"

"Sure you do." Jolene made a face at her husband. "It wasn't you she beat."

"No, but it was me who won. I got you." And he gave his wife a bend-over-backwards kiss right in front of everyone.

For once Jolene was speechless.

Grinning at his success, Reilly turned to me. "Can I get you something to drink?"

I never got to answer him because just then I spotted Edie coming in the front door. She was pale, not quite put together and plastered.

Mac saw her and swore softly. Reilly sighed. Jo took off across the room so fast that I practically had to run to keep up with her. We got to Edie just before she took her place in the receiving line.

"Ladies' room." Jo grabbed Edie's right arm.

"Good idea." I grabbed her left.

"Hey!" Edie wasn't quite certain what was going on. "Let me go. I wanna meet Mishter Mon'gomery."

"That's what we're afraid of," I muttered.

We got Edie into the ladies' room without incident, and once in there we claimed the sofa in the anteroom. Jo and I sat on the edge of the sofa on either side of the slumping Edie.

"I take it Tom hasn't come home," Jo said.

"Or called," I added.

Two big tears rolled neatly down the pathway made on Edie's cheeks by previously melted mascara.

"Ranny tole me to stay home."

"For once, Randy was right." I patted her hand. When in doubt....

"But I need to meet the new boss." She pronounced it bosh.

"I think not," Jo said. "You want your job come Monday, don't you?"

Two more tears. "I don't care." She was deeply into self-pity. "I just came for Mac. I want him to have his job."

"That was very thoughtful." I cringed at what a drunk Edie might mean to Mac's career.

"Thoughtful, schmoughtful." Jolene stood and stared down at Edie. "If Mr. Montgomery saw you now, he'd fire Mac for hiring incompetents."

Edie drew herself up, quite a feat when you're slouching on a sofa. "I'm not incompetent."

"You couldn't prove it tonight." Jolene stalked to the sinks, grabbed a fistful of paper towels and stuck them under the cold water. Then she walked purposefully to Edie.

Poor Edie never saw it coming.

Jolene was just finishing her forceful washing of Edie's face with Edie batting ineffectually when the door opened and Delia glided in.

Everyone froze for a moment. Then my stomach dropped and my hands turned cold. Of all the people who shouldn't see Edie, it was Delia.

She smiled nastily at Edie, who was too miserable to notice. "I see you still know how to pick your friends, Jolene Marie."

"Nice to see you, too, Delia." Jolene smiled regally, as if bathing snockered friends was the posh thing to do.

Delia walked to the mirror and checked her perfect make-up. She pulled out a lip pencil and colored her already perfectly colored mouth. Satisfied, she turned to leave. She looked at us and contempt oozed from every glamorous pore.

"Did you hear that?" I demanded as the door shut.

"What?" Jo asked, staring daggers in Delia's direction.

"Her silent sniff! I never heard anything like it."

"I heard it too," Edie lay her head on the back of the sofa. "She doesn't like us." Her sniff was very audible. "Where is he?"

Both Jo and I decided to treat the question as rhetorical.

Jolene reached into her little silver evening bag and pulled out a lipstick. She rubbed some on her index finger and then rubbed her finger over Edie's pallid cheeks. She did this until Edie looked healthy again. Then she carefully put some on Edie's lips. "I don't have any mascara with me, but we can't risk her crying it all over herself again anyway."

I reached in my little black bag and pulled out a tiny metal bristled brush. "Sit up, Edie. It's hair time."

While I brushed, Jo asked. "Do you think there's coffee out there anywhere?"

"Probably not." I pulled Edie to her feet. She barely swayed. I smoothed her green dress over her hips and tugged at the hem to get it to lie smoothly. It was a bit snug, but not as snug as the skirts she usually wore to work.

Jolene circled Edie and nodded in approval. "If one of us

is always holding her elbow, I think we'll be okay. Just don't let her near Mr. Montgomery."

"But I have to meet him," Edie said.

"Now's not a good time," Jo said. "We don't want him to get mad at Mac."

"No, we don't," Edie agreed. "We want Mac."

"Shoulders back, Edie." I took her elbow. "Here we go."

We walked back to the Brennan Room, and no one but Mac and Reilly even knew we'd been gone. I snagged a Perrier with a twist of lime and handed it to Edie. She took it eagerly until she realized it was Perrier and not champagne or some such thing. As we stood in a small knot near one of the floor-to-ceiling windows, I could have sworn I saw a man with a bicycle staring in. I blinked, and the impression was gone. It was a good thing I was a teetotaler. If I saw visions stone cold sober, what would I see if I drank?

Occasionally through the interminable evening, I glimpsed Curt in the distance, always with Delia hanging on his arm. She'd look up at him with an adoring look that made my stomach clench. I was the one who gave him adoring looks. Only me.

"I hear her local gallery is having its grand opening Wednesday night," Mac said as he watched me watch her.

"Her local gallery?"

"Sure. Intimations."

I stared at Mac in dismay. "Intimations is hers?"

"You didn't know?"

"Well, no. I mean I knew about Intimations. Curt's the first show and there's the gala opening and all kinds of exciting stuff. The owner has great connections in art circles." I studied my little black bag. "I just didn't know she was Intimations."

I pulled at a loose thread until I realized I would have little black beads bouncing all over the floor if I continued. I willed myself to let the thread alone.

Mac looked across the room where Delia and Curt were talking with Mr. Montgomery. "I never did like her much when we were kids, didn't miss her at all when her mother died and they moved away right after her graduation. But I've got to admit that she's done all right for herself."

"I don't like her much as an adult," Jolene said as Delia's laughter floated above the rumble of conversation. "Look at her, hanging on to Curt like she has a right."

Curt had been so low-key about the gallery owner he'd been working closely with that I hadn't paid any attention to the fact that she was a woman. I wasn't so small-minded that I reacted negatively to the fact he was working with a woman. I mean, I work with men.

But now I'd seen the woman.

SIX

The reception at City Hall dragged on forever. Every time I heard Delia's musical laughter play its tune across the room, I stretched my smile wider to hide my hurt.

"It'll be okay, Merry," Edie whispered after one particularly charming laugh floated across the room.

I blinked back tears.

When I collected my coat, resigned to the fact that Mac would be taking me home, Curt appeared at my side.

"Ready to go?" he asked as if we'd separated a mere five minutes ago. I gave him my most haughty expression, but he merely smiled down at me. I automatically smiled back, idiot that I was. I couldn't even stay mad at the man!

But as we drove home, I regained all my spleen and then some. By the time we entered the apartment, I was primed.

"You never even told me you knew Mr. Montgomery!"

Curt sank comfortably onto the sofa where Whiskers snuggled against him, purring and shedding white fur all over his black dress pants. I started pacing, flinging my arms and ranting, the very picture of what any man would want in a woman.

"You should have told me!"

"I thought you knew that the Montgomerys used to live in

Amhearst." He looked surprised at my outburst. "You always seem to know everything at that paper of yours."

"Well, I didn't know this little tidbit."

He waved his hand in the air. "It's no big deal."

"And I suppose Delia Big Deal-ia Montgomery is no big deal either?" Just thinking about her raised my internal temperature several degrees.

Suddenly it dawned on him that I was genuinely angry. And hurt. He looked at me cautiously. "Maybe."

"Maybe she's a big deal? Maybe?" I gave him the most scathing look I could manage. It was quite a stretch for the Saccharine Queen.

"Well, of course she's important."

"Ha! I knew it!"

He backtracked. "Well, not important important, of course. Not like you. Just sort of important. Merely a professional contact."

I glared at him. "Intimations. Intimations. What kind of a stupid name is that for an art gallery? Sounds like Imitations."

"I think the idea is 'intimations of greatness.'"

"Oh." Wouldn't you know there was logic behind that ridiculous name, and I'd been too blind to see it?

"Merry, honey, you're overreacting here. There's no need to get all in a huff."

"You think not?" I huffed. "You ignored me all evening!"

"I didn't."

"I had to spend the entire reception with Mac!"

He ran a frustrated hand through his hair, tumbling it into delicious curls. "I should have left you on the front porch in your undies."

"It would have been less embarrassing."

"What?" Suddenly he was standing, towering over me. "You're saying I'm an embarrassment?"

"Yes! No! Not you. Your absence."

"I wasn't absent! I was right there!"

"But not with me!" I clenched my teeth against my tears. He stared at me for a minute. "This is an idiotic conversation."

"It is not idiotic! It's important!"

"So I talked with Delia. Big deal!"

"You are so dense," I shouted. "If you can't figure out why I'm upset, then I don't want to talk about it anymore. And I don't want to talk to you anymore!"

I grabbed my coat and stalked to the front door. "Don't worry. I have my keys this time." And I stormed out.

I stomped to my car and drove off into the night. I did not have to put up with a man who had no sense of how he'd hurt me. I did not.

I was three blocks from home when it dawned on me that I had stormed out of my own apartment, leaving Curt behind with the warmth, light, food and comfort, to say nothing of Whiskers. I felt the flush of embarrassment envelop my entire body. Now I was not only furious and deeply hurt; I was mortified.

I pulled up to a stop sign and sat, trying to decide what to do now. A beep from a car behind me pulled me from my blue funk. I drove around a bit more, trying to find a graceful way out of my situation. I finally admitted I had only two basic choices. I could drive around all night, or I could go home.

The first was stupid; the second was humiliating.

I sighed. I pictured Curt and Whiskers, lying together on the sofa, eyes closed, gentle snores mingling harmoniously. It was such a peaceful scene.

I, on the other hand, was driving around town with no place to go, lonely and alone.

Dear God, what's wrong with me? How could I have done something this stupid?

I heard Stephanie Bauer say, as clearly as if she were sitting next to me, "The power of choice."

What choice, Father? He left me alone all evening!

"The power of choice."

I didn't deserve that humiliation, Father.

"The power of choice."

But I have the right to feel upset.

"The power of choice."

Yeah, yeah, yeah. You're saying that I can't choose how Curt will act, but I can choose how I act, right?

I sighed. I had chosen to put the worst possible spin on the evening. So Curt had left me alone. It wasn't very polite, it was embarrassing and it hurt me. But had he meant for me to feel these emotions?

In all honesty I had to admit that he had not. I had chosen to be embarrassed, to be jealous and nasty. I had chosen to be more concerned about my image and my evening than about Curt's professional opportunities.

Not that I didn't recognize that Delia was trolling for Curt, her hook cleverly hidden in the lure of a showing. But Curt had never given me any cause to doubt his affection for me. In fact he had declared it openly in front of Delia's father.

The truth, dear Father, is that I'm afraid. She's gorgeous. She comes from money. She has two galleries that can help Curt immensely. Why would he want me when he can have her?

"The power of choice."

So I choose to let my fear overwhelm me and make me do crazy things like run out of my own apartment. Or I choose to trust You and him.

I turned into the parking area beside my apartment, pulling in next to Curt's car. Thank goodness he was still here. A little of my tension drained away.

I squared my shoulders and walked to my door, pausing to

peek in the window. Curt and Whiskers were together on the sofa, but they weren't sleeping. At least Curt wasn't. He was stroking the cat who looked like he'd died and gone to heaven. Curt himself was staring into space, a frown on his brow.

I knew I had to apologize for my infantile behavior, but I now condemned myself so strongly that I couldn't imagine him forgiving me. I reached for the door and pushed it open. Curt must have vaulted off the sofa the minute he heard me touch the knob because he met me on the welcome mat. He grabbed me in a great hug.

"I'm sorry." I started to cry. "I'm sorry."

"No, sweetheart. It was me. You were right. I did ignore you. Please forgive me."

"But I was so nasty about it."

"But I should never have spent all that time with Delia. It was your night."

"Well, I should have been more understanding of how important she is to you and your career."

He pulled back and looked at me with a little half smile. "Now we're going to argue about who's the sorriest?"

"Yes." I snuggled close. "And I win. But you can be a close second if you want."

He laughed, led me to the overstuffed chair and sat, pulling me into his lap. He wrapped his arms around me again, coat and all.

We sat quietly like that for a few minutes.

"I was afraid," I finally whispered.

I felt him start. Whatever he'd expected, it wasn't this. "Afraid?"

"Of Delia."

His arms tightened. "Why?"

"She's beautiful!"

"She's attractive. You're beautiful."

"She's rich."

He shrugged. "You have a wealth of character."

I looked up at him. "You can say that after my performance tonight?"

He ran his knuckle gently down my cheek. "Everybody has little aberrations now and then."

"It's just she's part of your world in a way I can never be." I felt the fear flood me again. I clutched his arm. "That terrifies me."

He nodded. "She is part of my professional life, that's true. But you, my Merry, *are* my life, my heart."

"Oh, Curt." I cried into his pleated shirt.

He ran his hand over my hair. "I sat here after you left and thought about my life before and after you came along. I thought about you and your gallant heart, always out to right a wrong or write the best story or fix some problem."

"You think I have a gallant heart?" What a wonderful thing to say.

"And then I thought of all you've brought to my life."

I thought of all I'd brought too. "Stress, arguments, possessiveness, pettiness. Poor Curt."

"Shh, sweetheart." He laid his finger across my lips. "I'm trying to give you some compliments here."

I nodded and rested against his shoulder. "What have I brought you?"

"Joy. You make me laugh. I hadn't laughed for several years before you came along. And excitement. There's always something happening around you. And ulcers. All the excitement, you know."

"Ulcers!" I sat up and mock-glared at him.

He grinned and pulled me back against him. "See? Humor, too. And love." His voice became tender. "Most importantly, you've given me love."

After a few quiet minutes, I whispered, "I do love you."

"I know. And I love you." He looked at me solemnly. "You know what that means, don't you?"

His face was so serious I couldn't begin to guess what was on his mind. "What?"

He laid his hand on my cheek. "It means you're going to have to trust me, darlin' girl."

He knew how to go right to the heart of the matter. I sighed and nodded. "'Love always protects, always trusts, always hopes, always perseveres. Love never fails.'"

He nodded. "'Always trusts.'"

"But she's got her cap set for you, Curt."

He made a face. "I know. It's very awkward. But the show at Intimations is important. The invitations are out." He took my hand in his. "It'll only be four more days."

I lifted his hand to my lips and kissed each of his fingers. One for each day. "Only four."

I tamped down hard on the fear that threatened to gnaw holes in my trust.

Day One, Sunday, was a quiet day. I went to church and sat shoulder to shoulder with Curt. We were about to stand for the opening song when I felt a presence at the edge of our pew. In disbelief I looked at Mac standing there. He'd come to church three or four times since Christmas Eve and always with Dawn. Now he was alone. We slid over to make room for him.

"I don't know any of these songs," he grumbled during the opening bars of the first song.

"Then listen and learn," I encouraged.

"When they look in the Bible, I can never find where they are."

"Use the table of contents in the front."

"What do I do if there's Communion? Am I allowed to take

it? How do you do it here? Do you go up front or do they pass it? Never mind. I'll just sit it out if they have it. Then I can't offend anyone. Unless sitting it out offends someone. What do you think?" If he hadn't been so serious, he would have been comical in his extreme distress.

Curt looked at him with understanding. "Dawn's still at the hospital, isn't she?"

Mac clenched his jaw. "Long labor."

Just then Dawn appeared at the end of the pew. The transformation in Mac was immediate and amazing. Gone was the frown, the grousing, the tension. He smiled, he relaxed, he looked happy. Curt and I looked at each other and rolled our eyes.

After church the four of us went out for dinner.

"It was amazing." Dawn's brown eyes glowed. "I don't know how many times I've coached one of these kids through the birth, but every time is a miracle."

"Boy or girl?" I asked.

"A little girl with a headful of hair. Allison Ann. A very pretty baby."

"Aren't all babies pretty?" Mac asked.

Dawn looked at him with a wry smile. "They're pruney and red and their heads are misshapen."

Mac looked surprised. "When I see babies, they look pretty good. They all look the same, but they look okay."

"Then you've never seen them early on. You've been too long a bachelor, guy."

"Yeah." Mac looked at her with his heart in his eyes. "That may be true."

Dawn stood. "Excuse me. I need to visit the ladies' room."

"Isn't she beautiful?" Mac said as he watched her walk away. "Inside too."

"I didn't know you were looking for inside beauty in a woman." I smiled. When I'd first met Mac, I thought of him as Mac the Lecher and was careful to keep him at arm's length. "You're developing depth."

Mac pointed a finger at me. "She's smiling again. She's always smiling. It's unnatural."

Curt looked at me. "Not always. She can get pretty feisty when she wants to. Why just last ni—"

"Dawn smiles a lot," I interrupted. Mac didn't need any information about my unseemly fit of pique last night. He'd just throw it up at me later.

"Yeah," Mac agreed, readily forgetting whatever Curt was about to say. "But she's beautiful when she smiles."

"And I'm chopped liver?" But the man was so obviously smitten that I couldn't take offense.

"Do you know that she won't sleep with me?" He was genuinely astounded. "I mean, what is this? Everyone sleeps around. Just my luck I've fallen for the only girl on the planet who believes in premarital chastity."

"Not the only one," Curt said.

Mac looked at me. "You too?"

I nodded. "Me too." I pointed my finger at Curt. "Him too."

Mac stared at Curt. "What?"

"Me too," Curt said.

"Well, sure, if she won't."

Curt shook his head. "Not just because of Merry. I've always held that position."

Mac was incredulous. "You've never?"

We both shook our heads.

"But why not? Is there something wrong with you? I mean, who's it hurting?"

"There's nothing wrong with me, believe me," Curt said, grinning at me in a way that curled my toes. "I take this position because it's the Bible's position."

"Amazing." Mac shook his head. "I'm hanging around

with a bunch of throwbacks to the Victorian era. And I'm doing it on purpose."

"Why?" I asked.

He looked at Curt and me. Then he glanced toward the ladies' room. "You two I'm not sure about, but her?" He grinned. "I can't believe I'm saying this, but she's even worth a second virginity."

Wow! I wondered if Dawn knew her power.

When our salads arrived, she still wasn't back.

"Let me go get her," I said. "You guys can start if you want."

Curt shook his head as Mac picked up his fork. "We'll wait."

"Right." Mac quickly set down his fork. "It's only polite."

I found Dawn in the ladies' room staring at nothing. "Are you okay?"

She shook her head. "Not really. I'm scared."

"About what?" But I knew.

"Mac."

"He's crazy about you."

She smiled ruefully. "And I'm glad. That's what scares me."

I clicked my tongue against my teeth. "Dawn, you two don't have anything in common, certainly nothing important like faith."

She nodded. "Tell me something I don't know. He comes to church once in a blue moon, and he thinks that makes him 'religious.' He's got no concept of real faith. He thinks I go overboard, but he's willing to overlook it." She spun around, her sweet face full of anguish. "I don't want someone who's noble enough to *overlook* my faith. I want someone who shares it with me like Curt does with you."

Of course she did. Who wouldn't? "But you care a lot for Mac anyway?"

She nodded. "Too much. When I made that crack about him being a bachelor too long, I saw his face. And it reflected my heart." Her chin began to tremble. "I'm really scared, Merry."

I gave her a hug, giving her my patented pat on the back. *I'm scared for you too*, I thought.

She pulled free and turned to the mirror, checking under her eyes to make certain her teary moment hadn't made her mascara run.

"Now listen," I said. "We've got to get back out there. Dinner'll be on the table any minute, and the guys are going to start wondering what happened to us. But before we go, I've got a piece of advice. I spent six years dating the wrong guy before I met Curt. Six years. Don't make the same mistake, Dawn. The longer you see him, the harder it will be to let go."

"What if I can't let go?" Her voice was a whisper.

The romantic in me wanted to say, "Then hang on for all you're worth. It'll all work out for the best." Instead the realist in me spoke. "Never underestimate the power of choice. You can let go if you must. You tell that to the girls at His House all the time. You can't do any less than you ask of them."

She nodded. "I know." Tears sat in her eyes again. "But he's so wonderful!"

I thought about the Mac I knew and wonderful wasn't the word I'd choose. Crabby, demanding, driven, clever. But wonderful? No.

"Dawn, he'll only make you very unhappy."

She sighed. "But he's a great kisser."

I wanted to laugh at her expression, but I didn't. "That's because he's had so much practice."

She looked at me, hurt that I'd say such a thing. But it was all too true, and she needed to remember that.

"Dawn, you're a woman who has spent her whole adult life in ministry. Serving God has been your priority. You can't sell out for Mac. For that matter, you can't sell out for anyone!"

She closed her eyes. "You're right. I can't."

We were quiet for a moment. Then she straightened her spine. "Come on. Let's go eat."

I followed her to the table and watched Mac's face light up when he saw her. I could only imagine her expression.

Dinner was almost over when Mac pointed his fork at me. "I almost forgot. I got a phone call about you late yesterday."

"About me?" I laughed. "Good or bad?"

"Bad."

I blinked, surprised.

"I'm to keep you reined in, or the *News* will be the object of the biggest lawsuit we've ever seen."

SEVEN

I shook my head in disgust. "I know who the caller was."

"Good." Mac attacked his baked potato. "Then you can tell me. It was an anonymous call."

"I'm not surprised. He's a coward. His name's Bill, Tina Somebody's husband."

"Tina Somebody's husband." Mac looked at Curt. "And she wonders why I have to correct her copy before it makes the paper."

"There's nothing wrong with my copy and you know it." I cut the final section of my stuffed chicken breast into three neat pieces. "Tina is a woman I met at Freedom House yesterday. Well, I didn't meet her there exactly, but Stephanie put us in contact."

"Stephanie Bauer?" Dawn asked. "Isn't she great?"

"Yeah, yeah, she's great," said Mac, who had never met her. "But who's Tina?"

"A battered wife. I helped her move out yesterday and drove her to her parents'."

"And her husband came home and found her gone and somehow knew you were the culprit?" Mac asked.

I shook my head. "He was there when she left."

"You moved her out in front of the husband?" Mac was appalled. Curt didn't look any happier.

"Well, someone had to help her."

"Where are your brains, woman? What if he'd had a weapon?" Mac asked.

I shrugged. "Someone still needed to help her."

"Have you ever heard of the police?"

"It was for my story!"

"Oh." Mac was instantly mollified. "Okay."

"Wait a minute here," Curt said, veal cutlet halted halfway to his mouth. "It's okay for her to risk her life for a story?"

Mac raised his hand to quiet Curt. "But there wasn't any danger. She said he didn't have a weapon."

"She did?" It was Dawn. "I didn't hear her say that."

I laid my knife and fork carefully across my plate. "Listen, all of you. I will tell you what happened. But first I will tell you that I can make decisions about my safety on my own. Got it?"

I looked around the table, pausing as I looked at Curt. He and I had had "discussions" in the past about what he considered the risks I took in my work.

"Got it?" I repeated as I looked at him.

He looked grim but he nodded. "Got it."

I gave him a huge smile and said, "I think it's a matter of trust."

His eyes narrowed as I threw his own words back at him. He looked like he wanted to argue, and well he could. Trusting someone to remain faithful was a far cry from trusting someone not to get injured in the line of duty, especially when a second volatile person was involved.

I began talking quickly to forestall him. "Tina called Freedom House while I was there. She needed help. I helped her. Her husband was unhappy with me. He called Mac. End of story."

"How do you know that?" Curt demanded. "You don't even know his name, but he knows yours and where you work. It's a short step to finding where you live. And he's got a history of being violent."

"Only toward Tina."

"You know this for sure?"

I didn't. "If he calls again, we'll get worried, okay? In the meantime, I want chocolate truffle for dessert."

When we left the restaurant, we split up, Mac and Dawn each to their own cars and their own homes, Curt and I to his car.

"Let's drive up to Hibernia Park." I buckled my seat belt. "I need information about the mansion for my Great Homes article."

He looked uncertain. "I've got so much to do before Wednesday night's opening."

"What's an hour?" I leaned over and gave him a quick kiss on the cheek.

"Okay," he said. "But just a quick trip."

I tried not to feel guilty as we drove through the warm Palm Sunday sunshine and turned into the park between the white pillars with the lion heads embedded in them. We drove up the winding narrow road past the whitewashed cottages, some occupied, one boarded shut, over Birch Run Creek and past the fishing pond. We rounded the sharp S curve, and there sat the mansion, its coppery peach stucco a soft flame in the sunshine.

"Wouldn't it be fun to live in a place like that?"

"If you had lots of servants," Curt said practically.

We walked around the mansion with its slate front steps bordered by boxwood, its quarter-round turrets cuddled against the wings on either side of the main house, and I took lots of pictures. The white trim and red metal roof made the unusual color of the house more vibrant. I was disappointed the house was closed to visitors today.

We walked hand in hand to the beige building over the rise behind the mansion where the ranger's office was. Inside on the counter lay a collection of brochures on various features of the park, including one on the mansion. I picked it up and began reading.

I learned there had been an ironworks on the property from the 1790s to the 1870s. At the height of the ironworks there had been two iron forges, two heating furnaces, a rolling mill, a gristmill and at least sixteen men and boys working the facility.

I was impressed and turned to Curt to comment when a man in jeans and a flannel shirt walked in. "Yo," he called toward the offices in the back of the building.

A ranger walked out from his office. "Hey, Witt."

"We've got a visitor," Witt said.

The ranger glanced at Curt and me. "We've got lots of visitors."

Witt looked at us and shook his head. "This one's staying."

"As in overnight?"

I knew the park gates closed at dusk, so overnight stays were illegal.

"Pete found blood in the men's restroom early yesterday morning. He cleaned up the mess yesterday, but there was more today."

"A couple of visitors cut themselves."

Witt shook his head. "Not that badly two days in a row. We're talking lots of blood and bloody bandages, not Band-Aids. And Andy's lunch disappeared yesterday. And someone slept in the maintenance barn last night."

The ranger nodded. "I'll contact the police."

I grabbed Curt and dragged him from the office. "Do you think it's Tom?"

"The bleeding man? Of course not. If Tom were hurt, he'd go to the hospital."

"What if he stole the money?"

"Why would he hide here? He'd run."

"Maybe he's waiting for Edie to join him?"

Curt looked at me with his bemused I-can't-believe-you-said-that look. "Are you sure you don't want to be a mystery novelist instead of a journalist?" He glanced at his watch and grimaced. "Come on. I've got to get going."

I sighed and let him drive me home. It would have been such a great story even if I did feel guilty for suggesting it, like I'd betrayed Edie.

It was after four when I rang her doorbell. While I waited for someone to answer, I studied the daffodils nodding among the yews. Their heads bobbed in the soft breeze in time to a tune only Mother Nature heard.

I bent to the closest cluster and broke off a stem close to the ground, then another and another. I broke off some of the long, slender leaves too.

I was back on the porch with a fistful of yellow sunshine when the front door finally opened. "Hi, Randy."

He wasn't happy to see me. "I take it you want something besides my mother's flowers?"

"They're for your mother to cheer her up a bit." I smiled at him warmly. If I could drive Mac nuts with my smile, maybe I could do the same thing to Randy. "How's she doing?" I sounded as chirpy as a spring robin.

He shrugged and stepped reluctantly aside. My smile seemed to do nothing to him, good or bad. Oh, well. You can't win them all.

Edie was lying on the great blue couch much as she'd been the other night. Her face was a mask of misery with dark circles under her closed eyes and the lines from her nose to her chin deep and cruel. She huddled under the same blanket I'd gotten for her Friday. If I hadn't seen her last night, I'd have thought she hadn't moved since the body was discovered.

As usual I wanted to fix her hurt, and this time I truly had no idea how.

"Hey, Edie." I kept my voice soft in case she was asleep.

She wasn't. She turned to me immediately, hope in her eyes. When she saw it was only me, the hope died. Irrationally, I felt guilty.

"For you." I held out the sunshine I'd picked from her yard.

She took the bouquet and stared at it as if she'd never seen a daffodil before.

"I thought you might like some cheer." I grinned in what I hoped was an encouraging manner.

She smiled faintly. "I think I had too much of that yesterday, didn't I? Did I make too big a fool of myself?"

I knew she referred to her tipsy condition of last evening. "I've seen you in better shape," I said gently. "But no harm was done."

"Only because you guys took care of me."

"That's what friends do. Shall I put the daffodils in some water for you?" I took the flowers from her unresisting hand. "And while I'm in the kitchen, why don't I get you something to eat?"

"Not hungry."

"I'm sure, but that's not the issue. Have you eaten today?"

She frowned. "I don't know."

"She hasn't had anything." It was Randy. I hadn't realized he was still lurking in the doorway.

"But I haven't had anything to drink either." She turned her head and skewered her son with a sudden, fierce gaze. "Randy threw it all away."

The boy immediately began to excuse his actions. "Having a thief for a stepfather is bad enough. I'm not going to have a mom who kills herself and someone else driving drunk."

I realized with surprise that he was genuinely concerned about Edie beneath his facade of ridicule.

"You know, Randy," I couldn't resist saying. "It's okay to do nice things for people."

He looked at me as if I had a second or third head, made a disgusted noise deep in his throat and walked out.

I reminded myself that he'd had some rough knocks in life. He had the right to be testy.

The power of choice.

I promptly reversed my opinion. If the legal system could do it, so could I. Randy did not have the right to be difficult. All he had was the right to choose. And he was choosing wrong.

I turned back to Edie. "Do you have any chicken broth or instant soup?"

"I don't want anything."

"I'm sure you don't, but you're going to get it."

I found some Lipton's instant chicken noodle soup and heated it in the microwave. While it heated, I filled a vase and arranged the daffodils. Somehow they looked like pencils stuck in a jar, all weird angles and no grace. Sighing, I took the flowers into the living room and put them on an end table where Edie could see them.

I brought her the steaming cup of soup and a plate of saltines. "Sit up and drink."

She looked at me without moving, rebellion strong in her eyes.

"Edie, sit up. It won't be good if Tom comes home and finds you sick."

She pulled herself upright, grabbed the cup and took a small sip. She frowned as it burned her tongue, but she kept sipping. "I guess I was hungry after all." She inhaled a couple of saltines. Eventually the cup was empty and most of the saltines gone.

I took the empty cup and went back to the kitchen. I rinsed it and put it in the dishwasher.

"Did she eat anything?" Randy asked from behind me.

I turned and studied him. Because of my strong desire to

please people and fix everything, I had trouble comprehending someone like Randy, someone who purposely chose to hurt.

"What's the matter with you?" His tone was ice.

"Nothing. And yes, she ate. She had a cup of soup."

"Um." He turned to leave. "She wouldn't eat for me."

I tried to imagine a conversation in which Randy demanded Edie eat and she refused. The mind boggled.

"I'm assuming you've heard nothing from William," I said as I sat in my cushy chair across the room from Edie.

She shook her head. "Not a word. Now I wonder if I want to hear."

"Don't you want to know what's happened? I've always thought not knowing was terrible, worse than knowing, even when the information's bad."

"If the possible information was that your husband was dead, you don't want to hear."

"Do you really think he's dead, Edie?"

She slid back down on the sofa, and though her color was still bad, she looked more alert. The soup had been good for her.

"I've been lying here all day, thinking about just that question. One minute I think, of course he's not dead. If I had my heart torn out, I'd certainly know. Then I think, no, I wouldn't know. I'm not clairvoyant. I'm just a wife who loves her husband." She raised a shaky hand to her forehead and rubbed.

"Headache?" I asked.

"You wouldn't believe."

"Can I get you some Tylenol or aspirin?"

"Would you? Now that I've eaten the soup, I think my stomach can handle it."

"Where will I find them?"

"Upstairs in the bathroom off our bedroom. On the second shelf in the medicine cabinet."

I climbed the stairs and walked down the hall, carpeted

in nondescript, inexpensive beige, past two bedrooms and a bath. It wasn't hard to identify which room was Randy's. The door was open, and I could see every electronic device known to man or teen: wall-mounted plasma TV, CD system with the latest speakers and a collection of CDs that would make any disc jockey in the country drool, a computer with a slim monitor, a laser printer, a DVD player and a stack of DVDs, controls for computer games, a cordless phone, a scanner and an iPod. I even thought I saw a fax machine on his desk, though I couldn't imagine why a kid needed a fax machine.

Edie and Tom's room was at the end of the hall. I followed the beige carpeting across their bedroom to the bath. The cabinet hung above a small pedestal sink, and I easily found the Tylenol on the second shelf, just like Edie had said.

When I hurried back into the bedroom, I flinched and ducked as I saw someone rushing at me. Even after I realized I was looking at myself reflected in the mirrored doors of the closet, it took a while for my heart to stop pounding. Downstairs I went to the kitchen to get water for Edie. Her drinking glasses were just like mine, a blue-light special from Kmart.

Excess in the living room and dining room. Low budget in the rest of the house, Randy's room excepted. I frowned. Somehow Edie didn't strike me as the type to flaunt luxury in the rooms people saw when they visited. Tom either. Strange.

"I scared myself in your mirrored closet," I said as I returned to the living room and handed her the water and pills.

"Tell me. I scare myself every time I get up during the night. Tom likes them though." She smiled to herself. "He says he likes seeing multiples of me, if you can imagine that."

"That's so sweet."

She looked at me, smile gone. "You know, Tom has never told me if he has any brothers or sisters."

"Oh." I didn't know what else to say.

"Once when he was almost asleep and very relaxed, I asked him where he went to high school. Without thinking, he said he graduated from Audubon High School, hooray for the green and the gold. But every other time he was willing to talk about the past, he said he was from Camden. Later he denied he'd ever mentioned Audubon. I looked up Audubon and Camden on a map. Audubon is a town in New Jersey not too far from Camden, but you'd never live in one place and go to school in the other."

She closed her eyes and a tear ran down her cheek. "I don't understand what's going on."

Soon she was asleep. I stayed curled in my chair, thinking. I stood by my original sentiment that Tom loved Edie deeply. I could think of no good reason he wasn't calling home, and I could think of several bad ones.

Lord, if he's still alive, take care of him, okay? And let him come home safely. Please.

I heard Randy rummaging around in the kitchen and assumed he was making himself something to eat. Good for him. Maybe I had been misjudging him, and he would turn into a decent human being after all.

"There's nothing in this house to eat," he bellowed.

Nope, I hadn't been wrong after all. I ran to the kitchen. "Quiet! Your mother's sleeping."

"Like I care." He stalked down the front hall and out the door. I followed and watched out a window as he disappeared around the corner on his bike.

Did he often take off like that without saying where he was going?

My father always said, "Your mother and I tell you where we're going. You tell us where you're going. I don't care how old you are. Families talk."

At least some families talked.

When the wall phone in the kitchen rang, I raced to grab it before Edie awoke. "Hello?"

A man's voice growled in my ear. "If you say anything to the cops, I'll get you too."

"What?" I could barely push the word out of my throat.

"You heard me. I'll blow you away too. Just like your old man."

When the dial tone buzzed in my ear, I missed the cradle the first time I tried to seat the receiver. The second time I succeeded. I leaned against the wall and shuddered.

"Who was that?" Edie stood in the doorway, her face filled with the warring emotions of hope and fear.

"It wasn't Tom. I'm sure of that." I shuddered again. "But whoever it was sounded nasty." I dialed *69 to see what number the call had been placed from.

"This is your return call service. The last number that called is unavailable." Disappointed, I hung up.

"It was a threat?" Edie looked shocked.

"Big-time. We need to call William." I dialed his number.

"What happened?" he demanded. "Tom?"

"No. A threatening phone call. I tried *69. Nothing. Can you trace it another way?"

"We probably can't do much," William said. "Edie needs to call the phone company and get a special Call Trace account set up. If he calls again, we'll at least have a better chance."

I knew this service traced calls of an obscene or threatening nature, recording the number at the phone company where the police could obtain it. Edie herself would not be given the number.

"Let's go into the living room." I wanted to put off telling her the content of the call. "We can wait for William there."

She looked me in the eye. "What did the caller say?"

"He threatened me, though of course he thought he was talking to you."

"And he said?"

I knew I had to tell her. "'If you say anything to the cops, I'll get you too.'"

Edie lost what little color she had. "Too? He said too?"

I nodded.

"Was that all?"

I shook my head. "I said, 'What?' and he said, 'You heard me. I'll blow you away too. Just like your old man.'"

"Just like—" Edie gave a low groan and started to sway. I caught her just before she collapsed.

I laid her on the floor and ran to the sink. I grabbed a towel that lay on the counter, wet it and hurried back to her. I placed it on her forehead, grabbed her hand and began to rub.

Her eyes fluttered. "What hap—?" Then memory hit. "He's dead. Tom's dead." Tears filled her eyes.

"We don't know that."

"But you said—"

"I know what I said, but I don't know that he knew what he was talking about. Maybe he's just trying to scare you."

She pulled the cloth off her forehead with a shaking hand and sat up. "Well, he succeeded." She used the cloth to wipe her face. "I don't think I've ever been so terrified, not even with Randolph."

With Randolph? How did he get into the conversation?

She looked at me with sad eyes. "Tom's never going to come home."

"Edie! Don't say that."

"Don't ask me how I know, but I do. Tom Whatley's never going to come home."

EIGHT

I knew something was up as soon as I walked into the newsroom on Monday. The air pulsed with awed wonder.

"What's going on?" I asked Larry, the sports guy. He was standing by his desk staring in mute fascination toward the big picture window.

I saw nothing unusual. "Window cleaners are coming? The pigeons are having an open house and have invited us out to their sill? The African violets are being resettled?"

"Look again."

I studied the window and the windowsill and still saw nothing. My eyes drifted casually to the right to Mac's desk. "Oh, my!"

Larry looked at me with a raised eyebrow. "That's a mild expletive for the radical nature of the situation."

"As a nonswearer, I rarely get rawer than that."

"Remind me not to take you into the locker room after the home team has lost." Larry flopped into his chair, still staring. "Something big is up. The question is what."

I continued to study Mac's desk. It was neat for the first time since he'd become acting editor. "Does it mean he's been fired? Or does it mean he's trying to make a good impression? Or does it mean he's lost what little sanity he had?"

"He'll never find anything now. We'll be subject to fits of temper unlike any the human race has ever seen."

"You looking at something?" Mac asked softly from directly behind us.

I spun around, my face red as I recalled my crack about his sanity. I refused to even recall Larry's comment. I decided attack was my best defense. "It's bad enough when Randy sneaks up on me. You don't have to do it too!"

He studied me for a minute as I glared at him. "I think I like you better grumpy than smiley."

"Ha, ha." I opened my bottom desk drawer and dropped my leather shoulder bag inside. "How did you accomplish the cleanup between Saturday, when I last saw the indescribable mess, and this morning? And more importantly, why?"

He grinned. "I had help."

That grin could mean only one thing. "You asked Dawn to neaten up your desk? I thought you liked her."

"When she heard Mr. Montgomery was coming in today, she volunteered to help me. We spent yesterday afternoon working. Together."

I couldn't decide which concerned me more, Mr. Montgomery's impending visit or Mac's continuing infatuation with Dawn and its effect on her.

"Montgomery's coming to the newsroom?" Larry sat up straight, all nerves and rattled energy. It was obvious what was his major concern. "When? Maybe I've got time to organize my desk too."

We all looked at Larry's working space with its dog-eared books of statistics and well-read sports magazines, Internet printouts, handwritten notes, professional team mugs with dried coffee crusts and a new box of doughnuts that he might or might not choose to share. Then we looked at each other and shook our heads. Not a chance.

"But it's okay," I assured Larry. "Your job's not hanging by a thread."

"As is that of someone else we all know and love," announced Jolene as she plopped her handbag down on her desk and opened the Waterloo Gardens paper bag she had been holding carefully by the handles. She lifted out a basket of small flowering plants: primroses, tiny mums, tête-à-tête daffodils, grape hyacinths and cyclamen.

"Oh, Jolene." I stared at the basket, as bright as the spring it heralded, and promptly forgot all about Mr. Montgomery. "How beautiful. Did you arrange it?" I glanced at her face and knew by the satisfied look she wore that she had indeed clustered the flowers together and draped the graceful, airy Spanish moss around the edges to hide any holes or pots careless enough to show.

Mac studied the basket. "Not bad."

"Not bad?" She glared at Mac. "What do you mean, not bad?"

"It's great is what it is," he said hurriedly.

"Right answer. Now put it on the corner of your desk and maybe Mr. Montgomery won't notice the mess." She stopped cold. "Where's the mess?"

Mac reached for the basket. "How did you know Mr. Montgomery was coming today?"

"I didn't. I just knew that if I were deciding whether to keep you or fire you, I'd come see you in action. Now we'd better get to work, so that when he comes in, it looks like we actually do things around here."

The door at the back of the newsroom opened and we all spun, expecting to see Mr. Montgomery come to catch us all at our leisure. We breathed a collective sigh of relief when it was only Edie.

She looked terrible. Her face was pale, her eyes were puffy

and her skirt actually fit, a sure sign that she wasn't eating. I was willing to bet she hadn't had anything since the cup of soup I made her eat yesterday afternoon.

I hurried over to her, Jo right behind me.

"No word from Tom yet?" I asked.

She closed her eyes as if in pain.

"Edie." Mac held out the basket of flowers. "Take these and go home. You don't need to be here today."

"Please let me stay." Her face was desperate. "Please."

Mac blinked. "Sure you can stay. Whatever's best for you."

I was proud of him for his kindness. Sometimes I actually liked Mac a lot.

He still held out the flowers, ignoring Jolene's accusing look. "These can cheer up your desk."

She looked at them, then turned her head. "They look too much like something you might get if someone died."

I didn't think they looked like that at all, but I understood that she was terrified Tom was dead. I could hear her saying to me yesterday with desperate conviction, "Tom's never going to come home."

Poor Edie.

Wisely Mac took the basket and went to his desk, where he set it on the corner. Between the African violets on the sill and the basket on the desk, he looked like he was lost in a flowering jungle. He sat down and stared in bewilderment at his neat desk.

I thought Larry might turn out to be right about coming temper tantrums.

Edie went to her seat and began moving papers around. Jolene and I watched her out of the corners of our eyes, but she seemed all right. Gradually we relaxed and went about our own business. We did have a nine o'clock deadline.

First I called the police station for the latest on the body in

Randy's car. William wasn't in and wouldn't be until the afternoon. I spoke with Jeb Lammey, the cop who served as their press liaison and PR specialist.

"Nothing yet, Merry," he said. "We've sent fingerprints to AFIS—that's the FBI, you know—but who knows how long it will take to hear. It depends on how busy they are. And that's assuming the guy's prints are on file to begin with."

I turned my back to Edie and said as softly as I could, "What about Tom Whatley? Any word?"

"Nothing there either. We're making inquiries."

Ah, those all-encompassing, ever-convenient inquiries.

"Any idea why the man was in the Whatleys' garage?"

"None whatsoever."

"Jeb, you're not making this very easy for me, you know."

He laughed. "If it's hard for you, imagine what it's like for us! We have to find the answers. You only have to write about them."

We hung up, and I wrote a story that depended heavily on Jeb's quotes about the Automated Fingerprint Identification System.

The business of comparing the arches, loops, and/or whorls from the fingers of John Doe to the millions found in the FBI computer was amazingly quick, but requests for assistance from AFIS came from all over the world. On a busy weekend, a request might be one of hundreds and would have to take its place in line. When several similar prints were finally found by the computers at AFIS, the possibilities would be examined by a fingerprint expert. The final identification had to be made by human eyes.

I even ended up writing about Randy's birthday car, a gift from his father, damaged before it was even driven. How sad. I think I kept my personal feelings about a gift of this magnitude out of the article. I certainly meant to.

I reread my copy, pushed the right buttons and sent my stuff to Mac in his flowering jungle for approval and editing.

It was shortly after nine when I found time to call Tina at her parents' home.

"I'm just checking to see how you're doing."

"We're doing all right." Her voice was hesitant.

I leaned back in my chair, frowning. "What's wrong?"

"He came last night."

"Your husband? To your parents' house?"

"Yeah. He wanted to make me and the kids come home."

"Obviously he didn't." *Thank you, Lord.*

"But my father's in the hospital."

"Oh, Tina! What happened?"

She gave a little sob. "When he grabbed me, my father tried to stop him. Bill pushed him."

"What happened? Did your dad fall?"

"No. He had a heart attack."

I closed my eyes, wishing I could make all of Tina's pain go away. "Will he be all right?"

"We don't know." She took a huge shuddering breath. "Mom's at the hospital now, but I had to come home because of the kids. Oh, Merry, he's such a good man!" I assumed she meant her father, not her husband. "It's all my fault! I should have just stayed at home. I should have. Then Dad'd be all right and Mom wouldn't be crying and everything would be fine."

"Except it wouldn't be fine, Tina. You know that. You'd still be getting knocked around."

"But at least I deserve it!" And she began to sob in earnest.

I let her cry for a bit until the racking sobs became soft weeping. Then I said, "Now listen to me, Tina. You need to remember that you never deserve treatment like Bill's given you. Never."

"But neither does my father."

"You're right. He doesn't. It's just another sign that your husband is out of control. You need to get a restraining order to protect you and the kids from him."

"I don't know. I get so confused! My mom called the police when he showed up. They arrested him." She started to cry again. "They were putting him in the police car and he's yelling, 'I love you, Tina. All I want is for you to come home. I'll never touch you again in anger. I swear. I love you and the kids!' It was horrible!"

"Tina, tell me you're not going to go back to him!"

She said nothing, and I read a lot of bad things into that silence. I sighed. Another thing I couldn't fix.

"Will you let me interview you for the *News?*" I asked. "I won't use your name or anything. I'll protect you and the kids."

"You want to talk to me for the paper? Why me?"

"I'm doing an article on domestic abuse. That's why I was talking to Stephanie when you called on Saturday. I'd like to have your perspective on what it's like to be in your situation."

Tina stopped crying as she thought about the interview.

"Think of how you could help other women caught in situations like yours. Maybe something you say would help one of them be as brave as you and leave."

"I'm coming to Freedom House tomorrow," she said. "I could see you then. Is that too late?"

"No. That's just right."

"I have a black eye," she said suddenly, a touch of anger in her voice. "He clipped me last night when I tried to protect my father."

I thought of Curt holding me in his lap, comforting me even though I had been the foolish one.

Dear God, I don't even know how to articulate my thanks.

* * *

"Mac, I'd like to go to Audubon, New Jersey, and see what I can find out about Tom Whatley."

It was early in the day yet, not even ten. Audubon was a small town just across the Delaware River, and there should be plenty of time to get there and back before Sherrie showed up at 4:00 p.m.

"Why Audubon? I thought Camden was where he came from."

"That's the official line, but Edie told me that Tom once let slip that he had graduated from Audubon High School. He later denied he'd said any such thing. I looked in the Camden County phone book, and there are three Whatleys listed, all with the Audubon exchange. I called the numbers. One was an answering machine, but the other two claimed they didn't know anything about any Tom Whatley. They were awfully belligerent for not knowing him. Maybe in person they would talk to me."

Mac didn't even need to think about it. He just got a cat-who-ate-the-canary grin. "You've got good instincts, Kramer."

I hugged the rare compliment to myself.

He nodded. "Why don't you try the high school while you're there? Check the old yearbooks. Talk to the teachers."

I could feel the excitement thrumming. "Sure. There have got to be some who remember him."

An hour and a half later I climbed the front steps of Audubon High School, a solid-looking tan-brick building, went to the office and signed in. I had to show both my press card and my driver's license. I felt like I was trying to get through security at the airport. The school secretary directed me to the library.

"You want Mrs. Russo. She's been here forever, she never forgets a student and she'd love to help you. Just look for the lady with the curly hair."

When I walked into the library, several students were sitting at tables reading and several others were tapping away at computer terminals. I looked around and found Mrs. Russo immediately, a short, thin lady of indeterminate years. Hennaed curls stood out all over her head. Her red dress fought with her hair, but her personality beat both into submission. She was lecturing a linebacker-sized student, her finger wagging under his nose. He stood, patiently enduring, eyes on the floor.

I approached her, arriving just in time to hear her say, "You're a good boy, Jay Knowles. A bright boy. Don't you go doing something stupid like trying to get by on *Cliffs Notes* again. Read the whole thing, young man. *Never* settle for the easy way out."

"Yes, ma'am," Jay mumbled. He turned and walked to the table she pointed to, a sheepish grin on his face as the other kids smirked at him. He reached in his bookbag and pulled out a paperback copy of *Moby Dick* and began to read.

"Senior honors class," Mrs. Russo said to me, her sharp eyes watching the room to see if anyone dared challenge her lecture to Jay or tease him about receiving it. "They come in here each week for some sustained reading. Can't have them taking the easy way out. No, sir, we can't. They're too smart for that."

They don't make them like her anymore, I thought as I studied Mrs. Russo. And these kids don't know how lucky they are to sit under someone like her. Her eyes sparkled with a zest for books, for kids, for life in general. And she was definitely old enough to have known Tom.

"I'm trying to trace a man I think went to school here about twenty-three or -four years ago," I explained after I introduced myself and showed my press card.

Her eyes lit up at the idea of tracing someone. I was looking at a woman who thrived on research. "What was the man's name? I've taught here for almost thirty years, so I might well remember him."

Somehow I knew her comment was mere modesty. I bet she remembered just about everyone who had gone through this relatively small school since the day she arrived.

"Do you remember a student named Tom Whatley?"

Immediately she smiled and began shaking her head in the reminiscent way some people have. "Who doesn't remember Tom Whatley?"

I grabbed my tape recorder out of my purse. "Can you tell me about him?"

"Come on into my office where we can talk." She indicated a small closet of a room off to one side. She faced her readers and announced, "I'm stepping into my office with this young lady. I expect to hear no noise whatsoever while I am absent."

She walked ahead of me into the office, confident that the students would obey. I glanced over my shoulder and thought that they probably would. Nobody wanted a dressing down like Jay had gotten.

"Everybody knew Tom," Mrs. Russo said from her seat behind her desk. "He was one of those kids who was into everything. Football, basketball, track, National Honor Society, yearbook, class plays, choir. You name it, and Tom seemed to be involved."

Football? Basketball? Tom Whatley? Not only was he short. He was slight, even as an adult. As a teenager he would have been as substantial as dandelion fluff.

"All the girls had crushes on him, you know. So handsome. If I'd been a few years younger, he would have turned my head too."

I stared at Mrs. Russo. Maybe she wasn't as sharp as she seemed.

"Do you have old yearbooks that I could look at?" I asked.

"I'd like to see what he looked like back then." I'd like to show her she wasn't talking about the right person.

She got up from her seat. "Wait until you see how handsome he was." She shook her head. "I haven't thought about Tom in quite a while, though it must be about ten years, mustn't it? You doing one of those recap pieces?"

I mumbled something noncommittal as she led me to a shelf where years of books sat, the pictorial history of the school. A recap piece? Ten years? What was she talking about?

She went unerringly to a yearbook, flipped to the senior pictures and thrust the volume into my hands.

"There he is." She pointed to the picture of a young, handsome, very large kid down in the lower right-hand corner of the right page. I blinked and looked again.

The name read Thomas John Whatley, but he definitely wasn't Edie's Tom.

NINE

Comments like Class Everything, Ladies Man, Prom King, and Three-Letter Man were inscribed next to the picture of Tom Whatley. He had lots of dark, wavy hair and a killer smile. Hunk was the word that came to mind.

"Tell me about him. Anything and everything you can remember."

"Well, he was definitely a star in our little firmament." Mrs. Russo reached out and ran a finger across the picture. "And he was a nice kid too. I think he was as popular with the faculty as he was with the kids."

"What did he do after he left high school?"

"He went to Annapolis and played football for them. He did well his first two years, and then the trouble began." For the first time since we began talking, she wasn't smiling.

"What trouble?"

She looked out the window, squinting against the bright light or against the memories, I wasn't sure which. "From what I heard and read in the paper, he got caught up in drugs somehow and lost his place at the Academy. After that, he bounced around for several years, taking jobs but never sticking with anything for very long. It was quite sad."

"Did you ever see him during this time?"

She nodded. "Just once. I bumped into him down the shore one summer walking on the boardwalk. He was as charming as ever, but I realized for the first time that he was only charm, no substance. I remember wondering whether he'd always been that way and we'd all been blind to it, or whether he'd become that way as life got away from him. I still remember how sad I felt that night. The only time I felt sadder was the night I heard he'd died."

"He's dead?" My heart paused midbeat, though why I should be surprised, I didn't know. No one usurps the name of a living individual. The living individual tends to complain. "How did he die?"

"Again I don't know all the details, but it had something to do with a drug bust gone bad. I just remember that his best buddy was somehow involved."

"His best buddy?"

"Tom Willis. They were like brothers all through school. The kids used to call them the TomTom Twins." She shook her head and her hennaed curls bounced. "Most unlikely pair of friends you ever saw."

I pulled my fascinated gaze from her head. "Why?"

"Well, there was Tom Whatley, king of the school, and there was Tom Willis, nice little guy, but not even a princeling, let alone a king." She flipped the yearbook page. "There. That's Tom Willis."

Again my heart gave an irregular little beat. Smiling up at me was Edie's Tom, younger, slighter, full of innocence, but definitely Edie's Tom.

The comments beside Tom Willis's picture ran to the generic phrases reserved for the nonroyalty of high school, things like Nice Guy, Pleasant Personality, a Twin, Good Student.

I stared at Tom Willis and wondered how he got from being Tom Whatley's best friend to being Tom Whatley. What had possessed him to drop his own name? What had happened that night of the bad drug bust? Did any of this history have anything to do with Tom's present disappearance? And what would Edie say when she learned about this?

"Tom Willis surprised me," Mrs. Russo said. "I admit that I was so blinded by Tom Whatley's glory that I didn't see what, or I should say who, Tom Willis was. And he turned out to be quality. He didn't win any scholarships or appointments to prestigious schools. He went to Rowan University, a fine school but not in the same category as the Naval Academy. I think he studied psychology. After he graduated with honors while working two jobs to pay living expenses and help support his widowed mother, he went to the police academy and became a cop right here in Audubon. I ran into him around town not long after that time I saw Tom Whatley down the shore. Suddenly I realized what I hadn't seen earlier. Tom Willis was the man with substance."

I thought of all he was to Edie and nodded. But where was this man of substance?

"You know what saddens me?" Mrs. Russo was looking out her office door at Jay, who was diligently reading *Moby Dick*. "For some students high school is the peak of their lives. Tom Whatley was one of those." She turned to me. "Isn't that one of the saddest things you ever heard?"

I'd never thought about that fact before, being only eight years out of high school myself and just starting to find my place in God's scheme of things. Still, the thought that everything could be downhill from here was very sad.

Please, Lord, don't let it be true of me!

I looked back at the yearbook picture of Tom Willis. "How was he involved with Tom Whatley's death?"

Mrs. Russo grew thoughtful. "Again the details are hazy, but it had something to do with him being one of the cops in the drug bust, and Tom Whatley being shot and killed in the process." Mrs. Russo pondered a minute longer. "You know, now that I think of it, I've never seen Tom Willis since that time so long ago, not even at Tom Whatley's funeral. I know he quit the force, but he must also have left town."

And I knew where he'd gone, at least up until last Thursday. "Do the families of both or either of these men live around here still?"

Mrs. Russo turned, walked to a reference shelf and pulled a phone book off a shelf. She flipped to Whatley, then Willis.

"There are three Whatleys in the area, and they're probably related to Tom. And Mrs. Willis, the other Tom's mother, still lives right here in Audubon."

I shook Mrs. Russo's hand and thanked her for her help.

"It was nice to have you drop in," she confided. "It gets a bit dull when the high point of your day is confiscating *Cliffs Notes*."

"I want to be like you when I grow up," I said.

"You should be so lucky." And she winked.

I was still smiling when I climbed into my car and pulled out my cell phone. I dialed the three Whatley numbers. This time I got three answering machines. It was disgusting how no one stayed home these days waiting for phone calls from the press, specifically me. I dialed the Willis number, and a lady answered. I hung up without speaking and immediately drove to the address I'd gotten from Mrs. Russo. As I might have expected, her directions were perfect.

The Willis house was a typical Audubon bungalow, gray with white trim, the front porch closed in to make a sunroom. The sparse grass in the front yard was in need of a good lawn service, and the globe yews hadn't been trimmed in forever. The only bright note was a fat azalea full of plump buds just waiting to burst in spring's warm sun.

I rang the doorbell and waited. Finally the inside door

opened, and a little bird of a woman peered out at me. She must have decided I looked safe because she came across the sun porch and opened the door a mere crack.

"Can I help you?" she asked with a tremulous smile.

I gave her my best smile, the one that Curt loved and Mac hated. "Hello, Mrs. Willis. I'm Merrileigh Kramer and I think I know your son, Tom. And your daughter-in-law Edie."

Instantly the smile disappeared. "I'm not interested," she said in a desperate voice and began to close the door.

I quickly put my hand on the door. "I mean it when I say I'm a friend. I work with Edie. Please talk to me. I'm very confused."

The whole time I talked, Mrs. Willis shook her gray head. "Go away, please. Just go away."

"But Mrs. Willis, we need to find Tom. Edie's beside herself with worry. Do you know where he is?"

"Go away," she pleaded yet again. "I don't know anything."

I looked at the small woman, and I saw genuine fear in her face. I sighed and took my hand from the door. "Please."

Mrs. Willis shook her head, and the door shut in my face with all the finality of the gates of hell snapping shut behind an unrepentant sinner. The only difference was that I was on the outside while the sinner would be on the inside.

I arrived back at the newsroom shortly before four.

"How did Mr. Montgomery's visit go?" I asked Jolene.

"He never came, and if he doesn't hurry, Mac's desk is going to revert to its natural chaotic condition." She wrinkled her nose, showing her beautiful capped teeth. "We're all just waiting around practicing our paeans of praise about Mac."

I cocked my head toward Edie, and Jolene shrugged: *who knows?*

"I'm fine," Edie said tartly. "And I'm not an idiot. I know what this means." She jerked her head a couple of times.

"Sorry. I didn't want to bother you. You looked busy."

"I am. I'm a reporter, and I'm working on a story. And I'm fine."

"No, she's not." Jolene leaned back in her chair. "She wouldn't go to lunch with me. I even offered to pay."

Jolene might be a millionaire, but an offer to pay was a rare occurrence and a sign of the depth of her concern.

"I asked you to bring me a cup of noodle soup," Edie defended.

"Which you carried to the restroom and threw away when you thought I wasn't looking." Jolene's lethal nail pointed straight at Edie's nose.

"You are one nosy woman," Edie griped.

"I am," Jolene said proudly.

I turned to go speak with Mac about my story of a lifetime when William Poole entered the newsroom. The focused look on his shar-pei face as he approached Edie's desk made me think, *Uh-oh.*

"Edie, may I talk with you in private?" William asked.

Edie, who had watched his approach with trepidation, seemed to shrink into herself. "Is this about Tom?"

William nodded.

"Do I need a lawyer?"

William blinked. "I don't think so. This isn't an official interrogation or anything. We just need to talk."

She looked at Jolene and me in a panic.

"It's okay, Edie." I came and stood by her, putting my hand on her shoulder. "You can trust William." I shot him a look that said he'd better be trustworthy. "He's a friend."

But Edie wasn't having any of it. "Stay with me, Merry. You too, Jo."

"Like you could get us to leave." Jolene joined me beside Edie. Her expression dared William to tell her to go.

William looked exasperated. "Edie, I need to talk about some very private things with you. I don't think you want an audience."

"I have no secrets. I want them with me."

"There's a conference table over there." I pointed to the scarred collapsible table about the size of two card tables that sat along the far wall. It was so unstable that if Mac got angry during a meeting and pounded his fist, everyone's beverages jumped and spilled. "Why don't we sit around it?"

William looked unhappy but resigned. After all, he'd said it wasn't an official interrogation.

We paraded across the newsroom and clustered about the table, William at the head, Jolene and Edie on one side, me across from Edie. When Mac saw the parade to the table, he came to see what was going on. I'm sure Larry would have come too, but he wasn't here.

"What's all this, William?" Mac asked.

"I need to talk with Edie," William explained again, looking beleaguered.

"Oh, okay." Mac pulled out a chair and sat next to me.

William sighed deeply and cleared his throat. We all looked at him expectantly, me especially. I wondered if he was going to mention Tom Willis or if I had beaten him to the punch.

"Edie," William began, "do you remember when I questioned you about Tom's background?"

She nodded. "And I knew very little."

"Well, we've learned a bit more. By tracing Tom's Social Security number, his birth date and birthplace, we've learned a fascinating piece of information."

We all waited while he paused for dramatic effect.

"Tom Whatley doesn't exist."

"Oh, no!" Edie put her hands to her face and began to cry.

Jolene scowled at William like it was his fault Tom didn't exist. Mac frowned and reached across the table to pat Edie on the shoulder. You would have thought he had taken patting lessons from me. But he was alert enough to pick up on William's choice of words. "What do you mean, doesn't exist?"

I sat still and said nothing because I knew how right William was. A terrible thought struck me and knocked my complacency for a loop. Was he referring to the real Tom Whatley or Edie's Tom Whatley? "Is 'doesn't exist' a euphemism for 'Tom's dead'?" I blurted.

William nodded. "Tom Whatley is dead all right." He talked right over Edie's wail. "As a matter of fact, he's been dead for ten years."

As a conversation stopper, William's comment was one of the best I'd ever heard. I looked around the circle and tried not to smile at everyone's dropped jaws. I looked at William, who was looking at Edie.

She turned her earnest, tear-streaked face to William. "Then you haven't found my Tom's body?"

William shook his head, surprised. "Your husband's body? No."

Edie looked at the ceiling. "Thank you, God."

"But Tom Whatley's body?" William glared at all of us. "Yes."

Mac was having a hard time assimilating William's information. He was probably still hung up on *doesn't exist.* "Tom's not dead but you've found his body?"

"Edie's husband isn't dead, to the best of our knowledge," William agreed. "But Tom Whatley definitely is. We found his death certificate at the Camden County Courthouse dated almost exactly ten years ago."

Mac narrowed his eyes. "If Tom Whatley's dead, then who's Edie's husband?"

William nodded. "The question of the hour. We don't know

yet. I've sent Jeb out to Edie's house to get something with Tom's fingerprints on it. We'll begin a trace immediately through AFIS."

"Don't bother, William," I said. "I can save you the trouble."

Everyone looked at me, and I have to admit that I kind of liked the power of knowing what no one else knew. Childish, of course, but fun.

"Edie's husband is named Tom Willis."

Everyone looked at me in surprise, including William, who wasn't happy about being beaten to the punch. Edie dropped her head onto her chest, but was that relief I saw in her eyes before they closed?

"Tom Willis is from Audubon, New Jersey, and he's an ex-cop." I acknowledged William with a nod of my head as I passed on that bit of information. "He was somehow involved in the death of his best friend, Tom Whatley, in a drug bust. His mother—that is, Tom Willis's mother—still lives in Audubon, but she wouldn't talk to me."

"Edie," Jolene cried. "If Tom Whatley isn't Tom's real name, are you really married? If he signed the marriage certificate Tom Whatley, are you legal?"

We all turned to Jolene in disbelief. Talk about the least important issue at the moment.

"Well, is she married?" Jolene asked, refusing to back down.

Edie's married state or lack thereof didn't interest William. "What I need to know, Edie, is why your husband is calling himself Tom Whatley."

"I don't know."

"But you've been married for how long?"

"Five years."

"And you expect me to believe you don't know about the false identity?"

"I do not know why he calls himself Tom Whatley."

"Where would he go if he ran away after committing a crime?"

"He did not commit any crime!"

"Did you know he was using a false identity?"

"I—"

The back door of the newsroom burst open and Randy flew in, startling all of us.

"Mom!" His eyes went to her empty desk.

"Over here, Randy." Edie waved her hand.

Randy came charging over, his face full of anger. "The cops were at the house again. You'll never guess what they were after."

He skidded to a halt beside our table and for the first time noticed William. "Oh."

"Hello, Randy." William stood and indicated the chair at the far end of the table. "Would you like to join us? We're talking about your stepfather."

"Here," Jolene said. "Sit next to your mom." She got up and moved to the seat at the far end.

Randy collapsed into the vacated chair and, full sneer, made one of his patented statements. "That man is not my stepfather."

Sitting with his back to the room, he didn't see Sherrie enter to keep her appointment with me. I did, though, since I was facing Edie and Randy. I held up a finger to Sherrie to show I'd be a minute here. Sherrie nodded and sat in an empty chair along the far wall, patiently waiting until I was free.

Randy kept talking. "Just because he's married to my mother doesn't mean I have any relationship whatsoever with him. In fact, he makes me sick." The last four words were separate and emphatic.

"Randy!" Edie was embarrassed and distressed. She reached for his hand. He pulled it away, crossing his arms over his chest and tucking his hands into his armpits so she couldn't grab at him again.

I glanced at Sherrie, noting that her usually bright eyes were clouded with concern. I got up and walked toward her, keeping an ear tuned to the table.

"Hi," she said to me absently, her attention fixed on Randy just as mine was. "What's wrong?"

"The police are talking to Randy's mother about the disappearance of his stepfather."

"His stepfather has disappeared?"

"He's been missing since Thursday night."

Sherrie looked confused. "He said today that he had just gotten rid of a huge problem and was feeling light as a feather in relief." She turned to me. "You don't think he was referring to Mr. Whatley, do you?"

I thought the chances were about one hundred percent that he was referring to Tom, but I didn't want to upset Sherrie. "Maybe he had just finished a huge term paper or something."

Sherrie hitched her backpack higher on her shoulder. "Nice try, but I doubt it."

Just then Randy went wild again. He stood up abruptly and his chair, a rickety folding thing about as sturdy as the table, went flying. He glared at Edie.

"How can you defend him, Mom? How can you be so stupid?"

Edie said something we couldn't hear, her face pleading.

"He's a thief! And I bet he's a murderer too." Randy struck the table with the flat of his hand, the sound reverberating through the room like thunder. "I bet he killed that guy in my car just to make my life miserable."

I glanced at William, who was listening to the outburst with grave concentration. He was not going to interfere.

Edie's voice became a little louder in response to Randy's

harangue. "I doubt that anyone would kill someone just to make your life miserable, Randy. Especially not Tom. That was a very self-centered comment."

"Self-centered? Me?" He leaned into Edie, his nose mere inches from hers. "You leave my father and marry that man, and you call me self-centered? You've ruined my life!"

"Ruined your life? Me?" Edie stood, glaring at her son. "You're doing that all by yourself."

"You married a thief and a murderer!"

"I married a wonderful man!" She turned to sit down. But Randy wasn't finished yelling yet. He grabbed Edie and spun her to face him so fast she lost her balance. She reached out for Randy's arm to steady herself.

"Get your hands off me!" Randy pushed at her. With her previous loss of balance compounded by the push, she started to fall. She grabbed for Randy more desperately than ever. His face contorted with rage. "I said get your hands off me!"

He shoved her as hard as he could. Her chair flew, striking Larry the sports guy's desk with a great crash. She staggered, then went down hard, striking her head on the edge of the table as she fell. The table flipped, falling on her and pinning her to the floor where she lay absolutely still.

The incident happened so fast that none of us could intervene. Mac leaped from his seat and rushed to subdue Randy. William lurched to his feet and around the table with the same goal. Jolene screamed and I grabbed the phone on my desk to dial 911 and ask for an ambulance.

But the fastest responder was Sherrie. She raced across the room yelling, "Nooo!" She threw herself at Randy, beating William and Mac by a good five strides. She wrapped herself around him, pinning his arms to his sides. She was panting and crying and screaming, "How could you do that? I thought you were nice! You're just like my father! You're just like my father!"

Randy stared at his mother, his face white and his eyes wide with horror. "Mom!" He tried to move, but Sherrie, tears streaming down her face, hung on.

"Don't you dare touch her again!" the girl screamed. "Don't you dare! You're just like my father!"

Randy looked at Sherrie's tear-streaked face and shuddered. "No," he whispered. "I'm just like my father."

Into this chaos walked Jonathan Delaney Montgomery.

TEN

Mr. Montgomery, the epitome of professionalism in his navy blazer, gray slacks, light blue shirt and red-and-blue rep tie, brown leather briefcase clutched in his hand, took one look at the emotional tornado streaking through our newsroom and closed his eyes as if to deny what he was seeing. Then he turned very deliberately on his well-shod heel and left.

Just like that.

No "What's going on?" No "Can I help?" Not even "Do you need help?" The least he could have done, I thought critically, what with Edie lying there on the floor unconscious, was to ask, "Is she all right?" But nothing. Not one word.

It was abdication pure and simple. At least the Duke of Windsor had run because of the "woman I love." Mr. Montgomery just ran.

And, I thought ruefully, it is my great joy to work for this man.

I looked at Mac, who was watching Mr. Montgomery's exit with resignation and sorrow on his face. Obviously he felt his goose had just been cooked, and I was afraid he might be right. The unfair thing was that Mac was innocent of any responsibility for the chaos.

I caught his eye and smiled with sympathy.

He sighed, shrugged and took a deep breath. He turned to Edie and hunkered down beside her.

"Hey, Edie." He took her hand in his and began rubbing it. "Can you hear me?"

When she groaned and started to move, he said, "Shh. You stay nice and quiet. Help's on its way. Merry called the ambulance for you." He sat beside her, talking quietly and soothing her, until the ambulance arrived.

In the meantime I hustled the hysterical Sherrie back to my desk and pushed her gently down into my chair.

"How could he? How could he?" she kept saying over and over again. She looked shocked, her eyes wide and tear-filled.

I went down on my knees and threw my arms around her, holding her, patting her back. I didn't know what to say, so I said nothing. I wasn't certain she would hear me anyway.

Eventually the tempest eased somewhat though she was still hyperventilating when I called Stephanie.

"I'll be there in less than five minutes," Stephanie said.

After I hung up, I knelt before Sherrie again and pushed her hair back off her forehead. Her face was flushed and her hands shook.

"It'll be all right," I said, trying to comfort her. "Mrs. Whatley will be fine. You'll see."

She shuddered violently at my words. "No, it won't be all right even if Mrs. Whatley is fine." Her eyes overflowed with a new sea of tears, and I suspected that a lot of her own past, a past she probably thought she had licked, was flashing before her eyes. Her sorrow broke my heart.

"Tomorrow we'll try again to talk, okay?" I said for want of anything better to say. "It's even more important now, don't you think?"

Sherrie mumbled something that sounded like an affirmative. Then after a mighty sniff, she said clearly, "Is he still here?"

I nodded as I glanced at a distraught Randy. "He's very upset."

"Good!" She kept her eyes fixed on the floor so she wouldn't accidentally see him. "He should be."

Randy looked terrible, all white and wide-eyed, as he stared first at his mother, then at Sherrie. I wasn't certain which bothered him the most: his mother's injury at his hand or the blighting of his romance with Sherrie, again at his own hand.

"I'm sorry, Sherrie," he whispered a few minutes later in an anguished voice as, head down and taking care not to look his way, she left with her mother. "I'm so sorry."

"You ought to be, boy," William Poole said as he walked to Randy and took his arm. His voice was devoid of sympathy, and his eyes drilled a hole right through Randy. "And now you need to come with me." He reached toward his belt like he was going for his cuffs.

"No!" Randy looked frantic. "I don't have to! Mom? Do I?"

Edie lay on the floor, the emergency techs strapping her to a backboard. Her neck was already in a cervical collar. "Oh, Randy," she sighed and a tear tumbled out of her eye and rolled back into her hairline.

Randy sank to the floor beside her. "I didn't mean to hurt you! It was an accident!"

"Was it?" William asked coldly.

"Mom! Tell him! It was just that something came over me. I couldn't help it!" He grabbed for her hand, but one of the techs reached out and restrained him. Randy looked distractedly at the tech, then back to his mother. He balled his large fists awkwardly on his knees.

"The something that came over you, boy, is your own lack of self-control." William was giving him no quarter. "And the sooner you admit that you're the one to blame, the better off you and your mother will be."

"No," Randy cried. "I didn't mean—"

"Sure you did." William glared at him. "I've seen your kind for years, and you make me sick."

Edie made a protesting sound at the harsh words, and William looked at her, his gaze gentling. "Edie, don't be easy on him, or there's a lifetime of this treatment awaiting you and some woman foolish enough to marry him someday."

Edie smiled at him sadly and nodded. "I know," she whispered. "But he's my son."

"Don't let that get in the way of what needs to be done."

Edie looked at Randy again. Then she shut her eyes in pain. "Do whatever you need to, William."

"No, Mom! I love you. I do! I'm sorry." Randy's eyes were red, his nose was running and he looked more like five than fifteen.

"That's just what your father used to say, Randy." Edie looked hopelessly at the ceiling. "You're becoming just like him, and it breaks my heart."

"No! No, I'm not!" He grabbed for Edie's hand again, and this time he connected. "Don't say that! Please! I promise, I'm not!"

Edie smiled wanly at him and said nothing.

"Randy." Mac lowered himself to Randy's eye level. "We all care for your mother a lot, from Sergeant Poole to all the *News* staff. That you would dare touch her in anger upsets all of us. Not only were your actions morally reprehensible, but assault and battery is against the law."

"Assault and battery!" Randy couldn't believe his ears.

"What else would you call it if not that?" Mac asked quietly.

"Get up, son. We're leaving." William put a hand beneath Randy's arm and lifted.

It seemed impossible, but Randy's face turned paler, and he clung to Edie's hand.

I didn't know whether William could or would actually do

something official to Randy or if he was just trying a scare-him-straight type of thing. Either way, I thought Randy was a thoroughly broken young man, and I was pleased to see it.

Ah, God, use this to make something of him. May he turn to you for help.

"William, may I see You for a minute? Alone?" I motioned him to my desk.

He released Randy. "Don't you move."

Randy nodded, compliant. He was taller, younger and undoubtedly fleeter of foot than William, but all fight was gone. Besides, where would he have fled?

William walked across the room. "Yes?"

"He's underage and has no other family in town. If you need somewhere for him to stay tonight—you know, if they keep Edie at the hospital—he can come to my place. The sofa will be fine for one night."

"You're not afraid he'll hit you?"

I looked across the room at the boy in question. I didn't think I'd ever seen anyone so contrite, so forlorn. "Should I be?"

William gave a sad smile. "I don't think so. I just hope this is the kid's wake-up call. His mom'll forgive him even if the girl won't. He can still recoup things nicely if he's got a mind to." He looked at me. "But I'm not going to make it easy for him. I'm going to make him squirm."

"Just call me if you need me."

Finally only Jolene, Mac and I remained, and Jolene didn't stay long. She was itching to get home.

"Wait until Reilly hears! He thinks my job's dumb." She cracked her gum in delight. "This'll show him!"

I looked at Jo. The woman never ceased to amaze me at the way she saw things, always slightly skewed. Here I was, emotionally drained, and she was as perky as a high school cheerleader. All that was missing were the somersaults and splits.

"I don't think he thinks your job is dumb." Mac looked more weary than I'd ever seen him. "He thinks that you having a job is dumb."

"You mean because of the lottery money?" Jo asked.

Mac nodded. "Twenty-five thousand dollars a month for twenty years makes the idea of working as a general assistant at the *News* sort of redundant, doesn't it? It's not like you need the money."

"Well, I've got to do something with my life," Jolene said. "I can't just sit around all day getting my nails done. I mean I could, but come on. How boring is that!"

"What do you do with it all?" Mac asked, blatant curiosity compelling the question.

Jolene just looked at him. "That's a very personal question."

"And you won't answer it?"

She nodded and shot him with her forefinger. "You got it." She grabbed her purse and headed out the back door. "See you tomorrow."

I listened to their exchange as a brilliant, beautiful Easter lily of an idea, fragrant with possibilities, blossomed. I didn't know why I hadn't thought of it before. I just had to figure out how to pull it off without Jolene realizing she was being manipulated.

I left the hospital parking lot at 9 p.m. Edie was resting comfortably, and I hoped I soon would be too. I was driving on empty, both literally and figuratively.

The first problem was easy to fix, and I stopped at the gas station at Eighth and Main. The latter was also fixable, I realized, and I headed for Intimations. All I had to do was share my Audubon story with Curt, and I'd immediately feel better. He'd congratulate me and give me a great hug and kiss, and I could forget Edie's pain and Sherrie's tears and Randy's white face and bask in the glow of my love's approval. Already I felt brighter, refreshed.

I was grinning as I pulled up in front of the gallery and parked behind Curt's car. I looked at the quietly elegant sign over the door, unlit since the grand opening had not yet occurred, then at the picture tastefully displayed in the window— Curt's latest from which prints had been made. The picture was softly lit, its deep red barn and silo glowing in a setting sun that streaked the evening sky with soft pearl pinks and mauves.

I had to admit, albeit unwillingly, that Delia knew what she was doing. Intimations looked great. I sighed. I'd have liked it better if I could be mad at her for pulling Curt and his work down to some tacky level that diminished his abilities and threatened his reputation. The truth of the matter was just the opposite. She was going to be a professional godsend.

I walked to the front door. As I expected, it was locked. I knocked loudly, but got no answer. I peered through the door into the gallery, dark and falling away into black shadows except where dim light seeped in from a streetlamp. Way in the back of the room I saw a sliver of light peeking out from the bottom of a door. The workroom, I guessed.

I knocked again as loudly as I could and didn't stop until the closed door at the rear of the gallery opened and a woman dressed all in black emerged. As soon as she pulled the door closed behind her, all that showed was a glimmer of blond hair gliding across the gallery toward me.

She opened the gallery door a scant two inches, her elegant face set in a winsome, friendly cast.

"I'm sorry. We're closed." Her voice was gracious, her smile warm. "Please come back Wednesday night for our grand opening."

"Thanks." I smiled with equal grace and charm. "I'm looking for Curt Carlyle."

Her eyes narrowed for the briefest of moments as she suddenly recognized me.

"I'm sorry. Curt's not here."

"Sure he is. That's his car."

She followed my pointing finger with her eyes. Her lips compressed ever so slightly.

"It's not that he's not here." She backpedaled with an agility that came from long practice and made me wonder how seriously afflicted she was in the truth-versus-misleading-statements department. "It's more that he's not available." Again the smile, but all the charm was now gone. "He's working."

I nodded. "I'm sure he is."

"And he can't be disturbed." It was like she dared me to contradict her.

I accepted the dare. "Please tell him that Merry'd like to see him for a minute."

I knew she wanted to tell me to get lost, but she was saved from such gauche behavior when the rear door opened and Curt, bathed in a swath of light, stepped into the gallery.

"Hey, Delia, I've got an idea for the—"

"Curt!" I called before Delia slammed the door in my face.

"Merry?" His voice held both surprise and pleasure. It was all I could do not to look at Delia and smirk. He hurried across the room. "Hey, darlin' girl, how are you?"

Delia had no choice but to step back and let me in.

Curt covered the distance between us quickly and came to a stop well inside my private space. I was delighted to have it invaded, especially with Delia watching.

"I'll be in the back, Curt." Her voice was cool and impersonal for the most part, but in the end she couldn't quite keep her claws sheathed. "Don't be long. We don't want to waste too much time."

I think it was the slight emphasis on *waste* that made me look at her and smile sweetly enough to give cotton candy a run for its money. Mac would have ground his molars if he'd seen.

"We won't be long," Curt said as he took my hand. He found it full of my car keys and house keys. Without a second thought he took them from me and slid them into his pocket. Then he took my hand again and pulled me in for a quick hug.

Since he stood with his back to the rear door, he didn't see Delia pause in the doorway and turn. Of course if he had been facing her, the glare she leveled at me would have been a soft smile, I'm sure.

"You'll never guess what I learned today," I said, dismissing Delia Big Deal-ia as unworthy of my thoughts at the moment.

"You mean you didn't come just to see me?" Curt asked.

"Well, yes." I wrapped my arms around his waist and rested against his chest. "But I've got big news too."

"Me too. You should see how things are coming together for the opening. Delia really knows her business. And tomorrow—"

I pulled back enough to see his shadowed face. "Tom Whatley isn't really Tom Whatley," I said dramatically.

"Tomorrow," he continued as if I hadn't said a word, "Delia's taking me to some big lunch down in Philadelphia where I'll meet not only people from the art community in Center City but several down from New York."

"Nice," I said. "But listen. Tom Whatley is dead and our Tom Whatley is really Tom Willis. Edie's been married to an imposter!"

"I thought it would take me years to meet some of these people, if ever. Amhearst isn't exactly the center of the art world, you know, and these people aren't readily accessible to any old person. Imagine if I got my work hung in some New York galleries!" His eyes gleamed in the dim light at the wonder of it all.

I nodded, staring thoughtfully at his chest, about a foot from my nose. He wasn't listening to a word I said. "I beat the cops to the story."

"Mr. Whitsun from the Broughley Gallery is even thinking of coming back down from New York for the opening!"

The door in the back of the room opened, and Delia appeared. "Curt, dear heart, I need you."

He dropped his arms from about me and turned. "In a minute. I'm almost done here."

"Dear heart?" I looked at him with one eyebrow raised.

He flapped a hand negligently. "Sort of I-call-everybody-darling, only it's dear heart."

"Somehow that doesn't make me feel much better. Now did you hear me tell you that Tom Whatley is really Tom Willis?"

Curt squinted into the dark room, obviously trying to recast the conversation. He smiled brightly, his teeth white in the dusky gloom. "Yep. I remember. And this is supposed to mean something?"

I blinked. "Sure. Tom Willis was masquerading as Tom—"

Curt nodded. "I got that. But why?"

I shrugged. "It has something to do with the way Tom Whatley died in a drug bust, but we don't know exactly what yet." I grinned. "And I'm the one who discovered all this!"

He patted my shoulder. "That's great, Merry."

But it was more like patting your collie after he fetched for you about a hundred times in one afternoon and you wished he'd just give up and leave you alone. Curt wasn't really paying attention to me, but looking at something behind me with an intensity I wanted for myself.

I turned and looked but saw nothing except the window display. "What's wrong?"

"Not much. Don't worry. It'll be okay." He walked over to the picture in the window. He leaned into the display and shifted the easel upon which the picture sat about a quarter inch to the left.

"There. That's better." He stood back, satisfied.

If he had bothered to look at me, Curt would have seen my mouth hanging open. I'd expected congratulations, applause, acclamation, adulation. Instead, he was fixated on the stupid angle of his picture.

The back-room door crashed open. "Curt, are you coming?" Delia demanded.

"Be right there," Curt called.

"Right." Delia's sarcasm would have curdled the blood of a lesser man.

"Right," Curt repeated, unfazed.

"Well, hurry up, lover," she said, emphasizing *lover.* "There's still much to do back here." Somehow she made those words very suggestive.

"Lover?" I repeated, jaw clenched. "Is that like dear heart?" What I wanted to do was scream in the direction of the back room, "Don't you dare call him that!" That would be after I screamed at him, "Will you listen to me?"

Curt, unaware of my anger, shrugged. "What can I say? It's my charm."

"Charm, schmarm." I grabbed the door handle and gave him one last hostile glare. "You haven't heard a word I've said, have you?"

Curt looked bewildered. "Sure I have. Tom Whatley is— something. Missing."

"Try dead."

Curt looked surprised. "Tom Whatley's dead? Poor Edie."

"For ten years."

"What?"

"Curt!" The tattoo of Delia tapping the floor in frustration or anger cut across the gallery.

"See?" I scowled at him. "I knew you weren't listening!"

He looked down at me, his face thrown into sharp planes of dark and light from the open door to the back room. "And have you heard anything I've said?" His voice was hard.

"Yeah. You're going to lunch with her highness tomorrow." I pulled the door open. "Have fun." I slammed the door as loudly as I could. With luck, the glass pane would shatter under the tension.

Fat chance. Safety glass had been invented for protection against temperamental idiots like me.

I was in the car reaching for the ignition before I realized I'd left my keys behind. In Curt's pocket. I let my head fall back against the headrest. Not again! I thought of the humiliation of going back to Intimations and banging on the door and felt the heat rise. All my anger dissipated like mist before a strong breeze.

A knock on my window startled me. I swallowed a scream at the huge shape looming over me and reached out automatically to slam the lock down. I wasn't fast enough.

The door flew open and my keys dropped in my lap.

"I think you'll need these."

It could have been worse. It could have been Delia come to gloat.

"Thanks, Curt." I sighed. "Twice an idiot."

"Thrice," he corrected, ever the gentleman. "Move over."

I slid across to the passenger side and he climbed into the driver's seat.

"What happened back there?" he asked. He sounded genuinely perplexed.

"We had a fight?"

"But what about? Delia?"

"I don't think so, though I don't like her calling you dear heart and lover."

"It means nothing," he said, reaching for my hand. He began rubbing his thumb back and forth over my inner wrist. "At least it means nothing to me."

I felt better already. "I know."

"Then what? I wasn't excited enough about your story?"

"To the head of the class with you." I reached out and straightened his collar. Then I brushed back the curl that always fell over his eye. .

"But you didn't pay any attention at all to my good news either."

I was stung at his accusation. "Of course I did."

"You call your crack about lunch with her highness noticing?"

Now it was my turn to recast our conversation. Try as I might, I couldn't recall one nice comment about what was a great career opportunity for him. My shoulders sagged. "You're right. I'm sorry."

He smiled slightly. "I didn't mean to diminish your big news either. You did a nice piece of investigative reporting to discover something like that."

"Thanks." My eyes filled with tears. "And I'm delighted for your opportunity. Truly I am. I know how much it must mean to you."

I don't know who moved first, but as make-up kisses go, this one had to be among the best ever.

We sat silent for a couple of minutes, arms about each other.

"Are we too different?" I whispered. "Or is this type of mis-understanding typical of all couples?"

"If I had to hazard a guess, I'd say typical, but I don't know. I've never paid all that much attention to the dynamics of being a couple." He smiled and kissed my cheek. "I never had to before."

All the lights in Intimations erupted into the night, golden, brilliant and demanding. Delia.

"I've got to go," Curt said, pulling back. "Really."

I nodded. "Have a wonderful lunch tomorrow."

"How about dinner tomorrow night?" He squeezed my hand. "I promise to listen very carefully to your Tom story."

"And I to your luncheon report. Can Delia spare you for the evening?" I slapped my hand over my mouth. "I didn't say that last sentence. I didn't. Or at least I didn't mean it to be nasty."

"Give me a kiss, darlin' girl." He leaned in and I complied.

As I drove home, I told myself over and over that we'd get this communication thing figured out. We would.

Oh, Lord, we will, right? What we've got developing here is too special to lose.

Yes, we were different. We liked different things. We had different careers. But we were learning to love each other, and we both loved the Lord.

We could do this, I told my rapidly beating heart.

We would do this.

Right, Lord?

ELEVEN

"Merry, you said to call." It was William Poole.

I smothered a yawn as I looked at the clock. Almost eleven. "Randy?"

"Can you keep him for a couple of days?"

A couple of days? When I'd said he could come for tonight, I'd never given a thought to any longer. What would I do with him? What would I say to him? What if he lost it while here? I had visions of my furniture in kindling and the house ransacked. Then I remembered the quality of my furniture and the dearth of ransackable goods and acknowledged those thoughts for the excuses they were.

"Will Edie be in the hospital that long?" I asked for something to fill the stretching silence.

"I don't know. But even if she comes home tomorrow, which she probably will, she'll be in no shape to keep an eye on the kid."

"What does he say about coming here?"

"He doesn't get a choice. It's you, or I'm taking him to juvenile detention down in Lima."

Me or the juvenile facility. No pressure there. My heart beat against my ribs, and my stomach churned like a malted in a blender.

"I've got to go to work in the morning," I said.

"Take him with you."

"What about school?"

"There's only a day or two before Easter break. He can miss the time or you can take him and pick him up. I really don't care."

"Are you at the police station?"

"Yes."

I took a deep breath and jumped. "I'll be right there." *And Jesus, You'd better come with me!*

Randy was not the finest of companions as we drove to his house for clothes and necessities, which I was interested to notice included his iPod and laptop computer as well as a PlayStation and numerous cartridges. He was sullen, embarrassed and angry.

"Do you have school tomorrow?" I asked as he packed.

Grunt.

"Do you have homework and stuff?"

He swung his backpack before my nose.

"Do you want to go to school or to work with me?"

Grunt.

"Is your car okay?"

Grunt.

And just because I couldn't resist, "Don't forget clean underwear."

That didn't even rate a grunt. We left his house in silence.

Looking at the situation from his fifteen-year-old vantage point, I understood his attitude. After all, I'd seen him slug his mother, fall to pieces and get dragged off by the police. Our common experiences were hardly the stuff of meaningful conversation and deep friendship.

"Have you had dinner?" I asked.

He shook his head.

"McDonald's okay?"

He nodded.

I pulled up to the drive-through order mike. "What'll it be?"

He stared straight ahead without speaking for a few seconds, tumultuous emotions pouring from him in waves. It was as if he were so consumed by internal conflicts that he couldn't articulate a coherent thought.

Finally he growled, "Two Big Macs, two large fries, two large Sprites and two apple dippers. Don't forget the caramel stuff."

"Thanks, but I already ate," I said, trying to lighten the atmosphere.

He looked at me blankly.

The boy of ten who took my money was definitely more fun than Randy. He might struggle to reach the cash register, but at least he knew how to smile.

Randy wolfed down the food as we drove and left the paper sack stuffed with trash on the floor of the front seat when he climbed out at the carriage house. He stared at the place in disbelief long enough for me to collect his trash. He barely blinked when I shoved it in his hand.

"Trash basket's in the kitchen."

"What is this building?" he asked. "It looks weird. And it's not on the street. It's on the alley." I could definitely hear his lip curl in disdain on the last comment. I guess if I were getting a classy sports car for my sixteenth birthday, living on the alley would definitely look déclassé.

"It's an old carriage house that's been converted into four apartments. The mansion that it serviced was torn down long ago and those houses built where it used to be." I gestured toward the residences fortunate enough to be on the street. "My apartment's on the first floor. I hope you don't mind the couch, because that's what you've got."

He barely restrained a grimace.

"One thing you need to be aware of is that the bathroom has two doors, one in the living room—yours—and one in the bedroom—mine."

"So?" he said, ever charming.

"Neither door has a lock."

He looked at me like I had lost my mind.

We went inside, and I got out extra sheets and blankets and a pillow. From the linen closet I pulled a set of new, fluffy pink towels that I'd bought myself just last week. If he thought them unmanly, that was his tough luck. It was pink or use paper towels.

"This is Whiskers." I scratched the boy behind his furry ears. "I got him at the pound, but he has decided that he won't tell anyone of his lowly background. After all, he's already come a long way, living on the alley. He suspects that it's just a matter of time before he moves up to the street. Right, baby?"

Whiskers responded by butting against my shins. I stroked his back, and he purred in delight.

Randy held out a hand. "Here, cat." The command had all the grace of a drill sergeant telling his men to stand at attention, but for some reason, Whiskers responded. He wrapped himself around Randy's ankles, and the boy actually managed a smile.

I tried to think back to when I was fifteen. Had I been so sullen and withdrawn? Of course, my parents hadn't divorced, my father hadn't forgotten the date of my birthday, my step-father hadn't disappeared and I'd never flown into a rage and struck my mother, so it was difficult to make a comparison. I looked at the boy as he awkwardly petted Whiskers, and my heart broke for him.

Oh, Lord, he needs You so badly!

When I had his bed all arranged, I said, "You can watch TV if you want. Just keep the sound down so I can sleep, okay?"

He stared at me blankly in answer.

"Right." I gave my fist a shake, a little homeboy sign to make him feel comfortable. "Now I know you can easily walk out of here during the night." He started as I said that, making me wonder if he'd already been planning to leave. "However, let me tell you that I don't think it would be a good idea. Enough people are upset with you as it is." I looked him dead in the eye. "I'm trusting that you're smart enough to know what's the best thing to do even if it's not the most fun or the most exciting."

He looked over my left shoulder and out the window into the night, and made no response.

I bit back a sigh. "Tomorrow morning after breakfast we'll call the hospital and see if your mom's coming home. If she is, we'll arrange a time to go get her. Until she's released, you can come to work with me if you don't feel up to school."

At that pronouncement, he actually looked at me, and his pained expression showed clearly what he thought of my plan. Still, I got the impression that it was better than school. After all, he'd have to face Sherrie at school.

What would happen when Sherrie came to see me after school? I didn't even want to think about that scenario.

"I'll use the bathroom first and get out of your way." I spoke to the top of his head because he had dropped onto the sofa and was contemplating the floor. Whiskers was winding around his ankles, purring in ecstasy. "I'll let you know when I'm finished."

I turned and noticed for the first time the little blinking red light on my answering machine. Someone had called while I was getting Randy. Maybe Curt? With a smile I pushed the Play button.

"Stay out of it! It's none of your business! Or you'll get hurt!"

I stared at the phone in fascinated horror.

"Who's that?" Randy demanded.

"I don't know." I hit Replay. I grabbed a pencil and wrote

down the number displayed in the Caller ID box as the nasty male voice taunted me again.

"What did you do?" Randy was so curious that he forgot to be self-conscious.

I shrugged. Was it the same voice I'd heard at Edie's?

"What kind of pervert is stupid enough to leave messages?" Randy asked, stating my thoughts exactly. "Hasn't he ever heard of voice prints?"

I quickly called the police and reported the threat. It was only a matter of minutes before William called back.

"Can you identify the caller? Is it the same person who called Edie?"

"No, I can't identify him. And I don't know if he's the same guy. Maybe. I want it to be. How many weird callers does Amhearst need? But I don't know."

William sighed. "It'll be a phone booth. I'll bet you anything."

"What did he say?" Randy asked as I hung up.

"Phone booth."

He nodded and looked at me with interest. Then he walked back to the sofa and collapsed. Gathering Whiskers close, he buried his head in the cat's ruff and made believe I was no longer there.

I shrugged my mental shoulders and went into the bathroom. When I was sure I'd left no toothpaste spit in the sink or dirty foam on the soap, I knocked cautiously on the bathroom door that opened into the living room, then cracked it a couple of inches. I was surprised to see the living room in darkness.

"I'm finished, Randy. It's all yours."

"Thanks." It came out as a croak, and he quickly cleared his voice and tried again. "Thanks."

"You're welcome. I'm glad you're here." And I realized that was the truth. "Good night."

"Merry?"

I stuck my head back in the room. "Yes?"

"Will that guy hurt you?"

I tried to keep the surprise out of my voice. "The one on the answering machine? I doubt it. There's something sort of cowardly about a phone threat, don't you think?"

"Yeah," he said, contempt for the caller making his voice fuller, surer. "Yeah."

"Good night, Randy."

"Merry?"

"Yes?" I smiled, thinking of little kids coming up with some foolish questions to keep from having to go to sleep. But Randy wasn't a little child, and his questions weren't foolish.

There was a long pause. Then: "She'll be all right, won't she?"

"Your mom?"

"Yeah."

"I think so. I don't know why not."

He grunted, a sound that somehow conveyed relief. I was moving to close the door again when he said, his voice thick with apprehension, "Will she ever forgive me?"

Such unnecessary pain, I thought. For both of them. "Sure. Moms always forgive, especially nice moms like yours."

"Not Mom. Sherrie."

Ah, Sherrie. Different kettle of fish.

"I know Mom'll forgive me. She's like that. But I don't know about Sherrie."

"I don't know about Sherrie either, Randy. You behaved very badly in front of her, and you brought up some very unsettling memories for her."

He sighed. "Sometimes it's not good to have things in common."

Not when one of them was an abusive father. "She's only fifteen. You've handed her a situation that many adults couldn't deal with."

"I know. I wouldn't blame her if she never talked to me again."

Since he seemed freed to speak by the darkness, I flicked out the bathroom light and slipped into the living room, staying close to the door so he wouldn't feel crowded. "But Sherrie's a girl of uncommon grace and faith. Maybe in time she'll be okay."

"You think so?"

There was such yearning in his voice that I felt tears spring to my eyes. "I hope so, for both your sakes."

He seemed satisfied with that, as if recognizing that that was the best he could expect right now. We fell silent for a minute. Then he took a deep breath.

"Tom's not a terrible man." The words rushed out of him like water from a ruptured dam. "He's been nice to me always. I'm the one who's been terrible."

"I know."

"Yeah." He made a choking sound. "I haven't been very subtle about it, have I?"

"Mmm."

"I don't want him to be in trouble." There was an urgency in his words that underscored the truth of his statement.

"I know."

"My mom loves him. He's so nice to her. He takes care of her." There was wonder in his voice.

"Do you think that's unusual?"

I heard him shift on the sofa, the sheets murmuring in the darkness. "I used to think it meant he was weak. A real man made a woman fear him, not love him. That way he was always in control."

"And now?"

"I—I think I've changed my mind."

"Why?"

"I've seen how upset Mom is over Tom."

"I'm not sure I understand what you mean."

He shifted on the sofa again. "I think that if my dad had ever disappeared, Mom's strongest response would have been relief. I wouldn't want Sherrie to be relieved if I disappeared. I'd want her to care." His voice caught on a muted sob that he tried to swallow. "Not that she's ever likely to care about me."

The conversation had come full circle.

"Randy, how do you think God fits in all this?"

"God?" He sounded surprised.

"You know how important God is to Sherrie, don't you?"

"Sure. I mean, her mom's got a mission."

"Do you realize that if Sherrie forgives you, it will be because God gives her the strength to do it?"

I could almost feel him thinking. "Does that mean she talks to God about me?"

"It does."

"That makes me feel weird. Or special. I don't know which."

"Maybe both?"

He gave a half laugh. "Maybe both. I don't think anyone else talks to God about me."

"I do."

His surprise bounced off the walls.

"I have to admit that I used to pray mostly for your mom, that she'd survive you." *Oh, Lord, don't let that offend him so much he stops listening!*

He grunted.

"But from now on I will pray that you become the man that's inside you, the man that God would like you to become. And I'll pray that you realize that God's the only one who can help you become that."

I held my breath and awaited his reaction. Eventually I heard a muffled, "Thank you."

"Good night, Randy. Like I said, I'm glad you're here."

The next morning, Randy was back to less than monosyllabic.

"Cereal or toast?"

He pointed to the Captain Crunch my mother would never buy for me and which I enjoyed each morning in sweet rebellion. Then he pointed to the bread.

"Both?"

Nod.

"Whole wheat or oat?"

He pointed to the oat.

"Orange juice?"

Nod.

We listened to each other crunch while I tried to imagine several days like this.

WWJD, Merry?

I poured him some more Captain Crunch.

When we got to work, I settled Randy at his mother's empty desk. He pulled out his laptop and started typing away, ignoring me and everyone else in the newsroom.

I shot everyone a warning glance, especially Jolene, and got to work, calling the police station first thing. William wouldn't be in until afternoon. I spoke with Jeb Lammey, the press liaison.

"No identification yet on the body in Randy's car?" I asked. "Hasn't AFIS come through?"

"You know, I think they have." I could hear Jeb shifting papers around. "Here we go. The deceased was a petty criminal named Barnard Slocum. He has a list of priors going back twenty years, and all for small-time stuff like selling pot to an undercover agent or being bagman for a bookie or acting courier for a drug shipment."

"What does any of that have to do with Tom Whatley or Tom Willis?"

"We don't know yet. But my money's on drugs. Willis was involved somehow when Whatley died in that drug bust. I bet he's involved again."

At least he was no longer accusing Tom of taking the dealership money. "Is that a hunch or do you know something you haven't told me yet?"

"Strictly a hunch. Oh, and there is one more thing. There's a car missing from the Hamblin lot."

"What's that got to do with anything?"

"Every month they do an inventory of the lot to track and verify all the cars so none just sort of disappear. This was a special inventory done at our request, a between-times tabulation, if you will. Apparently a car could be borrowed off the lot between inventories, and no one would be the wiser. It just needs to be returned before the next count is taken."

"So what do you think it means that this car is missing?" I asked.

"Missing car, missing man, drug courier killed. Three guesses. And then there's the fact that Tom was the last to sign the car out."

"Sign the car out?"

"You know. When they let a potential customer drive a car or when they take a car home themselves to try it out."

"They have to sign it out?"

"And in."

"And Tom took the missing car? He signed it out?"

"But not in."

"And you actually think he'd steal a car he signed out? He'd put his name there confirming that he stole it? Come on. That doesn't even make sense."

"He took the money."

"Jeb! You don't know that. You don't know any of this."

"I can't take it to court, but I'll bet it's an accurate scenario."

I stared at my blank computer screen and wondered if he could possibly be right. "What do you think any of this has to do with Tom Whatley's death?" I asked.

"The Audubon PD faxed us a bunch of stuff late yesterday, but I'm not free to pass it on without authorization. I can tell you though that something was funny the night Whatley died, and Willis was right in the middle of the funny stuff. That's all I can say right now."

I knew I wouldn't get any more out of Jeb if he was in authorization mode. I disconnected and wrote steadily to get my Whatley/Willis article finished before deadline. I took one break to call Bill Bond, Tom's boss at Hamblin Motors, to see if I could get a statement from him about the inventory and missing car.

I had to call him at home because of the hour. Dealerships open later than newsrooms. All I got was an empty ring, not even an answering machine. Either this guy was online with dial-up or he was behind the times. I went back to writing.

When I sent the finished work off to Mac, I turned to Randy, who was doing who-knew-what on his laptop.

"I need to see a couple of people." I got to my feet and slipped on my navy blazer. "Bring the laptop and let's go."

Our first stop was Hamblin Motors. The dealership was finally open for the day, and I hoped Bill Bond would be around for me to interview.

Randy came to life as we walked into the showroom. His eyes roved lovingly over the models on floor display. Next thing I knew, he was sitting in a low-slung blue number, hands on the wheel, mind on the open roads.

I, on the other hand, was drawn to a display case filled with old-fashioned toy cars, the heavy metal ones from the 1920s and 30s. I know nothing about cars and have no desire to learn one from another, but I was fascinated by the cumbersome toys, mostly because they had been fortunate enough to es-

cape the great scrap metal drives of World War II. There was
no doubt that I was looking at a collection of some value.

"Wonderful, aren't they?"

I turned to find a salesman standing behind me, all smiles
and good will. His name tag read Howard.

"That's a Reo." Howard pointed. "And that's an early Cad-
illac. And that, of course, is a Model T."

"Of course," I mumbled.

He continued to name every car in the case and the case
against the facing wall.

"Mr. Hamblin himself collects these toy cars. He has more
than a hundred, though he only displays the finest."

I nodded as we walked to the center of the showroom and
the real cars. Howard's brown oxfords squeaked on the shiny
tile floor, and he should never have been allowed out of the
house in the deep green twill shirt he was wearing. It made
him look sick. Still, since it said Hamblin Motors over the
heart, he probably didn't have a choice. But he had nice eyes
and an earnest spirit.

"Are you interested in a nice car for your son?" he asked,
nodding toward Randy.

I looked at him sourly. He might have nice eyes and an
earnest spirit, but he had the brains of a nit.

Howard realized his mistake immediately, not a great in-
tellectual feat given my facial expression. "Your brother?" he
offered hesitantly. "Boyfriend?"

"I'm babysitting for him." The chill in my voice should
have had everyone running for tire chains due to icy condi-
tions. "He's a high school freshman."

The poor man wilted completely.

Taking pity on him, I smiled. "I'd like to see Bill Bond,
please. Tell him Merry Kramer from the *News* would like to
talk to him if he has a minute."

He nodded and all but ran through a frosted glass door in the middle of the room. In his haste to please he neglected to shut the door firmly.

"What did you do to him to make him run like that?" Randy stood just behind me.

"He thought you were my son."

Randy blinked in surprise, then started to laugh.

"It's not funny," I protested. "I'm only eleven years older than you!"

"Yes, it is," he managed between sputters of laughter. "It's hilarious. Does that make Curt my father?"

I growled at him, and he wandered off to find another car to mind-drive, happier than he'd been in days.

A voice that was anything but happy cut through the showroom silence. It came from the frosted glass door Howard had neglected to close.

"Who did you say?" It was a low roar.

I couldn't make out the answer. I assumed poor Howard was giving my name again.

"Tell her I'm not here." The statement was abrupt and emphatic. "I will not talk with her."

There was a rumble from the salesman again, then a resounding, "I said no! Just get rid of her. If she gives you any trouble, go get Joey."

I walked toward the frosted glass door. If Bill Bond was so anxious not to talk with me for some reason I couldn't begin to imagine, I was suddenly dying to speak with him. I was reaching for the knob when the door swung open and Howard emerged, effectively blocking my way.

"I'm sorry," he said, looking acutely uncomfortable. He pulled the door firmly shut behind him. "Mr. Bond isn't available."

"Sure he is. I heard him talking with you."

Howard blanched. "Oh, no. You must be mistaken. Mr. Bond isn't here."

I looked at him, disappointed that he lied so willingly. "Oh, Howard."

He flushed and looked away. "Mr. Bond isn't here," he repeated.

"Sure he is." I pointed to the car lot. Howard looked, just as I'd hoped he would. I stepped around him quickly, taking him by surprise, and threw open the frosted door.

"You can't go in there!" Howard cried in a panic.

"Sure I can." I walked into what was essentially a hallway with two small offices opening off it on each side, four all together. The first door had a sign that read Bill Bond, Sales Manager. The room was empty except for a desk and three chairs.

I hurried down the hall and pushed through the far doorway. I found myself in a great, cavernous space filled with cars of varying ages and descriptions, all with men and an occasional woman working on them in some fashion. Bill Bond was nowhere in sight. At least I assumed he wasn't. I saw no one with a shirt like Howard's.

A couple of the mechanics looked at me curiously, but none spoke. Between the blare of music and the whir of power tools, a conversation would be difficult. But worth a try, I decided.

I walked to a young woman who leaned over the front fender of a car, her arms lost in the bowels of its motor.

I tapped her on the shoulder and she jumped like I'd bitten her. I smiled placatingly.

"Have you seen Bill Bond?" I yelled over the pneumatic roar of the mechanic at the next car freeing lug nuts on a tire. "I think he came through here."

She shook her head and turned back to her motor, which was obviously more interesting to her than I was.

I walked along the wall, peering between cars and searching on my own. A person in a dark green twill shirt was nowhere to be seen.

I turned to go back to the showroom, disappointed that I wouldn't discover why Bill Bond refused to see me, when I saw a once-white door with a permanent black, greasy stain just above the chrome push plate that was supposed to prevent just such a stain. Men, the door read.

"See if he's in there," I ordered Howard, who watched me like a nervous mouse watching a hungry cat. I don't know what he expected me to do, but eating him would be too offensive to the palate.

"I can't do that," he said primly.

"Why not?" Randy'd do it, I thought. Where was the kid when you needed him?

"I just can't." He'd cast our little drama as an us-against-her scenario, and he wasn't going to do anything to help me.

I sighed. "Then I guess I'll have to."

He looked shocked, but he did nothing. He probably didn't believe I'd breach that male bastion. I took a deep breath and pushed the door open.

Squeezing my eyes shut against I didn't know what, I burst into the room. "Mr. Bond! I need to speak with you. You can't hide from me using this old ploy."

"Well, well," said a voice appreciatively. "What have we here?"

"Pretty little thing, isn't she? Obviously lost."

My eyes snapped open, and I stared at two mechanics who stared back, goofy smiles on their faces. Unfortunately Mr. Bond wasn't anywhere in the room. I know because the door to the single stall was hanging drunkenly open, and every other facility was right out in the open. I backed out quickly, my face scarlet, immensely grateful that the two were merely washing their hands.

I turned to flee back to the showroom and ran into the solid chest of Joey. I know it was Joey because the name was written on his blue Dickies workshirt.

"Can I help you?"

I looked up at him and wondered how he could say something so innocuous and sound so threatening.

"I'm looking for Bill Bond." I was pleased to hear myself sounding firm and rational in spite the fact that Joey made me very nervous.

"Who?" Joey growled.

"Bill Bond. The sales manager."

"Don't know him," Joey said. "Never heard of him."

Right.

"Is there another Joey here?" I asked, hearing Bill Bond's *if she gives you trouble, go get Joey.*

"Not hardly." He puffed out his already impressive chest. "One Joey's all this place can handle."

I could tell he expected me to be impressed, but I didn't play along. His face darkened.

"You need to leave, lady." He pointed toward the showroom. "It's dangerous out here. Lots of possibilities for accidents."

Again what should have been just a statement of the obvious sounded like a threat. Knowing I had no choice, I turned and left, aware of Joey's smirk and resenting it mightily. When we were back in the showroom, I spun to Howard.

"Tell me about Tom Whatley," I said, hoping my abrupt change of subject would take him off guard. It worked.

"Nice guy," Howard said. "I couldn't believe it when they said he stole all that money."

"Why do you think he stole the money?"

"I don't know. Maybe his wife's sick or something. He loves his wife. Always talks about her."

"I don't mean why, for what purpose. I mean why do you think he's the guilty one? Especially since you said he was so nice."

Howard looked at me like anyone could figure that out. "The money's missing and so's he and so's a car he signed out."

"Howard, if you were going to ruin your life, would you actually sign out the car you were stealing?"

"No, but if he didn't do it, then where is he? And where's the car?"

I stuck out my hand and shook his like I was congratulating him. "You're a genius, Howard. If we answer those questions, we solve the mystery, don't we? Will you call me if you think of anything that might help Tom? Or hurt him, for that matter." I handed him my card.

He stared at it a minute, stuck it in his shirt pocket and nodded. "I liked Tom."

"You should still like him," I said. "He's a nice man. Even his stepson says so."

Howard snorted. "Not hardly."

"Hey, Randy," I called.

He looked up reluctantly from his inspection of the motor in a black car.

"Do you like Tom?"

He nodded. "Nice guy." He abandoned the motor and climbed in the black car.

"That's Randy, the monster stepson?" Howard stared in amazement.

"He's recently had a change of heart." I waved my hand in the boy's direction. "Come on, Randy, we're leaving."

He climbed reluctantly out of the black car which had so many bells and whistles that its name was emblazoned o trunk in gold letters. While he schlepped across the floor to me, I turned to Howard.

"One last question. What's Joey's last name?"

"Alberghetti. Joey Alberghetti." He looked at me thought-fully. "Be careful." He walked away as Randy reached me.

"Come on, son. Time to leave."

He grinned. "Right, Mom."

To get out of the congested lot, I had to back up across the entrance to the service bays. I looked over my shoulder just before I drove off and there against the far back wall was Joey Alberghetti talking to a man in a green twill shirt. The man's back was to me, but I was willing to bet it was Bill Bond. He was sticking his finger in Joey's chest and gesticulating wildly with his other hand.

Bill Bond, if that's who it was, was upset with Joey Alberghetti.

TWELVE

As Randy climbed out of the car, he looked young and scared in spite of his height and the breadth of his shoulders. He gave a toss of the head that was supposed to appear casual but was more like a nervous jerk.

One part of me wanted to comfort him because he was still young. It was easy to forget how young because of his size and mature good looks. Another part of me thought that the nervousness, guilt and regret might be a good thing. Sweating out the consequences of his actions had to be a strengthening experience. Certainly anything that painful must produce character.

When we arrived at Edie's room, she was dressed and waiting, resting on her bed with a book she wasn't reading. To look at her, you wouldn't know there had been any physical injury, but her eyes were full of pain. I hugged her, willing my chin not to wobble.

Randy hung back at the door and peeked in. I don't know what he expected, but all he saw was his mom looking much like she did every day, just a bit more worn.

He walked awkwardly, hesitantly to the bed. "Are you okay, Mom? Does your head hurt a lot?" Then his eyes filled with tears. He stared at the floor, trying to control himself.

I watched Edie watch him. Her face was a study in love

and trepidation. She understood, even if he didn't, that he was teetering on the edge of good and evil. He would fall one way or the other, setting a pattern that would govern his life for years. Since neither of them thought much in terms of the place of Christ in their lives, I wondered where she got her hope. Maybe from her mother's heart that couldn't believe her kid would go bad.

When Randy finally lifted his head, his face was full of anguish. "I'm sorry, Mom. I'm so sorry. I can't believe I—" He couldn't continue.

Edie stood and wrapped her arms about her son's waist. He threw his arms around her, and his shoulders began to shake.

"I don't want to be like Dad."

"You won't be, Randy," she promised. "You won't be."

I left the room and waited in the hall, sniffing a fair amount myself.

It was ten more minutes before a nurse arrived with a wheel-chair. She went blithely into the room, unaware of the emotional breakthrough inside, and emerged in a couple of minutes with Edie in the chair and Randy, red-eyed but obviously lighter in spirit, walking beside her, carrying her tote bag.

When we were in my car, Edie gave a great sigh. "I hated being in the hospital."

"Most people hate the hospital," I said. "I'd worry about you if you liked it."

Edie nodded. "But I hated it more because Tom didn't know I was there. What if he tried to call me?"

But he hadn't called. At least if he had, he'd left no message. I watched her shoulders sag and the hope in her eyes dim as she checked her answering machine.

"He'll show up, Mom. He loves you too much not to."

Edie looked at Randy in surprise. I smiled. Apparently he meant some of the things he'd said last night in the darkness.

Together he and I set Edie up on the blue leather couch with everything we could think of that she might need. Finally she held up her hands.

"Enough, you two! I'm not dying here. I can get anything I need all by myself. Or Randy can get it for me."

Randy and I looked at each other.

"What?" Edie said, an edge to her voice.

"I have to stay with Merry." Randy looked apologetic. "Sergeant Poole gave me the choice of staying with her or going to juvenile hall."

"And he chose me." I tried to sound bright and positive.

Edie glanced from me to her son. "Well, at least you made the better choice. I don't mind telling people my son is staying with a friend."

"A female friend," Randy said, wagging his eyebrows.

"Hey, now," I groused. "It's bad enough that Howard thought you were my son."

"Your son?" Edie laughed out loud. "Howard, whoever he is, needs glasses."

Randy picked up his laptop and became very businesslike. "I've got stuff to tell you two before Merry and I leave." He had settled in the big chair I'd sat in the other night, and I noticed the chair fit him a lot better than it fit me.

"I've been online most of the morning looking for information about Tom," he said.

Edie gasped. "Randy!"

"Look, Mom, I figured we needed to find out all we could about what happened ten years ago so we could better defend Tom today."

"Better defend him?" Edie stared at her son.

"Yeah," he said, head buried in his laptop. "Somebody's got to speak for him since he isn't here to speak for himself."

"I thought you didn't like Tom."

"I didn't." His fingers flew over the keyboard. "Not at first. Then I couldn't admit I'd been wrong." He glanced at his mom. "It's dumb, but it's a teen thing, you know?"

Edie nodded weakly.

"But I've learned a lot these past couple of days, most of it about me and how stupid I've been." He fell silent as he continued to work over his computer.

Edie sat, poleaxed. I had to smile at her expression. Of course, she didn't have the benefit of hearing last night's musings as I had.

"Edie, I've got a couple of questions for you while we wait for Randy."

"Ask away."

"Was Randolph an abuser? Is that what Randy's referring to when he says he's afraid he'll be like his father?"

Edie nodded, brushing at the wrinkles in her slacks. "You'd think I'd have known better, being raised by an abusive father, but I stepped right into my marriage without seeing it coming."

"That's why you didn't want to write the article on abuse? It was too painful?"

"But to my surprise that's proven not to be true. I've found the writing has been cathartic."

"The other night," I said, "you referred to thinking your days in the paper were over. What did you mean?"

She shuddered. "We ended up in the police report in the paper a couple of times when I had to call for help. What an embarrassment! I hated it. But let's not talk about Randolph anymore, okay? He gives me the chills even now."

I cleared my throat. "Edie, I've got one more question. It's presumptuous, but I've got to ask it as a reporter and as someone who wants to find the truth."

Edie swallowed. "Go ahead."

"Your furniture in here." I waved my hand at the living room, dining room and entry hall. "It's gorgeous."

"And expensive, right?" Edie looked relieved. Obviously this was a question she could answer.

"It's from my father," Randy said without looking up from whatever he was doing. "When Mom left, Dad sold the house and got an apartment. He wanted all new furniture because he was starting over again. He was going to give all the stuff we had to the Salvation Army."

"He was going to give away all this beautiful stuff?"

Randy nodded. "He has money coming out his ears."

I thought of Randy's silver sports car, wherever it was at the moment. I guessed Randolph did at that.

"I talked him into letting me have whatever I wanted. I took the stuff you noticed and my bedroom stuff." He glanced at his mother, embarrassed, a kid about to make a confession. "I was mad at Mom then because I blamed her for the divorce, so I refused to get her anything."

"Oh, Randy," Edie said, shaking her head. "Don't worry about that. The last thing I wanted was the bedroom suite I shared with him." She fluttered her hands rapidly like she was trying to shake something sticky and unpleasant off. "Some days even the living room is a bit much."

Randy looked at the beautiful furnishings. "You can get rid of this stuff if you want. I don't care. I don't need it anymore." He spoke like it was a revelation to him, this not needing the furniture. "Just keep the pictures." He looked at the watercolors hanging on the walls. "I really like them."

"Me too," Edie said. "And I don't think we'll get rid of anything at all. It's a given that Tom and I will never be able to afford anything this nice." She ran her hand over the soft arm of the sofa. "I'm glad you asked about the furniture, Merry, what with all this talk about missing money. Our furnishings are definitely beyond our income level, at least in this part of the house."

I thought of the plain beige carpet upstairs and the Kmart glasses in the kitchen. There was no question but that the rest of the house was ordinary. Nice enough but ordinary. I was relieved to my toes to know the prosaic origin of the spectacular furniture, though I couldn't help but wonder what William Poole thought of the opulence when he visited on Friday.

"Okay," Randy said, "here we go." He cleared his throat. "Tom worked for the Audubon PD for ten years. He was a sergeant at the time of the drug bust. The Audubon PD cooperated with the Camden PD and the Drug Enforcement Agency to break up a ring that was using the mall on Black Horse Pike in Audubon and the park down the street from the high school like they owned them. Of course they were also working Camden like crazy. They had a DEA guy and woman go undercover, he with the gang, she in the high school. They set up the bust at a drop in an old warehouse in Camden."

He hit some more keys, and Edie watched him in total fascination.

"The cops surrounded the building and did their usual 'Freeze—it's the police' thing. But one of the drug guys panicked and started shooting. Gunfire was exchanged and when the dust settled, Tom Whatley was fatally wounded and one other guy, named Felix Estevez, was dead."

He looked at us. "That's all available in the newspapers and is general knowledge. I got it from the *Philadelphia Inquirer* and *Daily News* sites. Now comes the interesting part." He went back to his screen. "Tom—our Tom—"

Edie turned to me and mouthed, "Our Tom?" and patted her heart like she couldn't believe what she was hearing.

Oblivious, Randy continued. "Our Tom rushed in with the rest of the force, and when he saw Tom Whatley, he went sort of crazy. He fell on his knees beside the wounded Tom and kept saying, 'You aren't supposed to be here! You aren't supposed to be here!' His superiors thought that was an incriminating comment given the men's history, so they had Tom's involvement with Tom Whatley and the drug bust investigated. But before they could come to any conclusions, Tom resigned from the force and disappeared." Randy snapped his fingers. "Just like that."

"Nobody had any idea where he was?" I asked.

Randy shook his head. "He was just gone."

He went back to his story. "The Audubon PD found no evidence to indicate Tom had anything to do with trying to taint the bust. He was cleared in absentia. But the kicker is that the lab tests showed that the bullet that killed Tom Whatley came from our Tom's gun. It was one of many shots fired, but it was the one that struck. The police kept that bit of information quiet for several months before it was leaked to an *Inquirer* reporter. No one ever admitted letting the report get out, and the reporter refused to talk, protecting his source. But there's no question. Our Tom accidentally killed the other Tom."

Randy looked at Edie and blinked. Whatever he had expected her reaction to be to this news, he hadn't expected a smile. Neither had I. But her face was alight with joy.

"You've known this all along, haven't you?" I accused. "You've always known that Tom Whatley was Tom Willis."

She turned her smile on me. "Do you really think Tom would deceive me?"

Given what I and everyone else said about the depth of their affection, the answer was obvious. But he had deceived the rest of us, including Randy. And so had Edie.

Randy stared at his mother, confusion all over his face. "You knew all this? I did all this work for nothing? I even hacked my way into the Audubon PD system!"

Here was Randy's great gift offered in love—for the first time in who knew how many years—and it wasn't wanted or needed, and he was hurt. And ticked.

Oh, Lord, don't let this revelation undo all the good of the past day or so!

"Honey, you have done me one of the biggest favors of my life." Edie walked over to him and kissed him noisily on the cheek. "I thank you, I thank you. You have helped me more than you'll ever know."

Though still confused, Randy seemed somewhat mollified by her appreciation. *Thank you, Lord.*

"So when did you find out?" I asked.

"Tom told me all about Tom and the shootout before we were married, but he swore me to secrecy. It didn't really matter until Thursday when he didn't come home. I didn't know what to do. What if the truth would sort things out? Though I couldn't imagine how. I decided I'd just keep quiet until I had to tell. But it was killing me inside. Now, thanks to this wonderful kid who uncovered all our secrets—" and she glowed at Randy "—I can talk about everything with a clear conscience."

"Would you have kept quiet indefinitely?" I asked, still somewhat peeved that she hadn't shared what she knew.

"I don't know. It would have depended on what happened. But it's a moot point now." She smiled at Randy. "I'm free."

He didn't smile back. "Why did you go along with it at all?" Much of his pique was passed, but there was still a touch of starch in his question.

Edie sat on the sofa and clutched a pillow in her lap. "Tom was already known here in Amhearst as Tom Whatley when I met him. How do you tell people that you've been using a false name without them wanting to know why? And then all that pain would be raked up all over again. I mean, who wants to live through that twice?"

"How did he come to be known as Tom Whatley in the first place?" I asked.

"Ah. Now there's a weird story. I bet you didn't find that in your magic little machine, did you, Randy?"

"You know I didn't," he said. "Come on. Talk. Tell me why I shouldn't be mad at you all over again."

"I love you."

He rolled his eyes and slouched down in the chair.

Edie paused and ordered her thoughts. "You already know that Tom and Tom were best friends and had been for years. The TomTom Twins. My Tom—" she looked at Randy "—*our* Tom had done well, graduating from college and the police academy with honors. He was doing well on his job. Tom Whatley, the golden boy of Audubon High, had done poorly, getting kicked out of the Naval Academy, drifting from job to job, unable to cope when no longer the golden boy."

"The moral here," Randy said, "is that I should be glad I'm only second string JV and not one of the popular jocks in the starting lineup?"

His mother smiled at him. "You're popular with me, kid." She blew him a kiss.

His expression said clearly that while he might be having a change of heart about many things, being popular with his mother still didn't cut it.

I'd had enough mother-son bonding. "So Tom Whatley was a failure. I found that out in Audubon."

Edie looked sad. "He fell into drugs big-time. My Tom was never sure how it began. He asked and asked, but the other Tom was always frustratingly vague. But as the years passed, Tom Whatley became more and more heavily drug dependent. Tom put him in detox programs more than once, but the other Tom would always leave, sometimes before even one day had passed.

"Our Tom knew that the other Tom was going to die soon if something wasn't done. The problem was that the other Tom didn't seem to care. Then came the word that Tom Whatley was involved with the ring about to be busted."

"How did Tom hear that?" I asked. "A source on the street?"

"A comment from his chief, if you can believe that. 'A hero's going to fall in this one,' he said the afternoon before the bust. Tom asked what he meant. The chief was an older guy who had a son named Bobby who had graduated with the Toms. Bobby played football, and he always lost out to Tom Whatley for everything from quarterback to team captain. There may have been a bit of satisfaction in the chief's comment when he said, 'Such promise wasted, not like you and Bobby.' Right away Tom knew what the chief meant. It was his worst nightmare."

I could imagine. Talk about an ethical dilemma. He couldn't tell Tom what was going to happen because Tom might tell his associates. Then they would either disappear and set up shop elsewhere, or they would arrange an ambush. But how can you let your best friend get caught up in a situation that could lead to his getting arrested or shot?

"Our Tom went to the other Tom's apartment, by this time little more than a mattress on the floor in a horrible part of inner-city Camden. 'Don't go out tonight, Tom,' was what Tom ended up telling him. 'I'm worried about you. Promise me you won't go out and shoot up tonight.' The other Tom didn't even ask why. He just promised to make Tom happy, then did what he wanted. As Tom has said many times since, he should have realized that druggies will agree to anything, then do what they need to."

"So Whatley went to the drug drop." I found the story fascinating. "I take it he was financing his own habit by selling?"

Edie nodded. "He went and got shot, and my Tom still holds himself accountable."

"But it wasn't Tom's fault," Randy protested. "He told the other Tom to stay home. Besides, the other Tom was killing himself anyway."

Edie nodded. "Tom knows that, but the other Tom was still dead, and he had been unable to save the friend he loved better than a brother."

Randy looked thoughtfully at the rug. "Maybe I don't understand because I don't have a friend like that. But if something happened to Sherrie and I couldn't save her…." His face said it all.

I thought of Tom Willis, quiet, unimpressive, kind, living with all this hurtful history while he helped Edie overcome hers. And I looked at Edie, living with all these secrets, protecting the man she loved, helping him learn to cope. How much easier it would have been if they had known that God sent Christ to bear just such pain for them.

Dear God, help me help them.

Edie wasn't finished. "I'll say one thing for Tom Whatley. While our Tom was weeping beside him, knowing his wound was fatal but not knowing the bullet came from his own gun, Tom Whatley looked at him, smiled and managed to say, 'Thanks. You tried. Love you, man.'"

I thought about that for several minutes. "You tried." How would I react if someone I loved said that, using his last breath to free me from guilt?

"What?" Edie asked me. "You're shaking your head."

"'You tried.' I was wondering if that would free me. I don't think it would any more than it did Tom. I think that's one that only God can set you free from."

Edie looked at me with something like respect in her eyes. "Tom still has nightmares about that night."

"But it wasn't his fault," Randy said again. "It's not fair."

"It's not," his mother agreed. "But then life's not fair."

That's sure true, I thought. "By the way…" I smiled at Edie. "I met your mother-in-law."

She stared at me. "Mom Willis?"

"When I went to Audubon."

Edie stood and began to pace. "I don't think Mom understands all that happened to Tom. She just knows he's living here in Amhearst and using a different name. He visits her often, usually at night so there won't be questions from the neighbors, and he sends her money every month. Without it, she wouldn't be able to keep her home. I think she talks about him to her friends. I know she brags on Randy a lot."

Startled, Randy looked at his mother. "Tom's mom brags about me?"

Edie smiled. "I heard her once on the phone talking about her handsome grandson."

He blinked. "But I've never even met her."

"That doesn't stop Tom and me from talking about you. She's got your pictures plastered all over her refrigerator."

"If she thinks I'm nice," Randy looked uncomfortable as he spoke, "then you haven't been telling her the truth."

"Let's just say we're selective," Edie said. "You do well in school, you play a mean game of football and you are a computer whiz. We tell her things like that."

He blinked rapidly a few times. "Can I meet her?"

"When Tom comes home."

"She's a little, tiny lady, Randy," I said. "You could carry her around in your palm."

"Sort of like Tom." But he smiled, and there was no mockery in his voice.

"Yes," his mother said as she made her way back to the sofa. "Sort of like Tom."

Randy had shut down his laptop and closed its lid. He

leaned an elbow on it. "I still have two questions. Why or how did Tom Willis become Tom Whatley?"

Edie took a sip from the now lukewarm cup of tea I'd made for her. "It's one of those dumb things," she said. "Tom had gone to ground after the shootings, staying at a friend's cabin in the Poconos."

"Did the friend know he was there?" Randy asked.

"I don't think so," Edie said. "He'd stayed there before. In fact, he and Tom had stayed there a couple of times in failed attempts to get Tom clean. This time our Tom went to be alone and grieve. He stayed there for a couple of months in the winter, reeling with the pain, only venturing out to go to the store for the bare essentials. But come spring, he knew he couldn't live the rest of his life like a hermit, eaten with regret and what-ifs.

"He got in his car and began to drive. Somehow he ended up in Amhearst just as his car died. He coasted into Hamblin Motors prepared to buy a car. Mike Hamblin himself was the salesman he talked with, and Mike was impressed with Tom's knowledge of cars. 'I need a salesman,' he said. 'I need a job,' Tom said. 'What did you say your name was?' Mike asked. Before Tom could answer, Mike was called away for a minute.

"While he waited for Mike to return, Tom saw a newspaper on the corner of Mike's desk. The headline read Cop In Drug Bust Killed Best Friend. A picture of him in his uniform stared out at him. He wasn't worried about being recognized as the man in the picture. He looked much different than the rookie cop with the earnest face staring out at him from under the bill of his hat. Regret and sorrow had aged him, his hair was much longer and he looked a bit scruffy. But it was the first time he knew he had been the one to kill Tom."

My stomach clenched. What a terrible way to learn something of that magnitude!

"When Mike came back, Tom's mind was still reeling. 'What's your name?' Mike asked again. And because his mind was full of his friend, my Tom said, 'Tom Whatley.'

"'Well, Tom, what do you say? Willing to give us a try?' Tom opened his mouth to correct the mistake in the name when he caught the first two words in the article—Thomas Willis. What if Mike Hamblin made the connection? Besides, he only planned to be there for a very short time. All he wanted was a little ready cash, and he'd be on his way. Who cared if they called him by the wrong name?"

"But what about Social Security and his paycheck and all?" I asked. "How could he get paid in the wrong name?"

"When Tom Whatley died, none of his family came to the hospital. They had all washed their hands of him long before. So the hospital gave my Tom all the other Tom's effects. He kept all the things with him all those months, actually carrying the papers in his own wallet. If Mike Hamblin thought it strange that he had to pull his Social Security card and read his number, he didn't mention it. And of course —" she spread her hands "—Tom found out he liked Hamblin's and selling cars and Amhearst."

"And you," I said.

"Well, there's nothing very sinister in all that," Randy said, relief evident in his voice.

Edie collapsed against the arm of the couch, exhausted now that the story was told.

"You need to rest," I said. "This has been hard on you."

"Yeah," Randy added. "You need to get better for when Tom comes home."

Edie looked at her son. "You sound like you want him to come home."

"Well, yeah. Because it's what you want." He turned bright red but forced himself to continue. "So it's what I want."

Edie was still reeling from the shock of Randy's comment when he and I left.

"I still have one question," Randy said as we pulled out of the driveway. "What does all that long-ago stuff have to do with Tom's disappearance now?"

What indeed.

THIRTEEN

Randy and I arrived at Freedom House at two o'clock. I was looking forward to my interview with Tina, and he was cringing with embarrassment. What if he saw Sherrie? Or her mother, who had undoubtedly heard about the events of yesterday from Sherrie?

"It's called facing the music," I said as we climbed the steps.

"Yeah, I know. But the tune is so ugly." He tucked his laptop under one arm and looked around the porch. "So's this building. Why don't they fix it up?"

"Money." I thought of the quality furniture in his family's living room and the multitude of gadgets in his room and all the money those things represented. "Or lack of it."

He grunted as a young woman I'd never seen before opened the door. Not having enough money was a concept that was hard for him to grasp.

"Hi, I'm Karen." She stepped back to let us in. She was pretty in an overblown sort of way with lots of long curly blond hair and way too much makeup. Still, I could see the bruise on her right cheek.

She smiled like she hadn't a care in the world. "We're having Bible study now, but Stephanie's almost finished. She asked me to take you to her office."

I noticed that the collection of equipment and offerings for Like New had grown and was threatening to overtake the entryway. Randy stared with distaste at the clutter.

"Isn't it great?" Karen grinned as we stepped over two supersized plastic bags of clothes, their cinches pulled tight and tied in red bows. "Some lady Stephanie doesn't even know dropped these bags off just a few minutes ago. Word's getting around."

"Word about what?" Randy muttered in my ear. "That the place is the town's new dump site?"

Karen beamed as she stopped in Stephanie's office door. She touched the dark shadow on her cheek. "I'm going to be the first trainee at the store. I don't have any place to live yet and I don't have any money, but I know I'll be okay. I have hope." And she left us.

Randy stared after her, frowning. "Why's she so cheery? That bruise on her cheek looked pretty bad to me."

"She's got hope," I said.

"Yeah, I heard. But why? She hasn't got a place to live. She hasn't got money. She's got a husband who beats her."

"But she's got a way out."

He shook his head, confused.

"That stuff out there…"

"That junk?" Distaste curled his lip.

"That's her way out."

"She's the town's new trash man?"

I looked at Randy. He'd come a long way in a short time, but he still obviously had a long way to go.

"Do you think Sherrie's smart?" I asked.

He blinked at the change in topic but came with me readily enough. "I should do so well in school."

"Do you think she's got class?"

"Down to her fingertips."

"How about her mother and brother?"

"Very neat people. Fun. I like them."

"Then why do you assume that they're collecting trash? Why do you assume that the property is shabby on purpose?"

He didn't look very happy at the not-too-subtle reprimand. Too bad. If I had to cart him everywhere I went, I was going to tell him a thing or two as I thought best.

"Okay." His voice was cool. "Why the mess?"

"Many women don't leave their abusive husbands because of money. They have no way to feed and house themselves and their kids. Stephanie wants to help them learn a marketable skill. She's opening a secondhand store and training women in sales skills there."

"Oh." He looked slightly chagrined, but he rallied quickly. "But why the mess in the hall? Why don't they put the stuff away somewhere?"

"Priorities."

"What?"

"What's more important? Finding a place for Karen to sleep until she can care for herself, or a neat hallway?"

He looked at me in silence for a minute. "You're good, you know." He walked into Stephanie's office and collapsed on one end of the sofa from the mission in Allentown. "All of a sudden you've got me thinking that mess is a wonderful thing."

"That's nice, but what I really want is for you to take time to think first, guy. Don't jump to conclusions about things. Or people."

He slid so far down on the sofa he was almost sitting on his neck. "Me? Jump to conclusions about people?" His laugh was bitter and full of self-loathing. "Not me."

He ran his fingers over a particularly dark stain on the sofa seat, then slapped at it. Dust motes flew. "Why would anybody want furniture like—" He stopped and looked at me. "They don't necessarily want it, do they? They have no choice. There's no money."

Inside I felt like a proud mom cheering for her kid when he hit a home run, but I said very calmly, "You got it."

He nodded and stared at the stain a minute. Then he plugged in his computer and was basically lost to his surroundings and all conversation. The game he was playing had his entire concentration.

I knew when the Bible study finally ended because I could hear the women's voices, all talking at the same time, laughing, lingering. Stephanie came into the office while women still talked.

"They don't like to leave," she explained. "It's safe here."

She saw Randy, who looked up apprehensively when somehow through his game fog he heard her enter. She smiled a welcome. "Well, hi, Randy. Nice to see you."

He relaxed visibly at her accepting attitude, his fingers easing on the computer keys. He blurted, "I have to stay with Merry."

Stephanie looked a question.

"It was her or juvenile hall."

"Ah. And you chose her." Stephanie sat in the stuffed chair. "Wise choice."

"Is Sherrie okay?" Randy asked, flushing an even more painful red.

Stephanie nodded. "Not happy, but okay. She went to school."

Randy seemed pleased. "Good. I need to apologize to her for yesterday."

Stephanie eyed him thoughtfully. "Maybe not quite yet."

He nodded sadly. "She needs time. I understand."

Stephanie smiled at him. "I like you, Randy. With God's help, you're going to be okay, you know that?"

Randy was bowled over by this show of confidence. He went back to his computer to hide his self-consciousness.

Stephanie turned to me. Her smile fell away. "She isn't here."

My heart dropped. "Do you know where she is?"

Stephanie shook her head. "But I can guess. I've been down this road with so many women, including myself in the old days. I was just going to call her parents to see what they can tell me."

She walked to her desk and sat down. As she reached for the phone, it rang.

"Freedom House. Stephanie Bauer speaking."

She glanced at me and mouthed, "Tina." I nodded. I could hear a happy voice splashing through the mouthpiece like verbal sunshine, though I couldn't hear specific words. Maybe things actually were all right.

Stephanie listened a minute, leaned back in her desk chair and closed her eyes in dismay. So much for all right.

"Oh, Tina." More words poured out of the phone, but none of them eased Stephanie's fears. Then she said, "You had an appointment with Merry Kramer for an interview. Did you forget?"

Next thing I knew I had Tina in my ear. Stephanie could pass off a phone with all the finesse of a relay runner passing off the baton.

"Hi, Merry. I thought you'd be there." Canaries never sounded so chirpy. "I wanted you to know I didn't forget, but I can't meet with you after all."

Rats. There went some of the best content of my story. "Can we talk now? I can interview you over the phone."

"Can't do it," she said happily. "Bill asked me not to."

"Where are you, Tina?"

"I'm at home." As my heart sank, she bubbled, "Isn't it wonderful? Bill came for me and the kids this morning before work. He drove all the way to Phoenixville for us."

I drove all the way to Phoenixville for you, too, I thought darkly.

"He was so good with the kids, hugging them and kissing them. I could tell he really missed us and regretted what happened."

"Don't waste your time," Stephanie whispered across her desk. "She can't hear you at the moment."

I nodded. I knew she was right, but I hated it. "Look, Tina, you still have my card, don't you? If you ever have time to talk to me or if you ever need me, you just call. I don't care what time it is, day or night."

After I hung up, Stephanie and I stared at each other. Finally she shook her head and said, "One of the hardest things I've had to learn is that you can't help them if they don't want to be helped."

"But he'll do it all over again."

She nodded. "He'll do it all over again. We need to pray that he doesn't kill her in the process."

"It took my mother years before she'd leave my father," Randy suddenly said, looking from me to Stephanie. "And I know we went back several times. He could be very persuasive." And he went back to his game.

I stood. "Come on, guy. We need to go."

"In a minute. I just want to finish this one part, or I'll have to start all over again."

"Obviously a fate worse than death," I muttered and left the office. Stephanie followed. We were almost to the front door when I heard a key in the lock. The door flew open and in backed Rob and Sherrie, busy waving at a car driving off.

"You're home early," Stephanie said.

Rob nodded. "Don brought us home. He's got a car for the rest of the week because his dad's in the hospital. His mom told him he could drive to school if he promised to go visit his dad every night."

"Sounds like a deal." Stephanie grinned.

Rob grinned back. "I think Don likes Sherrie."

Sherrie looked appalled. "Oh, no."

"Oh, yes."

"But he's too old!"

"He's my age. That's only three years."

"I don't mean in years."

I looked at Sherrie with respect for her insight.

"Ah," her brother said. "Experience. Yep, Don's had a lot of that. But he's still a nice guy. All the girls love him."

Sherrie frowned. "And that's supposed to be a selling point?"

"Oh, yeah," Rob said. "I forgot. You like them tall and blond and shy."

Suddenly Sherrie's frown became real. "Shut up, Rob."

"Rob," his mother cautioned.

Speaking of tall, blond and shy, where was he? I looked back to the office and watched as he came sailing out, laptop in hand, unaware of the ambush awaiting him.

"Hey, wait for—" He slammed to a halt as he saw Sherrie.

Sherrie went absolutely still too.

Randy swallowed a couple of times. "Can I talk to you for a minute?"

"Oh. I don't—" She looked at her mother for help, then back at Randy. "You weren't at school today."

He brightened because she'd noticed. "We brought my mother home."

"How is she?"

"Fine. She's at home now, resting."

Sherrie fell silent. As the silence lengthened, she grew embarrassed. She lowered her head, her black hair falling forward to guard her face.

"Can we talk?" Randy asked again, probably trying to not sound like he was pleading, and failing. "Just for a minute?"

There was no sign she heard him except for perhaps a more rapid rhythm to her breathing.

He accepted her silence as a no. "That's okay." He tried not to let his hurt show. "I understand. I wouldn't want to talk to me either. I was pretty awful."

Her head came up, her eyes uncertain. "It's not...I don't... You're not..." She looked at Stephanie again.

Stephanie stepped into the breach. "Sherrie, I know you're supposed to talk with Merry this afternoon. Why don't you two take the office? Randy, why don't you come upstairs with Rob and me, and I'll get you guys something to eat while you wait for Merry."

"You're here with Merry?" Sherrie asked, her head once again lowered.

Randy nodded jerkily, then realized she couldn't see him. "Yes."

"I thought you came to see me." Her voice was a whisper, and I couldn't tell if she was relieved or disappointed that Randy had come with me.

"I'd always come to see you if I thought you'd see me." It was a declaration straight from the heart.

Stephanie and I looked at each other and smiled. It was so sad and so sweet. This time Rob saved further awkwardness.

"Come on, Randy. Mom and Sherrie baked snickerdoodles last night. It was their mother-daughter ritual to help Sherrie cope." He started toward the stairs. "You might as well benefit from their activities." He stopped and grinned impishly over his shoulder. "After all, if it hadn't been for you, there'd be no cookies."

Sherrie gasped, but she didn't look up. Randy flushed at the gentle, precise jibe.

"Rob," Stephanie cautioned as she stood at the foot of the stairs and waited for Randy to precede her. With a last look in Sherrie's direction, Randy resigned himself to cookies instead of his love and followed Rob.

Taking a deep breath and letting it out slowly, Sherrie led the way to her mother's office. I took the sofa again and she the easy chair. I got out my tape recorder and my note tablet.

She sat and stared at her clasped hands for a minute, and I let the silence continue. She needed time.

"I still like him." She said it as if she was admitting she liked Internet porn.

"So do I. He's a nice person with lots of possibilities."

She looked at me then, clearly confused with herself. "But you saw what he did."

I nodded. "And he scared himself very badly."

"Badly enough to change?"

"I think there's a good chance."

"Can he do that without Jesus?"

"Maybe." I rubbed at the stain Randy had noted earlier. "Some people do."

"But lots don't."

"You know what that means, don't you?"

She thought about that for about two seconds, then grinned. "We've got to pray he finds Jesus."

I smiled at her. "I'd already been thinking about inviting him and his mom to church on Easter to hear you sing. Now I know I will. You pray that they come, okay?"

She nodded, excited. "I will. Oh, I will."

"Good girl. I knew I could count on you. Now let's get to work."

We talked for almost a half hour, and she did have some very good ideas for my story.

"Kids in an abusive home have one of two experiences," she said as she tucked her legs under her. "Either they end up getting hit too, or they observe it happening. Mom calls it 'pointed behavior' when the abuse is leveled at the child and 'modeled behavior' when the child only sees the abuse. Each has its own special terror. But either way, they think this is normal. They don't have any other gauge for family life, especially when they see it from a little kid on up."

"So you thought your dad's temper and beatings were normal?" I couldn't quite keep the surprise out of my voice.

"Sure. It scared me, but I thought that was just the way life was. I'd wake up to Mom screaming and begging and him roaring and cursing. I'd cry in fear because I didn't understand what was happening. I hid under the bed more than once, terrified I'd be next."

"Did your father ever hit you?"

She shook her head. "He never hit either Rob or me. And he hit Mom most when he'd been drinking or had a real bad day at work. Then he'd apologize and fall all over himself saying how he'd never do it again." She blew out a disgusted breath. "What a lie."

"What would you like to tell parents in abusive homes?"

She didn't have to think for even a moment. "I'd tell the moms to get out before the kids are scarred any worse. Every day you remain makes it harder for the kids to be normal adults. I'd tell the fathers to think what they're doing to their kids. They're making them scared and full of fear and teaching them that violence is an okay way to live. Go get help for the kids' sakes."

I smiled at her appreciatively. She was a good interview, her ideas organized and clear. "Why do you think moms stay?"

"They keep hoping it'll be different. They're ashamed. They don't have anywhere to go. They don't have any money. They don't have any job skills. They think God wants them to stay. Their pastor tells them they should stay." She shrugged. "All or any of those, and there are probably more reasons I haven't thought of. Take Mom. She's an optimist. She wanted to believe my father every time he said things would be different. She's a fixer-upper. She wanted to fix him. So she stayed."

"What would you tell girls your age to help prevent them from marrying someone like your father?"

"I'd tell them to be wary of anyone who has a temper. I'd tell them not to think they can change someone just by loving him. So many of the women my mom works with had a savior complex. They were going to love this man so much he'd become emotionally healthy. Love would make everything fine."

I looked at her earnest young face. "But that sounds good."

"The trouble is that he doesn't know what love really is. He only knows what control is. Love yields. Love cares. Love desires that the other person be happy or comfortable or pleased."

"But some guys are frauds, able to play the game until after the marriage." I wanted to hear her answer to that familiar problem.

She readily agreed. "Some guys are frauds. And the younger you are, the more likely you are to be taken in by a fraud. But in the long run there are no guarantees about anyone."

"How'd you get to be so smart?" I asked.

"Around here," she said, "all you have to do is listen."

"If there are no guarantees, what hope can you give a young woman?"

"Make certain the guy's a Christian. That's not a guarantee either, but it's the best I can offer. Make certain the guy loves God because God's love will change his heart, just like it'll change yours. Make sure he's dealt with any problems in his background. Make sure he's kind to his mother. I kid you not. The way he talks to his mom and grandmom is probably the way he'll talk to you. And he should be nice to animals and to old people too."

She fell silent, looking at me expectantly.

"Anything else?" I asked.

"Nope." She uncurled from the chair. "I think I said everything I wanted to."

I stood and collected my equipment. "Shall we go upstairs and get a snickerdoodle? I hate to think of those guys getting them all."

Sherrie immediately became hesitant.

I smiled gently. "Life's a lot harder than theory, isn't it? My suggestion is that you be pleasant but distant. Sort of like he's your pesky though handsome brother. He likes you a lot, which shows he has good taste." She blushed. "But right now he needs to take care of his own problems, not focus on you. Maybe in a year or two."

"Or three or four?"

"Or three or four," I agreed.

Slowly she relaxed. "A brother. Three or four. I can handle that." She nodded. "Let's go get some cookies."

FOURTEEN

I started when the doorbell finally rang and glanced at my watch. Ten p.m. Curt was only three and a half hours late getting back from Philadelphia.

Randy looked up from the TV we had been pretending to watch. "I'll get it."

I nodded.

Okay, girl, I said to myself for the thousandth time. *You have a choice. You can be a shrew or you can be kind. Like you told Randy this afternoon, don't assume.*

Randy had just reached the door when the phone rang. I picked it up as Curt crossed the sill. He smiled slightly in Randy's direction, but his eyes immediately sought me out. They were filled with the unlikely combination of excitement and apprehension. I didn't know why the excitement, but I sure knew why the apprehension. I hadn't been exactly understanding recently.

Choice.

I smiled a welcome. After all, there might have been a giant pileup on the Schuylkill Expressway and he'd been held up while they cleared the roadway of the myriad bodies or the oil slick or scores of little pigs freed by the collision.

Or he'd been with Delia.

My smile soured somewhat.

"Merry?" The word in my ear was so soft I almost didn't hear. It was also slurred, indistinct.

"Who is this?" I asked. The last thing I wanted was another threatening phone call.

"It's me, Tina."

I could barely make out the words. "Tina? What's wrong?"

Her answer was a ghastly, gurgling sob.

"Tina!" Curt and Randy were both at my side, reacting to the horror in my voice.

"Help me. Please." Then more sobs.

"Are you at your house?"

"Yes."

"Is your husband there?"

"He went out to get some booze. Help. Before he comes back. Please."

"Are the kids okay?"

"Scared. Crying."

Poor little mites. I'd be scared and crying too. "I'll be right there."

I disconnected and reached for my purse even as I dialed 911. Curt's tardiness for our special dinner had become the unimportant item it was.

"You're not going alone," he said clearly and with authority. "We'll take my car. It's parked behind yours."

For once I didn't argue. I wanted his size and protection.

We raced out the front door, and it wasn't until we were pulling out of the parking lot that I realized Randy was with us too.

"She sounded bad!" I was shaking so hard that I had trouble getting my seat belt on. Finally I heard the click.

Curt took my hand. "She'll be okay. We'll get her out."

I nodded, but I felt overwhelmed with guilt. If I'd argued more effectively, if I'd somehow been able to convince her of her danger, this beating wouldn't have happened.

Randy leaned over the seat. "It's not your fault, Merry. You tried. You told her all the right stuff. She just didn't listen."

"Thanks, Randy." I patted his hand resting on the seat by my shoulder.

When Curt pulled in to Tina's drive, I sighed with relief when I saw there was no sign of another car. Her husband was still out.

The front door opened even before Curt turned the motor off, spilling yellow light onto the little front porch. Jess, looking small and vulnerable in his pajamas, threw open the storm door as I ran up the sidewalk.

"Merry!" He launched himself down the steps and ran toward me. I reached for him.

He froze midstride as he became aware of Curt and Randy coming up behind me. I thought how two tall men must appear to a little boy who was already afraid.

I knelt on the sidewalk. "It's all right, Jess. This is Randy. And this is Mr. Carlyle. They're my friends, and they've come to help me help your mom."

"Hi, Jess." Curt went down on his knees beside me. "Are you all right?" He laid a gentle hand on Jess's head.

The boy flinched as he saw the hand coming in his direction, glanced at me doubtfully but stood his ground. When he felt the gentleness of Curt's touch, something in him gave way. He started to cry.

"It's my mom," he sobbed. He wrapped his arms around me and buried his face in my neck.

"Where is she?" I asked, standing with him still held close. He wrapped his little legs about my waist.

He mumbled something into my neck, now wet with his tears and, I suspected, the phlegm from his runny nose.

"Say that again?"

"I'll show you." He wiggled to get down.

I set him on the ground, and he led us into the house,

across the living room with its toppled lamps and upended coffee table and upstairs to a bedroom. That room was a shambles too, with shattered fragrance bottles and wall mirrors, a bed with the linens ripped off and thrown helter-skelter, a closet with clothes ripped from hangers and thrown on the floor. Shards of what had once been a porcelain figurine lay at the base of one wall beside a library book with its spine broken.

But the most terrible sight was Tina, lying on the bed with her eyes closed, a wide-eyed, apprehensive Lacey curled beside her, holding her hand.

One of her eyes was swollen shut and already turning black. The other was ringed with green and purple from the shiner she'd gotten in the skirmish between her husband and her father Sunday evening. Her nose was bleeding slowly, and she sniffed periodically, gagging as she swallowed the fluid. Her lip was split and swollen, and she couldn't shut her mouth. Saliva kept sliding out, and she was too despairing to care. It ran down her cheek and pooled by her ear next to the raw spot where hair had literally been pulled out by the roots.

The kids had drawn a comforter over her, covering her other injuries, but I knew there must be more.

"Tina," I called softly as I knelt beside the bed. "Tina, it's me, Merry."

When she didn't respond, I was filled with momentary panic until I saw the steady rise and fall of her chest.

"I got her that ice pack out of the freezer," Jess said, coming to stand beside me. He pointed to the chemical ice packet Lacey was holding to Tina's eye.

"That was very wise," I said. "You did well."

Jess straightened his frail shoulders. "I called 911 too."

"Very well done," Curt said, standing behind us. He made certain to keep his voice soft and friendly.

Jess still eyed him with distrust but nodded, accepting the compliment.

Just then we heard a vehicle pull into the drive behind Curt's car. Jess turned white and Lacey began to whimper.

"It's okay," I said, sitting on the bed beside Lacey. I leaned in and gave her cheek a kiss. "Even if it's your father, it's okay. He can't hurt you or your mom with all of us here. We're going to see your mom gets to the hospital, and you get someplace safe."

The kids looked at each other, and some message flew through the air between them. Jess nodded and Lacey calmed a little. She went back to stroking Tina's hand.

Randy looked out the front window. "It's the ambulance. And the police. I'll go let them in."

Jess climbed onto the bed beside his mother and sister. He knelt, leaning over Tina. "It's okay now, Mom. Merry's here. And so is the ambulance. And the police. It's okay now."

Tina, who hadn't moved or seemed aware previously, relaxed at his words. I could see it in the movement of her shoulders and hear it in the deep sigh she gave. A hand snaked out from under the quilt and touched Jess lightly, then Lacey, before falling heavily to the pillow.

Curt, Randy, Jess, Lacey and I sat on the living room couch and waited as Tina was prepared for her trip to the hospital. Lacey's little body shook as she leaned against me, and I ran my hand soothingly over her head. Jess sat alert, listening for anything that might go wrong. I thought with sadness that things going wrong was a regular part of his life.

The most amazing and unsettling thing to me was that every one of the emergency responders, police and medical personnel alike knew Jess and Lacey. One of the EMTs stopped at the couch and knelt in front of the children. "I'm sorry we took so long to get here, you guys. We were out on another call and came as soon as we could. Are you okay?"

Jess nodded for both of them.

"You're a good man, Jess," the EMT said as he stood. "And you're a sweetie, Lacey." He chucked her gently under the chin, and she smiled shyly.

With a quick nod at Curt and me, he disappeared upstairs. How many times, I wondered, had these people been here in the past to be on such friendly terms with the kids?

And why had Tina stayed with the villain who was her husband?

As the EMTs wheeled Tina across the living room, she made a feeble motion for them to stop. She looked at me, fighting to stay alert.

"The kids," she said in a barely audible voice.

"I'll take care of them. Don't worry."

"Jess, Lacey." When she reached out a weak hand to them, I stepped back. "I love you. Go with Merry."

"I'll call your parents if you want. Is your father still in the hospital?"

"Home. Very sick. Tomorrow." It was all she could manage. Her eyes lost focus and slid shut.

"I love you, Mommy," Lacey whispered, her voice desperate.

I picked her up and held her tightly as Tina was taken from the house. "She loves you too, kitten." I kissed the little girl's cheek. "She loves you a lot."

I looked at Jess, the little boy who was forced to react like a man. "And you too, Jess. She's so proud of you for all your help."

He looked at me, his big eyes uncertain. Curt laid an encouraging hand on his shoulder. This time the boy barely flinched.

We loaded the kids and their hastily packed suitcases in the backseat with Randy. Lacey clung to a battered, fuzzy, once-pink blanket, holding it to her face and rubbing it back and forth between her fingers. Jess had a teddy bear with a missing ear and a dangling eye tucked firmly under his right arm. They leaned into each other, and I almost cried when I saw Jess pat his little sister on the shoulder.

Just before I climbed into my seat, Curt looked at me over the roof of the car. "You want to go to the hospital to see how Tina's doing, don't you?"

I nodded.

"What about our little friends?" He glanced down at the car.

"I don't know. We certainly can't leave them. They need us as much or more than Tina."

Randy leaned out the window. "Mom and I can take care of them. Take us to our house. We've got a guest room they can stay in."

I looked at Randy, uncertain.

"Call Mom. She'll tell you to bring them."

I went back inside to call Edie so we could talk out of earshot of the children. She needed to be able to say no if having the kids was too much for her right now, but I didn't want Jess and Lacey to overhear and think no one wanted them.

"Oh, my goodness, bring them," Edie said without hesitation. "And bring their mother if they don't keep her at the hospital."

"You're sure? This is a tough time for you."

"People stepped in to help Randy and me back when we needed it. I have to step in now. One thing I learned all those years ago, help is needed when it's needed, not when it's convenient."

I thought about how I'd hesitated to help Randy and felt a strong kick of shame. Maybe one of the great drawbacks to an orderly, happy life like I'd experienced was that you didn't understand immediate and desperate need. You'd never had it.

After I explained to the children that they were going to stay with Randy and his mother, they huddled against the far door. They stared silently and skeptically at Randy across the backseat. Lacey hugged her blanket more tightly and Jess pulled his bear against his chest.

Oh, Lord, please let them be okay with this plan.

Finally Jess spoke. "Aren't you big to live with your mom?"

I blinked, startled. I don't know what I expected the boy to say, but that wasn't it.

"I'm not so big," Randy said. "I still go to school."

"You do?" Clearly Jess equated size with maturity. "College? Big guys go to college."

"Not yet." Randy smiled. "Someday."

The kids continued to study him. He sat still and let them stare. Every so often he smiled at them, but their solemn little faces didn't respond.

"I used to have a father like yours," Randy blurted as we turned onto Main Street.

"Yeah, right." Disbelief vibrated about Jess like sound waves about a tuning fork.

"I did." Randy held his hand up like he was taking an oath and bent all his fingers but the last. "Pinky swear."

The kids blinked, looked at each other and giggled. "Pinky swear," Jess whispered, like it was the funniest thing he'd ever heard. They giggled again.

"I had to call 911 for my mom too," Randy continued. "Once my father threw her down the stairs and broke her leg."

"That's bad," Lacey said, giggle gone.

Randy nodded. "Very bad."

"Did she get a cast?"

"She did. And crutches."

"Does she still got them?"

He shook his head. "She's okay now. That was a long time ago, when I was little like you."

Lacey stared, obviously overwhelmed at the idea of big Randy being little like her.

"What did you do?" Jess asked. "When he did it, I mean." He was back to looking out the window, but trembling with the need to hear Randy's answer.

Randy looked out the window too. "Nothing." He swallowed. "I couldn't. I was too little."

Jess gave a great sigh. "Yeah," he said sadly. "Too little."

"But you called 911," Lacey said to Randy. "Like Jess. That was good."

Randy smiled at her. "You're right. I did. Thanks for making me feel better."

She smiled back and stuck her thumb in her mouth.

He looked at Jess. "My mom said it was okay that I didn't do anything more."

Jess glanced at Randy, then away. "My mom too."

"But it still hurts. Even today it hurts."

Jess stared at Randy. "But you're big."

"There are some things you never forget, Jess. You just learn to live with them."

"Oh." He thought about that for a few minutes, his chin resting on the teddy's head. "Oh."

I caught Randy's eye and nodded. He smiled slightly. I was not surprised to see that within a few blocks Jess and Lacey were leaning against him like they'd been leaning against the far door a few minutes ago. Carefully, cautiously, he slid his arm around them.

In the emergency room I finally learned Tina's last name. It was on her insurance cards that the ward clerk handed me when I approached her to ask how Tina was.

"She's in x-ray," the woman said. "That's all I know."

As I automatically took the proffered cards, I wondered how many broken ribs they'd find.

I looked at the cards, and there the name was. William Bond. William. Bill. "Bill Bond! Curt, Bill Bond is Tina's husband!"

"And that's significant how?" he asked as he led me to a seat.

"Bill Bond is Tom Whatley's boss at Hamblin Motors! No wonder he wouldn't talk to me when I showed up at the dealership. He thought I was there about Tina, about the phone call to Mac, about his threat, when all I wanted was to talk about Tom."

"Didn't you recognize him when you saw him at Hamblin's?"

"I never saw him."

As I sat leaning against Curt, my head on his shoulder, I thought about how small the world could be sometimes. While I hadn't known whom I was seeking an interview with, he had known who I was, thanks to my giving my name when I rescued Tina and the kids from him on Saturday.

But if Bill Bond was Tina's husband, then the man I had seen lecturing Joey Alberghetti as I pulled away from Hamblin's was someone else entirely. I'd have recognized Tina's husband, even from the back. Who he was was probably unimportant, but his identity piqued my interest for all of five seconds before questions about Bill Bond took over, questions like where was he?

Surely he realized Tina needed medical treatment. He might be reprehensible, but he wasn't stupid. Even bullies understood the need to show up, to protect themselves by spinning their story of falls down stairs or trips over curbs.

I shuddered. Enough of Bill Bond. I turned to Curt. "Tell me about your evening. In all the excitement, we haven't had a chance to talk yet."

He smiled a half smile. "Somehow it doesn't seem quite so important anymore."

"But it is important." I took his hand between mine. "At least it's important to me."

His eyes began to sparkle, and I knew I'd said exactly the right thing. No more mistakes like the other night at the gallery.

"Oh, Merry, it was great!" The joy and happy disbelief in his voice made me smile. "Delia lined up the most incredible people for me to meet."

Delia. It suddenly became harder to rejoice for him.

Oh, Lord, I'm so petty! I'm jealous!

And I knew it wasn't just Delia herself that upset me, in spite of her blond beauty and sophisticated style. I was jealous because Delia could and would do for Curt things that I couldn't. She could give him a gallery showing. She could introduce him to important people. She could open doors to the art community that I didn't even know existed.

And what could I do? Nothing. Nada. Zero. Zip. Zilch. I sighed.

Curt heard and stopped mideffusion. He looked at me, questions written in his eyes.

"Sorry," I said hastily. "It sounds like you had a wonderful time. I am truly glad for your chances to make all these professional contacts."

He grinned knowingly. "It's okay." He leaned over and kissed my temple. "I still love you the best."

I stared at him. He had an amazing heart.

"What?" I could see him going back over his words, looking for his mistake. When he thought he knew what was wrong, he grimaced. "You *only* is what I meant. I still love you only."

I smiled. "I know what you meant. And I'm not worried about you. You're the good guy. She's the shark."

"And I'm the itty-bitty fish waiting to be devoured?"

I looked at him, all broad shoulders and athlete's body. An itty-bitty fish wasn't exactly appropriate. If indeed he had been an itty-bitty fish, I doubt Delia would have been interested, no matter how fine an artist he was.

"I'm jealous," I confessed in a rush. I never could keep a secret.

"Whatever for? You're ten times more appealing than she'll ever be."

"Really?" It was obviously time for his glasses to be changed, but what joy his comment gave me.

"It's true," he said, seeing my expression. "She may be sleek and lovely in her own way, but you're real. You have a heart that cries and cares and loves."

"But she can give you so much that I can't!" There. I'd said it. My worst fear. The core of my jealousy.

Curt looked at me and nodded. "You're right. Professionally, she can open doors for me and save me years of trying to establish myself."

How depressing.

He ran his finger down the side of my face. "However, for real life, for quality, character and spunk, you win hands down. You beat Delia without even having to try."

I looked into his eyes and saw that for him this was the truth.

"Trust me on this, darlin' girl," he whispered as he bent and nibbled my ear. "I know what I'm talking about."

I shivered and giggled and nodded.

"Excuse me." It was the ward clerk.

I drew away from Curt and hoped I wasn't too red in the face. I simply wasn't used to being caught in public with a man nibbling on me. Or in private for that matter.

"Mrs. Bond is ready to go home," the woman said.

We hurried into the emergency treatment area and found Tina sitting in a wheelchair with a physician standing beside her. The doctor's name tag read Sondra Blanchard, MD.

"Are you caring for Mrs. Bond?" Dr. Blanchard asked.

"We're taking her to a place where she'll be safe."

The doctor nodded. "See that she stays in bed for a couple of days. She looks worse than she is because the injuries are so visible. She has a pair of cracked ribs, but that's about it below the neck. Her face will become a veritable palette of rainbow shades over the next couple of weeks. Nothing to worry about. We stitched up the split lip on the inside, and there should be minimal scarring."

Curt and I nodded, thankful the injuries were not more serious.

Sondra Blanchard looked at Tina but spoke to us. "I told Mrs. Bond that I don't want to see her in here again." She smiled to take the sting from her words. "I want her to contact the authorities tomorrow and have a restraining order executed against her husband. One of these times he's going to do damage that isn't repairable."

Tina, full of pain medicine, gave a wobbly smile but said nothing.

The doctor patted her on the shoulder and disappeared down the hall, but not before I saw the worried expression on her face. How she must hate cases like this.

"Kids?" Tina managed as we got her settled in the car.

"They're at my friend Edie's. When we left, they were curled together in her son's big bed. He was reading to them, and they were about thirty seconds from dreamland."

"Why?"

Why might be all she could say, but I knew she meant, "Why are the Whatleys willing to take us in?"

"You know Tom Whatley from Hamblin's, don't you? Edie's his wife. She works with me at the *News,* but more to the point, she was an abused wife in her first marriage. She wants to help you because people helped her."

"Her son?"

"Randy. He's fifteen. He's taken Jess and Lacey under his wing. He knows what they're thinking. He's been there."

We showed Tina Jess and Lacey, teddy and blanket hugged close, cuddled together in Randy's bed. Randy lay asleep on the floor beside them, wrapped in a green sleeping bag.

"He wanted to be near in case they woke up scared," Edie whispered as we all stood in the bedroom doorway, Curt still holding Tina after carrying her up the stairs. Her head leaned wearily on his chest and tears fell silently at the sight of her sleeping kids.

We turned and entered the room across the hall. Edie had made up the bed with peach-and-yellow floral sheets, a cheery pattern that welcomed Tina.

"You sleep, Tina," Edie said as she stroked Tina's hair. "You're safe here, and I want you to stay as long as you want. This is your home."

Once again, Edie's hospitality and heart humbled me.

When we turned out the lights and left the room, Tina was still crying silent tears.

Curt drove me home, kissed me at the front door and left, as weary as I. I stumbled to the bedroom, fell into bed and slept four glorious but inadequate hours before it was time to get up and face the day and its many demands.

I needed to call Edie and find out how the various Bonds had survived the night. I needed to make certain Bill hadn't come near the place.

I needed to find out if the police had located and arrested Bill. I needed to send Stephanie to talk to Tina.

I sighed as I pulled open my car door. I climbed in and screamed.

I had found Bill Bond, and he was never going to bother Tina or anyone else again.

FIFTEEN

Blood, now congealed, had flowed from the wound down Bill's front and onto the seat and the floor. Sitting somewhat slumped in my passenger seat, he looked remarkably similar to Barney Slocum sitting in Randy's vehicle.

"Probably on purpose," William Poole said as the police swarmed over my car. "Probably the same killer, same gun, same warped reasoning."

"But why my car?" I wailed. As I heard myself, I thought wryly how much I sounded like Randy.

William shrugged, then smiled at me slyly. "You know you're going to lose your car for a while, don't you?"

I nodded in resignation. I'd been down this road before with other cars. "Scene of the crime. But you don't have to enjoy it so much."

I wandered back to my apartment and called Mr. Hamish, the car rental man. In the short time I had lived in Amhearst, he and I had become good friends.

"What is it this time? A murder? An accident? A deer?" He said the latter like he still didn't believe that story no matter how many times I tried to convince him.

I sighed. He'd read about it in the *News* anyway.

"There was a body sitting in the passenger seat of my car this morning."

"How awful," he said in a thoroughly delighted voice. "I'll get a car to you within fifteen minutes. Is that soon enough?"

By which he meant, will the cops still be there in fifteen minutes?

"That should be fine," I assured him.

When he arrived, I grabbed the keys and left while he settled down to watch the excitement.

As I drove, I called Edie.

"Everyone's fine here," she said. "In other words, they're all still asleep, including Randy."

"You would have been proud of him last night, Edie. He was wonderful with those children."

"Sort of scares you, doesn't it? You wonder when he's going to revert." I could hear the combination of hope and fear in her comment.

"Edie, bring him to church Sunday morning. He'll find a stability there that he can't find anywhere else."

Edie made a noncommittal noise.

"Come on," I coaxed. "It's Easter. And Sherrie's singing with the bell choir. He'll like that."

"I'll think about it," she said.

God, please help her do more than think!

I took a deep breath. "I've got some hard news for you. Bill Bond, Tina's husband, was found dead in my car this morning."

There was a moment of startled silence. Then, "Dead? In your car? Bill Bond?"

"He was shot."

"Like the guy in Randy's car? Oh, my!"

"Tell me about it."

"Do I have to tell her when she wakes up?" Edie was fading in and out by now, but I could hear the distress in her voice. I made a mental note to recharge my phone as soon as I got to work.

"No, don't you say anything. You've got enough to deal with without having to handle announcing to someone that she's a widow. The police will come out soon to tell her."

We disconnected to static.

I called Curt as soon as I reached the newsroom and listened to his wonderfully soothing comfort. Then I brought Mac up to date on the latest death and began writing about Bill Bond. I had to stop and hit delete a number of times because I found my adjectives and adverbs were noticeably negative and entirely prejudicial.

Partway through the article I called Hamblin Motors. I didn't know if they'd be in yet, or if they were, whether they'd heard about Bill, but I needed a quote from Mike Hamblin.

"What?" he shouted in my ear when I finally reached him. "Bill Bond is dead? How can that be? He was fine yesterday!"

"I'm sure the police will have more information than I do," I said primly.

"The police! Why the police? Don't tell me his crackpot wife finally did something to him!"

I thought of Tina, barely able to move last night because of what Bill had done to her, and wondered cynically what Bill had said at work about his wife. "I was wondering if you had any thoughts on Bill that I could include in my article on him."

"Like a tribute or a eulogy, you mean? Well, he was a genuinely nice guy."

Sure, I thought. That's why he used Tina as a punching bag.

"And a wonderful sales manager. The customers liked him a lot. They trusted him, you know. We will miss him terribly!" I heard a grunt, a noise of disbelief. "I still can't take in that he's dead!"

If you're surprised, I thought, *imagine how I felt when I found him in my car!*

"Can I come see you, Mr. Hamblin? I'd like to ask you some detailed questions about Mr. Bond, see where he worked, that kind of thing."

"Well…" I could hear reticence in Mike's voice.

"I was thinking I could do something more in-depth if I could talk with you. A genuine profile rather than a standard obituary. Don't worry. It won't put Hamblin Motors in a bad light. Not at all."

"Oh." Relief. "Well, why don't you come at about six-thirty tonight? I have appointments all day that I cannot get out of, even for something this important."

The trouble was Curt's opening was at seven. "Can you make it a bit earlier?" I asked.

"I'm sorry—I can't. I would if I could." I heard the flutter of pages like he was checking his Day-Timer. "Six-thirty's the best I can do."

It wouldn't take long to ask my questions. I could be at Intimations well before seven-thirty. That wouldn't be too bad. "All right. I'll see you at six-thirty."

Shortly before noon I grabbed my notebook, preparing to leave a morose Mac and the oppressive atmosphere of the newsroom to spend my lunch hour at Hibernia Park.

"If Mr. Montgomery doesn't do something soon," fumed Jolene as she yanked a dead leaf from the jade plant, "I'm going to march right up to his mansion and demand he rescue poor Mac—and all the rest of us—from rampant despair." She glared at Mac like his job instability and resultant melancholy were by his choice.

"Will you do me a favor?" I asked as I slid into my blue tweed blazer.

She looked at me suspiciously. Most people who asked her for favors these days wanted money. Well, so did I in a roundabout manner.

"You remember Sherrie Bauer?" I pulled my purse from my bottom drawer.

"The kid who had hysterics?"

I nodded. "I've been interviewing her and her mom and learning all about Freedom House for an article. I'm very impressed with them and what they do. Could you make Stephanie one of those wonderful baskets of flowers like you made for Mac?"

"Sure." She waved her hand like it was no great matter. "I'm going to the garden shop over lunch. I'll get the stuff then."

"Could you do me an even bigger favor and drop it off at Freedom House? I don't know when I'll see Stephanie again, and I'd like her to have the flowers before Easter, sort of a holiday gift, you know?"

Did that sound as much like an imposition to her as it did to me? Surely if I wanted to give someone a gift, I should take it myself.

Oh, Lord, please let her bite! And please move her heart when she sees the place and meets Stephanie!

"Sure. Why not?" She grinned. "I'm trying to learn to be nice."

I left before she could change her mind and stopped at Ferretti's for a BLT, a bag of chips and a Diet Coke, all to go. Then I drove to Hibernia Park, passing between the black lion heads set in their white pillars, and down the dirt road toward the picnic grove.

I noticed that three out of the four little whitewashed cottages along the road were occupied. Why was the fourth boarded shut? I wondered. Was it just too small for any modern family to live there, or was there some structural damage? But the sight of the mansion made the little white houses fall from my mind. The warm coppery-orange building was, quite simply, beautiful.

I found a picnic table sitting in a stream of sunlight. I tore my paper bag open and spread it on top of the table. I stood on the bench, turned and sat on my bag. I ate slowly and thought as I chewed. Then I just sat in the sun and thought some more.

Eventually I forced myself to climb out of my sunbeam. I walked slowly across the lawn to the ranger station.

"Hi," I said to the woman named Lori who sat at a desk behind the counter.

"Can I help you?" She rose and came to stand opposite me.

"I was here the other day looking for information about the mansion."

"Oh, yes," she said, quick to smile and reach across the counter to the brochure that I had gotten on Sunday. "This tells you all about it."

I took the brochure and thanked her. "When I was here over the weekend, the ranger and another man were talking about the fact that someone was staying in the park in an unauthorized manner."

She looked at me curiously.

"I'm Merry Kramer from the *News,* and I was just wondering if this person was still around. It might make a good story, you know? A homeless person staying in the park or a runaway trying to hide here."

Lori's face cleared. "It would make a good story, but I haven't heard anyone talk about seeing anyone who shouldn't be here."

"No more blood in the bathroom? No more stolen lunches?"

"What?" She obviously had no idea what I was talking about.

I felt disappointed. I handed her my card. "If you hear anything from anyone, will you call me? I still think it would make a great story."

Lori nodded and I let myself out, careful to take my

brochure with me. I sighed. There was no story here, just some tramp who'd been and gone.

I was driving through the exit at the far side of the park when a lightning bolt hit me. Of course! Of course!

I drove around the perimeter of the park to get back to the entrance, muttering to myself about the curse of one-way roads. After driving between the twin lions again, I slowed at the little boarded-up cottage, edged my car off the road and parked.

I looked around at the peaceful scene, the towering poplars and beeches with their branches still leafless against the blue sky, the creek tumbling and creaming over rocks behind the cottage.

You're crazy, Merry, crazy!

But I walked around the cottage anyway, listening, looking, trying to think like a man who needed to disappear for some reason I didn't yet comprehend. Even so, I almost missed what I was looking for. If I hadn't tripped over a stone hidden under the leaves and put out my hand to steady myself against the cottage, I wouldn't have seen the small smear of dried blood. Rusty red against snowy white.

My heart began to pound. I looked carefully at the side of the house and saw another smear. Now that I knew what I was looking for, the trail of blood smears stood out against the pristine whitewash like flares against a night sky. I followed them to the back of the cottage. There I found a window with the shutter torn free and a large rusty stain defacing the sill.

With the hairs on the back of my neck prickling in anticipation, I made my way to the window. There was no glass, and I looked directly into darkness.

Well, I shouldn't say directly, because the ground fell away behind the cottage, and the window was higher than I.

"Tom?" I called. "Tom, are you in there?"

There was no answer, but somehow I was aware that the silence had suddenly developed a listening quality. I was also aware that I had decided the man within was Tom Whatley. It fit somehow. That is, if there was a man within.

"Tom, it's me, Merry Kramer from the *News*. I'm Edie's coworker. You remember me, don't you?"

No one answered, but I thought I heard a slight noise coming from that stygian interior.

It could be a mouse, I told myself. Or worse yet, a rat. Or a snake. There were copperheads in the park. I shuddered at the thought of tangling with one of them.

But none of those critters would make that smear of blood on the windowsill or the smears on the whitewash.

I raced around the cottage to the front door. There the padlock mocked me, but I grabbed the latch and tried anyway. The door didn't even rattle under my assault, let alone open. I ran around back again.

"Tom! Can you hear me? Tom!"

I was feeling unhappy about the lack of response from inside when, very distinctly, I heard a weak moan. Then a hand appeared, gripping the windowsill. Dried blood stained the fingernails and light denim shirt cuff.

"Tom!"

As quickly as it had appeared, the hand disappeared, followed by a groan. Then nothing.

Heart pounding, I reached in my bag and pulled out my cell phone. I jabbed 911 but nothing happened. Then I saw the flashing notice: low battery. I felt like screaming in frustration when I realized that with the confusion over Bill Bond this morning, I'd forgotten to recharge.

Muttering all kinds of invectives at myself, I searched madly for some way to raise myself to window height. Tom, if that was Tom, needed help and immediately.

I started for the road. I'd drive my car back, park it under the window and stand on the trunk. That'd give me plenty of height. I'd only taken a few steps when I dodged a poplar and realized with keen disappointment that the trees were too close to allow for the passage of the car.

The shutter! I swung around hopefully. It wasn't a shutter like I usually thought of them, two pieces that met over a window. This shutter was one large piece of wood painted green, boards nailed across it in a Z pattern to make it sturdy. It lay on the ground, flat as the proverbial pancake. It would raise me all of two or three inches.

But, I thought, becoming twitchy with excitement, I could turn it on its edge and rest it against the house. I grabbed it and pulled, all set to drag the thing to the cottage and prop it against the wall. Surprise sped through me as my hands slipped. I staggered backwards and fell right on my rump, overset by the unexpected weight.

"It's okay, Tom," I called like he knew or cared about what was happening. "I'm coming. It'll just be a minute."

I pulled myself to my feet and eyed the shutter with a new respect. I took a deep breath and tried again. No matter how hard I gripped, my hands slid.

I stepped back and studied the shutter again. I reached my arms as wide as I could, stepped close, bent way over and gripped the far edges. I could just grasp them. I lifted.

Again all I could manage was a couple of inches, and my back was not happy about either the weight or the awkward angle. I took a baby step backwards and dragged. The shutter followed. I would have cheered if I weren't panting from the exertion. Step. Drag. Step. Drag. The blood rushed to my head from leaning over so far, and my hands ached. My back kept complaining with unkind little jabs like electrical shocks, and my calves threatened spasms. I gritted my teeth and reminded myself of the absurd folk truth no pain, no gain.

After forever, my backside finally bumped into the cottage. I stood, each vertebrae creaking.

"I'm here, Tom. I'm here."

Not that it did Tom much good. The shutter was still flat on the ground, only now it was flat next to the cottage instead of halfway across the yard. How was I to get it against the cottage? Inch by inch, I thought sadly. There was no other way.

So I moved it inch by inch. Lift it a bit on one side and prop it against the house, run around to the other side, lift it a bit, prop, run back to the first side. Lift. Prop. Lift. Prop. All the while, between the oofs and the out-of-breath puffs, I kept up a commentary for the sake of the wounded man inside.

"Hang on, Tom. I'm moving the shutter into place. Edie's been mad with worry. You should have called her, you know. But she never lost faith in you. Even Randy has confidence in you. Can you believe it? Oh, Tom, I'm almost there!"

Finally the shutter rested against the side of the house at an angle that wasn't too steep for me to run up, yet should be high enough to let me at least see into the cottage. That is, if the shutter didn't slip and collapse onto the ground as soon as I tried to mount it.

I ran to the creek and looked for a couple of rocks that were both good sized and carryable, not an easy combination. After trying several that were simply too heavy, I managed to carry three back to the shutter and space them against the edge digging into the ground. I tried to make them wedge tightly, like putting something in front of a car's tires to prevent the car from rolling.

I put a foot on the shutter and waited to see what happened. Nothing moved. I slowly put my full weight on that foot. Still nothing moved. I started to walk up the incline and felt the shutter slip. My stomach flipped and I screamed, "Please, God!"

The sliding shutter hit a bump in the stones beneath the whitewash and stopped its downward movement. I stood still, arms outstretched like that would hold the shutter steady. When there appeared to be no further slippage, I took another step and another. Soon I was at the window, and it was waist high.

"Yes, Lord!"

I grabbed the windowsill and peered into the room. Everything was so dark after the light of the wonderful spring day that I could see nothing. I threw a leg over the sill and waited an agonizing couple of minutes until I could distinguish shadows. It was a good thing I waited that long because Tom was huddled at the bottom of the window. If I had climbed in immediately, I would have fallen or stepped on him. As it was, I had to push myself off to the side to avoid him.

As soon as I was inside, I fell to my knees beside him. He hadn't reacted in any way when I had jumped down, and that fact frightened me not a little. I reached out and touched him. No response, not even a moan.

He couldn't be dead! Not in the last ten minutes! *Please, God!*

I felt carefully until I found his face. Immediately my hand stilled as I caught my breath in dismay. He was burning with fever. But that was a good sign, wasn't it? He wouldn't still be hot if he were dead.

I slid my hand to his neck and felt for his pulse. Beneath the hot flesh I felt the shallow but steady beating of his heart.

Tom moved his head and groaned softly. "Edie."

"No, Merry."

"Edie, don't leave me."

"Just for a couple of minutes to get help."

"Edie!" He became agitated and began clutching at me.

"Don't leave!" He could barely speak, but the anguish in his voice broke my heart.

"It's Merry and I won't." Though how I'd get help and keep that promise I didn't know.

"I love you," he whispered. "I love you."

I gave up on the Merry business and said simply, "I know."

He quieted, and I wondered again how I was going to get help.

In the distance I heard a car and wished I had a means of communicating with it. I'd just have to wait until Tom fell asleep again and then go for help. Hopefully that amount of time wouldn't do him any more harm than the time he'd been here already.

Loud bumps sounded from immediately outside and the light from the window overhead was blocked.

"No," I cried, visions of the shutter being replaced dancing like a nightmare through my head. "We're in here."

I lay Tom's head gently on the floor and stood. I sagged with relief when I saw not a shutter but a large man in a tan uniform at the window.

"Who's we and why are you here?" The voice was full of authority and no sympathy. "These windows are boarded shut to keep people out."

"We need an ambulance," I said. "There's a seriously injured man in here."

A flashlight shone in my face. I closed my eyes against the assault and stood still, letting the man look at me. In a short time the beam moved away and focused on Tom.

"Are you Merrileigh Kramer?" The man's voice was abrupt but no longer unkind.

"Yes. How did you know?"

"Your purse is out here."

I remembered dropping it when I started working on the shutter. "Get an ambulance, will you?" I asked. "He's been hurt somehow, but I can't see how in the dark. He's burning with fever. And call the police. Ask for William Poole. Tell him it's about Tom Whatley."

He hesitated, then grunted and disappeared. While I was sorry to lose his presence, I welcomed the sunlight that flowed again into Tom's little cell.

It wasn't too long before the front door of the cottage was opened, admitting more light, and shortly thereafter the police arrived in the comforting person of William Poole, then the ambulance for Tom.

"Have you called Edie?" I asked William as the EMTs worked on Tom. We stood outside in the fragrant fresh air.

"I'm just about to."

"When you're finished, can I talk to her for a minute? I need to know what she wants to do about Tina and the kids."

"What kids?"

"The ones she and Randy took in for the night."

"Randy's home?" He looked none too pleased.

"He went home with the kids. He had to. He slept with them. Oh, William, you'd have been so proud of him last night!"

He didn't look convinced. "I don't think I want to know about this now." He reached for his phone. Edie was crying with relief and joy when he finally passed it to me "for one minute only."

"What about Tina and the kids?" I asked, cutting through her thanks. "Are they all right? Should I come over so you can go to the hospital?"

"Tina's mom picked them up about fifteen minutes ago. Merry, how is he?"

"I don't know, Edie. He's unconscious."

"He's truly alive? You're not just telling me that, and then I'll get to the hospital and they'll tell me the truth?"

"Edie! You've been reading too many novels."

William held out his hand.

"I've got to go. William wants me off the phone. And he's fine. Well, not fine maybe, but certainly not dead."

And with those happy words, William took the phone. I waited until Tom left for the hospital, never regaining consciousness, then turned to walk to my car.

"Where's she going?" the ranger asked William. "Don't you need to question her?"

"Don't worry about her," William Poole said. "We know where to find her."

I frowned at him. "You make me sound like I'm one of your regular troublemakers."

He grinned, the furrows on his brow undergoing a seismic shift.

SIXTEEN

I walked into the newsroom feeling as weary as I'd ever felt. The poor night's sleep and the fatigue following the adrenaline high of finding Tom combined to make me crave nothing more than sleep.

I was shocked awake by the great rainbow bouquet of balloons soaring above my chair and the huge vase of velvety red roses sitting in the middle of my desk.

"What's all this?"

Jolene leaped from her chair. "Oh, Merry! Congratulations!" She threw herself into my arms.

"Thanks," I said somewhat breathlessly. "But what for?"

In answer, she giggled.

I watched a grinning Mac stride toward me. Grinning. Mac. Those words rarely went together these days. "You're happy," I told him. "What's wrong?"

"Nothing's wrong. You're just a pessimist."

I rolled my eyes. Talk about the pot talking to the kettle!

He grabbed me in a bear hug and shouted in my ear, "You did it, girl!"

When he released me and I could hear again, I put my hands on my hips and demanded, "Okay, what is going on here?"

He held out a Web site printout.

I grabbed the paper and read. I read it again. I looked up in shock. "Me?"

Mac grabbed me again, dancing me around my desk. Any residual fatigue vanished as it hit home. I'd won a Keystone Press Award! Me, Merrileigh Kramer! I'd won for the articles I did last winter on His House, Dawn, and the pregnant girls who lived there.

I began to giggle just like Jolene and doubted I'd ever be able to stop.

"We're saved!" Mac hugged me again. "You saved us!"

Jolene flicked one of the balloons. "Mr. Montgomery can't very well fire a reporter who has just won such a prestigious journalism award, or the editor who came up with the assignment, now can he?"

"Are these from him?" I indicated the balloons and flowers.

Mac shook his head. "He doesn't know yet. At least I don't think he does."

"We thought we'd tell him tonight at Curt's show," Jolene said. "Nice and publicly."

I wasn't sure about that idea. "But it's Curt's show. We can't distract from him."

"Yeah, we can." Jo waved that consideration away just like she did everything she didn't want to think about or agree with. "He's so nice he won't care."

She was undoubtedly right, but still...

Mac grabbed my arm. "You can tell Monty what a wonderful editor I am—"

"Monty?" Jo and I said together. He ignored us.

"—and I can tell him what a sterling reporter you are, a veritable paragon of prose, a princess of perspicacity, a woman of wondrous wisdom."

"And he can't possibly fire any of us!" Jo finished triumphantly.

I shook my head at the two of them. They were both clever to a fault, unbelievably frustrating more times than not and incredibly dear to my heart. What if I'd chosen to stay safe in Pittsburgh instead of risking a life in Amhearst? I'd have missed these two wonderful, nutty people, to say nothing of Curt.

"Curt!" I said. "I have to call Curt!"

I grabbed my phone and called his home number, his cell phone and finally Intimations. No answer anywhere, but today it didn't bother me. I'd won a Keystone!

"The balloons are from me," Mac said, unable to keep the news of his thoughtfulness quiet any longer.

"Balloons," sniffed Jolene. "Flowers are the proper gift, you idiot."

"Flowers wither."

"Balloons deflate."

"Flowers die."

"Balloons crawl on their bellies on the floor."

They were crazy, both of them, but my life would be so flat without them. I grabbed them about their necks, one in each arm, and hugged.

"By the way," Jo said, rubbing her neck after I released her. "I took your basket to Freedom House." She looked at me sternly. "That place is falling down."

"True," I said, "but you don't need to frown at me. It's not my fault."

"Um." She studied me cynically. "You sent me there on purpose, didn't you?"

"Sure. I needed the flowers delivered."

She snorted. "Don't think you can charm me. I know a setup when I see one."

"And?" I waited expectantly. *Oh, Lord, let her help! Please let her help!*

"The least I can do is buy decent furniture for her office."

It wasn't what I'd hoped for at twenty-five thousand dollars a month for twenty years, but it was a start.

I hugged her. "Thanks, Jolene. That's kind of you."

"And maybe see that the place gets painted and fixed up."

I grinned. "That's even better!"

"And maybe pay the rent for the first year so they can get Like New up and running."

"Jolene!" I was overcome.

She raised an eyebrow. "Is that enough?"

I pulled a rose out of my bouquet and handed it to her. "You are wonderful."

She leaned over and put the rose back in the vase, smirking all the while. "That's what Reilly always says."

My phone rang as I tried to think of a comeback.

"Thought you'd like to know," William Poole barked in my ear, "Whatley's main problems are blood loss and dehydration. He should be fine in spite of a nasty shoulder wound."

"Thanks, William. That's wonderful news."

At the name William, both Mac and Jolene stiffened like a pair of spaniels on point.

"The doctors said that if you hadn't found him when you did, he'd have been in big trouble. Not that he's not hurting anyway, but at least it's not life threatening. We're waiting for him to gain consciousness and tell us what happened."

"How's Edie doing?"

"She hasn't stopped crying since she got here."

I was laughing when I hung up. So many wonderful things happening all at once!

"What does Poole want? And what's it have to do with Edie?" Mac demanded.

"You know how Tom's been missing?" I began.

"He's been found?" Jolene clapped her hands.

"Where? How? By whom?" Mac demanded, ever the newspaperman hot on the scent of a good story.

"Hibernia. By following a blood trail. Me."

"You? You found him?"

I glared at my editor. "You don't have to act so surprised."

"I'm not surprised. I just can't believe you didn't say anything sooner."

I glanced at the flowers and balloons. "I got sidetracked."

Mac barely gave my gifts a glance. They were fluff. The story was all. "So give, woman. Tell me every single detail."

So I did, ending with the news that Tom was in the hospital, still unconscious, with Edie at his side.

"But he's going to be okay?" Jolene asked.

"So William said."

"Flowers," she said, completely in character. "We'll send a huge colorful bouquet of spring flowers, including irises and lilies and daffodils."

Mac nodded approval. "Good, Jolene. Tell them to put a balloon or two in the arrangement. Merry, you get that story written. I've got to call Dawn. She's been praying."

Jo and I looked at each other in amazement. Poor Mac. He was well and truly smitten. And he certainly had good taste, finally, after years of chasing everything in skirts. But I still had reservations.

I made quick notes about my adventure with Tom, then turned off my computer and gathered my belongings. My brain was mush. It was time to go home, regroup for a few minutes before going to see Mike Hamblin and then moving on to Intimations. I gathered my balloons and roses.

"Don't worry. I'll bring them back," I assured Mac, who frowned as he watched me try to shepherd the uncooperative floaters through the door.

Whiskers loved my flowers.

"Get away from them!" I shouted, shoving him to the floor from the bureau where he sat trying to eat them. "Go bat a balloon."

In fact the balloons scared him as they hovered and shifted and twisted in the drafts. He eyed them fearfully and wouldn't go near them. With an eye to saving my roses, I wrapped the balloon strings about my jewelry box and pushed it next to the roses.

Whiskers sat on the bed and looked longingly at the fragrant flowers, then fearfully at the balloons. He made no move to approach either. Safe for the night.

I pulled on my black dress, nothing as classy or expensive as the one Delia, Miss Little Black Dress herself, was certain to be wearing. Still, as I checked myself in the mirror for cat hair, I didn't think I'd shame myself or Curt. I thought I looked as sophisticated as I'd ever get with my black hose and shoes and my one piece of good jewelry—a miniature portrait on ceramic that my great-great-grandmother had painted—pinned to my shoulder.

As I pulled into Hamblin Motors at 6:23, I was listening to KYW, the all-news station out of Philadelphia. I wanted to know if there were any reports about Tom Whatley being found. I didn't think the news had leaked yet, but I wanted to know before I talked with Mike Hamblin. One thing was sure: I wasn't going to be the one to tell prematurely. There was too much at stake, like finding the bad guys responsible for whatever had happened to Tom.

I found an empty parking slot near the front door of the Hamblin showroom, no mean feat with the limited open space on the lot where cars, vans and pickups sat cheek by jowl. Hamblin's sat on Route 30 just east of Amhearst, and the four-lane highway passed mere feet from the showroom. Down the road about a quarter of a mile was a well-lit shopping center with my favorite bookstore. I reached for the keys when a knock on my window made me jump. Howard the salesman peered in at me.

I rolled down my window. "Hello, Howard."

He smiled with what he thought was charm. Today he was wearing a cream twill shirt with Hamblin Motors over the heart. He looked much healthier.

"I'm sorry, but we're closed," he said. "Our colleague died this morning, and we're closing early in memory of him."

I nodded. "Bill Bond."

Howard seemed surprised. "Yes."

I pushed my car door open and stepped out. I flipped the lock switch down and closed the door, feeling virtuous about how well I was caring for Mr. Hamish's car. "Mr. Hamblin is expecting me. It's all right."

Howard didn't look convinced and followed me to the glass doors. I pulled the doors open and walked into the showroom. Howard followed.

"It's okay, Howard. Truly. I promise not to steal any of the cars, toy or real."

He frowned at me. Obviously humor wasn't one of his strong points.

"Say." I paused. "Do you guys wear denim shirts one day a week?" I pointed to the Hamblin Motors logo on his cream shirt.

Howard looked disconcerted by the change of topic. "Yes," he said hesitantly. "On Thursday. We have a different shirt for each day of the week. Today's is cream twill, and everyone wears that, even Mike. All except Bill. He likes…" He swallowed convulsively and looked suddenly sad. "Liked to wear a dress shirt and tie. Mike let him since he was sales manager. It set him apart."

"Was Bill good to work for?" I asked gently.

Howard nodded. "I liked him a lot. Every so often he'd get

temperamental, but mostly he was fun. He was good at his job." He sighed deeply. "It's so sad!"

I made a noncommittal noise. How could a man be one kind of person at work and another at home? I made a mental note to ask Stephanie if this was a common phenomenon.

Howard led me to a handsome man with dark curly hair standing by the toy showcase against the outside wall of the showroom. The front of the showcase was open, and he had been rearranging the contents, trying to make room for something else by the looks of it.

He smiled warmly when he saw me. "Merry Kramer? I'm Mike Hamblin."

We shook hands while Howard stood watching.

"It's all right, Howard," Mike said, dismissing his salesman. "She and I have an appointment."

Howard nodded, though he still looked at me suspiciously. "Then I'll see you tomorrow, Mike." He turned and walked away.

Mike watched him go. "He's a nice enough guy," he said like he had to explain Howard. "Lots of our customers like his slow, thorough service. He makes them feel safe."

I nodded, not really interested in what the customers thought of Howard. "What did your customers think of Bill Bond?"

"Come on back to my office where we can talk more comfortably," Mike said.

I nodded and followed him across the showroom to the door that Howard had prevented me from going through on my last visit.

When we entered Mike's office, I was immediately taken with a large toy car sitting on his desk. It was about two feet high and three feet long, much larger than any of the toys out in the showcases. It had a long hood, a flat roof and a rumble seat. Spare tires were mounted on the running boards on both sides just behind the hood. The door to the driver's side was open, and I could see the seats had upholstery that looked as good as new.

"That's one big toy," I said.

Mike laughed. "It's not a toy. It's a showroom sample. I found it at an antique show over the weekend. Some guy sold it to me for a thousand dollars." Mike laughed. "Poor chump."

I looked at the scarred metal of the car. "A thousand dollars sounds pretty pricey to me."

He shook his head. "A model this size is probably worth between twenty-five and thirty grand."

I looked from him to the car in disbelief.

He grinned. "Amazing, isn't it? But I know what I'm talking about when it comes to cars, whether toys, samples or the real thing."

"Do you have any real antique cars like Model Ts or anything?" If he did and Mac thought it would make a good story, I'd give it to Larry, the sports guy. He actually knew one model of car from another, unlike a certain charming journalist who shall remain nameless.

We talked about his antique car collection and the huge garage he'd had built at home to house all ten of them. Rather, he talked and I listened. He told me about the shelves that circled his garage for the huge toy car collection he had, everything from a Stutz Bearcat to the latest Matchbox.

"What you see out there are not necessarily my finer pieces." He waved toward the showroom. "They're the ones my customers like and recognize. The bulk of the collection is at home." He grinned. "I love cars of any size!"

Then he described his security system to protect his collection in much more detail than I wanted to know. As he talked, I thought that the retail car business must be more lucrative than I'd ever imagined. We were talking a big-bucks hobby.

Finally we got around to Bill Bond.

"Wonderful, wonderful man," Mike assured me. "Such a tragedy."

"Have you any idea why someone would shoot him?"

He gravely shook his head. "I can't begin to imagine. What is it they always say? *Cherchez la femme?*"

Sure, I thought cynically. Blame it on some poor woman.

I sat forward. "Do you think Bill had a woman tucked away somewhere?" And did he beat her too? I wanted to ask.

Mike quickly held up his hands in denial. "No, no. Bill was not the kind of man to have a girlfriend on the side. I was referring obliquely to his wife."

"His wife?"

Mike looked uncomfortable. "She's…" He paused. "Let's just say she's unusual."

"How?" I asked bluntly.

He shook his head. "I'm sorry. I shouldn't have said anything. It's all speculation."

I waited a minute, but it was obvious he wasn't going to talk about Tina anymore. Had he just suffered a slip of the tongue, or had he meant to cast doubt on her character, to turn the eyes of people to her as a probable culprit? I wondered what he'd say if I told him that at the time of Bill's death she was trying to sleep off the battering given by the man everyone at Hamblin's seemed to consider so wonderful.

Mike took me into Bill's office where a picture of his family sat prominently on his desk. Tina smiled warmly at the camera, Jess and Lacey leaned against her legs and Bill sat behind her, arm lovingly about her shoulder.

A picture's worth a thousand words, they say. Sometimes pictures lie.

"He was a dependable man, always here when I needed him," Mike said, staring at the picture. "We're going to miss him!"

"Did he ever lose his temper with your salesmen?"

"Never. Now why do you ask that?"

"With the customers?"

"Absolutely not."

"So you don't think he had a temper problem?"

"I'm not sure what you're insinuating, but I don't think I like it."

I smiled and changed the topic. "Tell me some Bill stories so I can get a feel for him."

"The customers liked him because he told them jokes and made them laugh."

I waited expectantly, but that was it.

I tried again. "I understand he liked to wear a shirt and tie instead of the staff shirts."

"He had good taste in clothes and liked to dress formally."

I hated interviews like this one where the person appeared polite and cooperative but gave me nothing. The question I had to ask myself was whether the stonewalling was on purpose or not. I made another leap in subject matter.

"How did Bill get along with Tom Whatley?"

Mike blinked. "They got along fine. Why wouldn't they?"

"Bill was sales manager, but Tom was top salesman."

"Bill was proud of Tom."

"No resentment? No jealousy?"

"Bill was a wonderful, wonderful man."

Yeah, yeah, so you've said. "Do you think Bill's shooting has anything to do with Tom's disappearance?"

Mike looked surprised. "I hope not. I do. If they're linked, I'm going to start thinking that Hamblin Motors is the object of some strange vendetta."

I tucked that highly speculative comment away for later thought. "Have you heard from Tom since he went missing?"

Mike shook his handsome head. "Of course not."

That line at least had the ring of truth.

"Why do you think Tom Whatley has disappeared?"

"Men run away for all sorts of reasons." Mike smiled hesitantly. "I'd say *cherchez la femme* again, but this time I wouldn't mean the wife."

I forced myself to smile back, thinking of Edie and her pain. Another woman, ha!

After a half an hour, I bid Mike adieu and walked thoughtfully to my car. I thought of the various things he had told me about Bill, bothered by the fact that none of them had substance. Where were the "I'll never forget the day that Bill…" stories?

I turned as I walked across the macadam lot and looked back. Mike had returned to his toy showcase as soon as I walked out the door. As I watched, a big man came from the back of the building and joined him in front of the showcase. I realized I was watching the same two men talk as I had on my previous visit. Mike Hamblin, owner, and Joey Alberghetti, head repair guy.

Something was definitely off-kilter here at Hamblin's. I knew it. I just didn't know what it was yet. Was it Mike? Was it Joey? Was it Bill and his meanness still polluting the air? My great hope was that when Tom regained consciousness, he could tell us things that were now unclear.

I put my hand on my car door handle and pulled. Nothing happened. Locked.

I reached into my purse and began rummaging for my keys. I couldn't find them. I dumped the bag onto my trunk lid and swished things around, searching. No keys.

I thought back to my arrival at Hamblin's. I'd pulled into the lot. Parked. Turned off the motor. Jumped like an idiot at a knock on the window. Smiled sweetly at Howard. Stepped out. Pushed down the door lock.

A chill slid up my back. I peered into the car and there,

dully reflecting the parking lot lights, hung my keys in the ignition. When Howard knocked on the window and I began talking to him, my pattern was disrupted.

I'd climbed out without the keys.

SEVENTEEN

Without much hope, I tried my other car doors. All locked. Why did I have to pick this evening to become responsible? Now I'd really be late for Curt's shindig.

I walked back to the showroom. Surely Mike had one of those long pieces of metal that slid down into a door and popped the lock. I pulled the showroom door open.

Mike and Joey, their backs to me and their attention on the showcase, didn't hear me. I paused as I tried to think of how I might ask for help without sounding like an idiot.

"You found a good deal this time, Mikey." Joey was patting the showroom model that Mike had brought from his office. "Is there a shelf that's high enough for it? It's one big baby. You know we're going to have to kill her."

"The shelves are all adjustable. We can make one high enough with no trouble. Why should we kill her?"

"Because she's going to figure it all out any minute now."

"Her? She's just a cute little chickie. Nothing to worry about."

Joey shook his head. "Don't you read? She's that reporter who already solved a couple of crimes."

"Her?" Mike was aghast. "That little thing?"

"Her." Joey polished the front fender of the model.

"Don't you think someone's going to start noticing that all

these dead people have a connection to Hamblin Motors? If she can figure it out, so can the cops."

"All the bodies have to do with the *News*, Mike! Except for Barnard, but he don't count. Besides he was found in a *News* reporter's house. With the girl dead too, that's where the cops'll look."

"You hope."

"She goes, Mikey." Joey's voice was steel.

My skin crawled and I looked at the door. Could I risk opening it again?

Mike stared at Joey. "You like killing, don't you?"

Joey thought about the idea for a second. "I don't think I like it so much as I don't mind it."

"You're sick."

Joey grinned. "If you say so."

"I still wish you hadn't done Barnard. He was the best courier we ever had. Dumb and dependable is a hard combination to find."

"He was trying to get out, Mikey. He kept muttering about how his kid was doing drugs. He couldn't deliver them anymore now he saw what they did. All his wife did was cry. Garbage like that. He was even starting to go to church!"

"Church?" There was horror in Mike's voice. "Barnard?"

Joey nodded. "To pray for the kid, he said."

"Pray." Mike's voice was full of disgust. "I hate it when a good man gets a guilty conscience."

Joey nodded. "I put him in Tom's garage as a warning, you know? I mean, I had to put him somewhere, right? And no one knew he ran for us. It's not like anyone'd think, aha! Barnard, Tom, Hamblin's, drugs."

"You'd better be right about that." Mike looked at Joey. "But explain to me how you ever saw a warning in dumping the body."

"The body said, this is what happens to people who mess with us. People who start to think about talking." He ran a gentle finger over the roof of the model car. "Are you going to have it restored?"

"I haven't decided. I kind of like it like this, but collectors are used to restored pieces."

"So restore it then. Not that you'll ever sell it." They both laughed.

"Just be careful, Joey. It's dangerous playing games with oblique threats."

"She knew what the threat meant," Joey said softly.

Mike looked up from his showcase. "She?"

"Tom's wife. I called her."

"What?" Mike stared openmouthed. "You're crazy! What did you say?"

"I told her that she shouldn't say anything to the cops or else."

"Or else what?"

"She'd get what her old man got."

Mike stared until Joey began to fidget.

"Don't worry." Joey's manner was defensive. "She didn't know it was me."

"You're an idiot!"

"I'm not!"

The men glared at each other, and I could feel the waves of their animosity wash over me. If politics made strange bedfellows, apparently crime made stranger ones still.

Drugs! Hamblin Motors was somehow a center for drug trafficking. And the dead man in Randy's car was a courier, a dumb but dependable courier who'd developed a conscience. Unbelievable!

Taking a deep breath as if to calm himself, Mike turned back to his cars. "Look at the detailing on the interior of this baby. That's why it's so valuable. Be careful, Joey. I don't want to be taken down because you decided to play games."

Once again Joey's gentle hands played with the model. He gave a short laugh of pleasure. "Look! The front seat tilts forward! Don't worry, Mikey. I'm careful. And we're still going to have to kill her."

Mike sighed. "It's a shame. She's sort of cute, you know? So serious when she asks her questions."

I was afraid to move, afraid any motion would attract their attention. But if they turned…

"We wouldn't have to do her if you hadn't gotten carried away last night." Mike rubbed the roof of his model with a soft cloth.

"Well, you should have seen him last night. He must have gone after his wife again. His knuckles were all bloody and he had blood stains on his shirt. But it was the gun he was waving that made me sort of nervous."

"Bill had a gun?" Mike was incredulous.

"He said it was to keep that Tina in line. She wanted to leave him and take the kids and he wasn't going to let her."

"He should have let her go and gotten someone he liked."

"Mikey, for a smart man, you're dumb. It was the beating he liked."

Mike shuddered. "That's sick."

"Maybe, but it's power. And so was the gun."

"The man was a miracle at selling cars, but he couldn't keep his hands off his wife. And he was going to shoot her too? Nuts."

"He was falling apart before my eyes, needing a fix so bad he was shaking and sweating. Ugly." Joey snorted. "And the gun. Any fool can pull a trigger. It was me or him, let me tell you. The guy was going to shoot m— Hey, the trunk opens too!"

"That's a rumble seat, buddy, not a trunk."

I listened, unable to believe what I was hearing. Models and murders—and my murder!—discussed in the same casual tone of voice.

"Rumble, schmumble," Joey said. "If you move that Model T and that Oldsmobile on the second shelf to the other case, you could lower that shelf and have plenty of room for the model. Our weak link, besides that girl—and she's easy to fix—is Tom. If he shows up, we're in deep trouble, and I mean deep!"

"I don't think he's going to show, not after all this time. He's dead somewhere."

"You wish." Joey reached into the case and pulled out two of the cast-metal cars. "I know I hit him—I just don't know how bad."

"Next time you'll shut your office door before you hand out any bags."

"How was I supposed to know he was still here? He should have been long gone. Instead he drives that car off the lot and into the garage as cool as you please. He pulls up right next to my office. 'Hey Joey,' he calls out the window. 'This car's got a knock like you wouldn't believe. You'd better fix it before we show—' Then he realizes what he's seeing. Me and Bill and him stare at each other for a minute, sort of frozen like. Then he hits the gas. I run after him and take a shot. I know I got him because the car swerves into that light post out there." He jerked his head toward the lot.

Mike grunted. "He'd better be dead, Joey. I'm not taking the fall for your stupidity."

Joey straightened to his full height and glared at Mike.

"Don't try and threaten me with your size, Joey. I'm in charge here, and don't you ever forget it. You're a rich man because of me."

"If it hadn't been for me, you'd never have made the original contacts, and don't you forget that," Joey countered.

Mike grunted as he set the glass shelf on the newly positioned supports, then took his prize and slipped it into the case. "Nice." He nodded with satisfaction.

"Nice," Joey agreed. He handed one of the toys to Mike and they started to turn.

Suddenly reality slapped me across the face, and I dropped to the floor, hugging a sports utility vehicle of some kind. If they found me, I knew all too clearly what would happen. The only question was whose car they would put my corpse in.

I could hear the men walking across the showroom to the other toy showcase. Under cover of their footsteps, I slipped under the SUV, thankful for the high-slung chassis. I crouched against the inside of the front passenger tire, making certain that nothing like a foot or the hem of my new red coat stuck out. All I had to do was stay here as quiet as a mouse until they left. Then I could get out of here, call William and report what I'd heard.

It seemed such a good plan when I made it.

"Hey, Mikey," Joey called in an excited voice. "She's still here."

My heart stopped midbeat.

"What do you mean, she's still here?" Mike's voice had a chill that froze my blood.

"That white Sable out there?" I could just imagine him pointing. "I saw her climb out of it, talking to that imbecile Howard."

"Then where is she?"

I pressed myself against the tire and prayed. I heard the two of them moving around the showroom, looking in all the sales cubicles, opening the door back to Bill Bond's office.

"We've got to check the garage area," Joey called as he went through the door to the offices.

I strained to hear whether both of them had left the showroom or if it was just Joey. I didn't have to wait long before I heard the click, click, click of Mike's feet as he slowly circled the showroom once again.

As he moved away from me down the inside wall, I dared to turn and study the distance between my hiding place and the door to the outside. Surely I could make it to and through the door when he was at the far end of the room. All I had to do was make the parking lot and run screaming into the street. There was enough traffic that I would be safe.

I rolled to my knees, preparing to making my mad dash. I shook off my coat on the theory that in my black dress I'd be harder to spot as I ran. I glanced back over my shoulder to see where Mike's feet were.

And looked directly into Joey's eyes.

He was crouched on the far side of the SUV, and fast as a striking snake, his large, calloused hand fastened about my ankle.

I screamed. I hate screaming women. I read about them in novels all the time, and they always sound so wimpy. I joined their ranks without a second thought.

And when he began to pull me inexorably toward him, I screamed again. I also began kicking at his hand with my free foot, landing more blows on my own ankle than his hand. Once he hissed in pain, and I felt a surge of victory. Then I missed and the heel of my dress pump rasped over my ankle, shredding my stockings and drawing blood. He saw and smiled nastily.

Suddenly both ankles were imprisoned by those cold hands and I was pulled ignominiously from beneath the car on my stomach, my little black dress rutching up to my thighs, getting all wrinkled and dusty, certain to make Curt feel less than proud when he saw me. Not that it probably mattered. I was in grave danger of not making it to Intimations or anywhere else ever again.

I grabbed frantically at the front tire of the SUV as I slid past. *Oh, dear Lord, help!*

I dug my nails into the rubber, wrapping my hands about the back of the tire where it met the hub. I managed to slow Joey down, and then, to my surprise and relief, bring him—or rather me—to a stop.

He released my legs, and I began to scramble back under the car, hope burgeoning. How premature. With daunting ease, he stood, leaned over and grabbed me about the waist.

My body jackknifed as he tucked me under one arm. The air rushed out of my lungs like I was a leaky balloon. My fingers lost their precarious hold on the tire, and I tore several nails as I scrabbled for another grip. I slammed the back of my head against the lower edge of the driver's door, striking hard enough to paint a field of stars and red flashes behind my eyelids.

Joey walked across the showroom with me dangling at his side like Raggedy Ann. He dropped me unceremoniously in a heap beside the showcase where Mike was waiting.

"It worked, Mike. Dumb woman thought I'd left the showroom just like we knew she would." He sneered down at me. "She was so easy."

Joey was obnoxious even when he wasn't filled with overweening pride, but I found him particularly repulsive at that moment. I pushed myself to my knees, refusing to lie at his feet like an overcome Victorian maiden. My head ached fiercely, but I wasn't going to go gently into that good night. No, sir, I was not.

Mike looked down at me with disdain. "She's yours, Joey. Kill her. Just don't put her in my car. I don't want the cleanup bill."

They both laughed at Mike's clever repartee while I dragged myself to my feet by holding on to the shelves of the showcase.

"And, Joey." Mike's voice became steely, reminding both

Joey and me that he was the man in charge. "I don't want any possible connection to the dealership."

Joey nodded. "Not to worry, Mikey. Not to worry."

I stood, swaying gently. My hand closed around the roof of one of the toy cast-iron cars as I grabbed for a handhold to keep from falling. My shoulders slumped and my head hung.

"Get rid of her," Mike ordered again and turned his back, his contempt for me written boldly in every line of his body.

Joey was grinning broadly at what easy prey I was when I swung the cast-iron toy clasped in my hand full at him. The collision with the side of his head startled and rocked both of us. Shards of pain raced up my arm and across my shoulder, but Joey fared worse. His eyes went vacant and he slid silently to the floor, unconscious.

Mike turned at the sound of the blow, and I felt a thrill of satisfaction at the disbelieving expression on his face. Then his eyes narrowed, and I felt a jolt of fear.

OhLordohLordohLordohLord!

I turned and raced for the door. I pushed it open and ran into the parking lot, his footfalls pounding behind me. I sped toward the street and the traffic with the drivers and the passengers who would be there to save me.

But there was no traffic. Not one single car. Where was a traffic jam when you needed one?

I knew I couldn't outrun Mike. After all, I had on dress shoes and my legs were much shorter than his. But I ran for all I was worth as my side began cramping and my lungs filled with fire.

What if he has a gun?

That thought ratcheted up my panic several notches. I tried to judge how close behind me he was, to hear his footsteps slapping the street, but I was breathing so harshly that I could hear nothing. I fought the urge to glance back, knowing it would only slow me down and frighten me further.

When I heard a car, I wanted to sing with relief. I turned and stood, waving my hands and shouting, "Help! Help!"

My relief turned to terror when I realized that the car was driving full speed straight at me. I raced for the side of the road and the great sycamore that stood there, desperate for its protection. I dived behind it, my pulse pounding, my blood thundering in my ears. I screamed as the car roared past, inches from the bole of the tree, inches from me.

My hands ground painfully across the gravel at the base of the tree until I slid to a halt, spitting dirt. My knees fared no better, but I didn't care. He'd missed me!

As I lay there gasping and thanking God I was still alive, a deep rending noise sent up gooseflesh all over my body. Mike had missed me and the sycamore, but he hadn't been able to avoid a large rock just beyond. He had driven right over it, and it had promptly ripped the undercarriage of the car to shreds.

I pushed myself unsteadily to my feet and stood weaving as I waited to see if the car burst into flames or self-destructed in some other way. Nothing happened, unless you count a swearing and apparently uninjured Mike climbing from the ruined car. He balanced himself against the side of the car and began searching the darkness for me.

As I began to run again, my goal was the shopping mall down the road. People and safety! I heard Mike's footfalls pounding behind me.

OhLordohLordohLordohLord!

After a seeming eternity I dashed down the grassy swale that separated the road from the mall parking lot. The bright lights of the stores beckoned to me, offering hope and protection. I ran straight toward them.

I risked a glance over my shoulder and screamed. Mike was mere feet behind me. I swerved suddenly, running between two parked cars. I heard Mike slap one of the cars as he attempted to make the same abrupt turn I had.

I danced around an abandoned shopping cart, then stopped. I whirled, grabbed the cart and shoved with all my might. It careened down the narrow alley between the cars right into Mike, catching him in the stomach. He and it tangled and fell as I raced away.

Directly ahead was Chester County Best Books, its lights ablaze, and I could see a clerk at the sales counter. I raced the last few yards with my skin twitching in expectation of a hand falling heavily on my shoulder. I yanked open the store door and raced inside, so out of breath I could barely speak.

"Help!" I managed between gasps as I all but fell onto the sales counter. "Call the police! Help me!"

The clerk, a middle-aged woman with a soft jawline and wary brown eyes, stared at me.

"Police! Please," I begged as I glanced over my shoulder. I gave a little scream. Mike was standing on the sidewalk just outside the store, staring at me through the great storefront window, his expression a mixture of malevolence and uncertainty. I bolted instinctively, dodging between bookshelves until I got as far from the front of the store as I could. I ended up in the last aisle, crouching in Inspirational/Religion. There was no one there except me.

Help me think clearly, Lord. You said that if I walked through the flood, You would be there and the waters wouldn't overwhelm me. You said that if I went through the fire, You'd protect me. Well, I'm pretty wet, and the flame's awfully close! Be with me now.

Feeling much calmer, I moved to the end of my aisle and peeked out. I couldn't see Mike, and I didn't think he'd followed me into the store. Now that I was reasoning instead of reacting, I knew he wouldn't dare come in. Too many people, too much light. I was safe as long as I stayed here.

I took a deep breath and walked purposefully toward the front of the store with its lights and customers. I reached the counter just as the salesclerk replaced the phone in its cradle. "The police?" I asked.

She nodded and looked at me cautiously. I couldn't begin to imagine how I must look to her, all torn hose and desperate eyes.

"Thanks." I smiled and hoped I looked saner than I had a few minutes ago when I'd rushed in screaming.

"They said they'd be here as soon as they could, and you should remain in the store until they got here." She folded her hands on the counter in front of her.

"Thank you." I held out a hand to shake hers and saw for the first time the scrapes and cuts on my palms, the blood and broken nails. I was stunned. I hadn't realized I'd been injured. Also for the first time, I became aware of the burning pain.

I glanced down my body and grimaced at my dress, dirty and wrinkled, a trip to the dry cleaners its only salvation if I discounted the three-corner tear near the hem. I stared silently at the ruins of my hose and the bloody abrasions on my knees which had suddenly begun hurting too. My ankle, swollen and bruised, throbbed where I had kicked myself as I'd tried to get away from Joey.

But I was alive, safe here in the store, and I had a story that would jolt Amhearst. Hands, knees and ankles would heal, and compared to what Tom Whatley had been through, my plight was nothing.

I was smiling at how fortunate I'd been when it suddenly occurred to me that standing here in front of huge plate-glass windows was not the wisest thing I could do. Mike stood to lose both his legitimate business and his illegitimate one, his reputation and his much-loved cars, both big and little, when I told my tale. In exchange he'd gain an orange jumpsuit with a number stenciled on its back and a compact little room without a seat on its toilet.

That might well be enough to drive a man to shoot.

A large support pillar reaching from floor to ceiling stood nearby. After an apprehensive glance out the front window, I quickly moved behind it. The sales clerk watched me much like an animal trainer might watch an escaped lion. "I'm going to get you a damp cloth and some Bactine."

I smiled my thanks and leaned against the pillar.

"Come on, William! I know who shot him and why."

EIGHTEEN

When the police arrived at Hamblin Motors, they found Joey sitting on the showroom floor holding his head. He was sent to the hospital where they determined he had a concussion. Tomorrow morning he would be on his way to jail.

"You did good, Merry," William told me. "Real good."

"Thanks," I said wearily. "Can I please go to Curt's showing? I need to be there for him. If you need to talk to me more, you can do it later, can't you?"

"You might want to stop home first to change."

"William, are you telling me I don't look lovely?"

"Uh." He thought for a moment. "Yeah. That's what I'm saying."

I gave a little laugh. "An honest cop, just when you don't want one." I patted his arm. "Thanks for the offer, but there's not time. I've got to go as I am, or it'll be over before I even get there."

I almost fell asleep as Jeb Lammey drove me to Intimations because I was without a car again. When the dealership became a crime scene, my rental was included. Mr. Hamish would love it.

"Remember, Merry," Jeb cautioned as I climbed out of the patrol car. "No dark alleys. But don't worry. We'll catch him in no time."

He pulled away, and I walked toward the gallery. I had almost reached the door when an arm slid around my waist and a desperate voice hissed in my ear, "Don't make a sound or I'll hurt someone."

Even as I tensed, a smart-mouthed response echoed inside my head: "Hmm, I wonder who that would be."

Oh, Lord, it's fire and flood time again. Protect me!

"Don't do this, Mike." I twisted to look over my shoulder at him, thinking that looking him in the eye might make killing me harder for him. "You don't want to be tried for murder. Drug trafficking is bad enough."

He made a sound that could have meant anything.

"It's over, Mike. Joey's in custody, and you know as well as I do that he'll say anything to try and get off. Turn yourself in. Tell your side of things. Make it easier for yourself."

"Shut up! Don't tell me what to do." His voice shook, and he refused to look at me. "I've got a gun in your back." He poked me to be certain I felt it. I did. "Move! Into the alley over there."

"Over there?" I asked, pointing.

"Yes." He released the pressure around my waist and gestured with the gun.

Instead I turned to face him full on.

"Move," Mike ordered again.

"No. I'm not going with you." I folded my arms and stared at him.

He blinked and raised the gun.

I squared my shoulders and continued to eye him defiantly. "If you want to shoot me, you're going to have to do it here where all the people in Intimations will hear and come running and with me looking straight at you."

Mike waved the gun in my face. "I mean it when I say I'll kill you."

"Maybe you do and maybe you don't, but I'm not making it any easier by going down a dark alley."

Behind me the door to Intimations opened, and a burst of noise filled the street. The owner of a local real estate business and his wife exited the gallery amid vociferous goodbyes.

"Turn yourself in, Mike," I said even as I turned my back on him.

"Hello, Mr. Ellis. Mrs. Ellis," I said loudly and made a run for them, my back twitching once again. "You know Mike Hamblin, don't you?" I gestured in Mike's direction.

"Who?" Mr. Ellis asked.

Mike was gone.

I let out a breath and pulled the door to Intimations open. My knees hurt every time I took a step. I was limping on my swollen ankle, and I ached from head to toe. But this was Curt's night, and I was going to share it with him if it killed me.

I was thankful for the milling crowd that hid me. If I could get to the ladies' room before anyone noticed me, I could wash my hands and knees and get rid of the blood. I could comb my hair, brush the dirt off my dress and get rid of my ruined stockings. I looked for the restroom sign.

I spotted Curt near the back of the room, his dark curls gleaming in the state-of-the-art lighting the gallery boasted. He looked wonderful, his handsome face alight with vitality and life, his intelligent eyes behind their glasses intent on the person to whom he was speaking. The intervening crowd prevented even a glimpse of the person beside him, but I would have been willing to wager that I knew who it was. And I knew she was lapping the attention up like a thirsty pup did water.

I located the restroom sign and was about to sneak off in that direction when the crowd between Curt and me suddenly separated as neatly as a block of butter when someone draws a warm knife through it. He lifted his head and looked directly at me.

And smiled. Full wattage.

My stomach did a somersault, and I smiled back with all my heart.

He gave a little come-here jerk with his head, and I began walking toward him.

It was an act of faith, that walk across the gallery. I was choosing to believe he meant it when he said, "You beat Delia without even trying."

The contrast between the two of us women would never be greater than right now. She looked beautiful in a sleek black floor-length dress whose simple lines screamed big bucks. Her blond hair was pulled back in a sleek knot at the nape of her neck, not an escaped wisp in sight. Marvelous gold earrings danced in her ears, her only jewelry. She was her own best ornament.

But Curt was smiling at me

By the time I reached Curt, the pleasure in his eyes had been replaced by concern. I realized he hadn't been able to see how disreputable I looked when I was back by the door. Now I stood before him in all my wretched glory.

Delia shuddered gently and did her best to ignore me. She indicated the man across from her. "Curt, Mr. Whitsun has a point about…"

But Curt wasn't listening to her. He was watching me. He took a step in my direction, pulled his hand from his pocket and reached for me.

"Are you all right?" he asked in a gentle voice.

Nodding, I put my hand in his. My heart pounded with joy. He had spoken truly about loving me. He had chosen me. I couldn't stop grinning.

Then he gave my hand a squeeze.

I gasped and tried to pull away.

He eased his grip and, turning my palm up, looked at the dirty, bloody mess.

"I took a dive behind a tree and skinned my hands and knees," I explained. "But I'm okay."

"Are you sure?" It was Mr. Whitsun, looking unconvinced. He was staring not at my hands but at my legs with their ruined stockings, brush burns and blood. "If this were New York, I'd say you'd just been mugged."

"It's just surface injuries." I grinned. "You should see the other guys."

Mr. Whitsun laughed companionably.

Curt wrapped an arm around my shoulders. He seemed oblivious to Delia hanging on his other arm. Even she was finally struck with the obvious: Curt had chosen. She pulled her hand free, and immediately Curt wrapped his other arm around me too.

I rested my head against his shoulder and thought how utterly weary I was and how wonderfully sturdy he felt. I began to relax, a dangerous thing when you're as beaten up as I was. I ordered starch back into my spine and hoped I could continue to remain upright.

I smiled prettily as Curt introduced me to Mr. Whitsun, the man from the Broughley Gallery in New York.

"Mr. Whitsun is going to take four of my paintings," Curt said, pride and satisfaction filling his voice.

"Oh, Curt, how wonderful! I'm so glad for you. You've made a wise decision, Mr. Whitsun."

Curt turned to the fourth member of the group. "Mr. Montgomery, you remember Merry, don't you?"

Mr. M was looking at me with as much favor as his daughter.

"Good to see you again, Mr. Montgomery," I said. "I didn't get a chance to speak to you at the *News* when you stopped in for that brief visit the other day."

I heard myself and flinched. It must be post-trauma stress. Rather that than that I was just too dumb to keep my mouth shut.

Mr. Montgomery looked at me, appalled. "You work for the *News?*"

I nodded.

"I thought you were just a friend of Curt's," he said, making it obvious that "just a friend of Curt's" could be ignored, but if I worked for the *News,* he'd have to pay attention to me, if only to decide to fire me.

Curt heard the insult and gave my shoulders a squeeze. "Merry's a lot more than just a friend, Mr. Montgomery. She's the love of my life."

His easy statement took my breath away and sent color flooding my face. Mr. Whitsun smiled indulgently at me while Mr. Montgomery looked sharply at Delia. Poor Delia.

"Merry! You're late!" Jolene rushed up to me, took one look and said in horror, "Where have you been? You look terrible!"

"Jo, ever tactful." Reilly stepped up and gave me quick hug. "You know Merry always looks wonderful."

"I know." Jo was still staring aghast. "She's one of those cute-as-a-bug's-ear girls who are so adorable it makes your teeth ache. Usually."

"But not tonight." Mac had appeared behind Jolene, Dawn on his arm. "What happened? Who did this to you?"

I grinned at him. "Have I got a story for you!" I said at the same time Curt said, "She fell."

Curt looked at me with one eyebrow raised. "Didn't you?"

Before I could explain, the front door to Intimations flew open, and William Poole stalked in, looking as official and authoritative as I'd ever seen him. People stepped quickly out of his way as he moved purposefully toward us.

He stopped in front of me. "He turned himself in."

"Good." Satisfaction coursed through me.

"He said you told him to."

"I did."

"When he had a gun in your face."

I heard several gasps, but Curt's "Merry!" was the loudest by far.

"Who had a gun in your face?" Mac demanded.

"Mike Hamblin."

Jolene gave a little scream. I ignored her and looked at Curt. "But I knew he didn't want to use it."

"And just how did you know this?"

"He hadn't killed anybody before. It was Joey who murdered Barnard Slocum and Bill Bond."

Curt glared. "There's always a first time."

I waved away his concern. "I'm fine."

"But Mike Hamblin?" Mac wasn't about to lose the main story line over concern for me.

"Mike had a drug ring working out of his business," I said.

"And he's down at headquarters singing away, telling us all kinds of interesting things," William said with satisfaction.

"What's he saying, William?" I knew I'd get a fuller explanation at a later time, but for now I wanted to get some holes filled in. "I know they were trafficking in drugs, but I haven't the vaguest idea how. I know they used Barnard Slocum—"

"Who?" Jolene demanded.

"Barnard Slocum. You know. The guy found dead in Randy's car."

Everyone nodded except Delia and Mr. Montgomery, even Mr. Whitsun who hung on every word. Both Mr. M and Delia looked like they'd eaten a very sour grape.

"You know they inventory the lot monthly." William looked at us to be sure we were with him. We all nodded. "Well, between inventories, Slocum would take a car off the lot with a temporary tag and drive the drugs wherever he was told. The car would reappear back on the lot a day or two later, no one the wiser. They would use a different car for each run, so there was never a pattern or a particular vehicle the authorities could look for."

"Is that what happened to the missing car you thought Tom might have stolen? When this Slocum was murdered, the car never made it back?" Mac asked.

William shook his head. "No, Tom did take that one."

I nodded. "But he only took it because Joey was shooting at him."

William nodded. "So Tom told me."

A surge of joy shot through me. "Tom's awake?"

"And well," William added. "A bit weak and beat up, but all things considered, he's fine."

"What did he say about the missing money?" I asked.

"He didn't say anything, but Mike admitted it was all a hoax to pin suspicion on Tom so that if he was found, his word would be doubted."

"So you're saying Tom Whatley stumbled on this drug ring, and that's why he was shot," Mac clarified. "He never took the money, and he's completely innocent of any wrongdoing."

William nodded.

"Well, I just knew he hadn't walked out on Edie." Jolene's tone of voice said that being shot wasn't nearly as surprising as walking out on his wife would have been.

"Why didn't he just go to the hospital or the cops?" Mac asked.

Ah, the big question. We all looked at William.

"He said that he was afraid for Edie and Randy. They wouldn't be in danger unless he was near them. He felt he had to stay away, had to hide. He said all he could think about was the bad drug bust where his best friend was killed. He said he panicked. He drove to Hibernia, hid the car well then hid himself. Then before he knew it, he was too weak to do anything."

"So how did you find him?" Curt asked.

"Merry found him."

Curt turned one of my hands over and ran a finger gently over the scrapes. "That's how you got these?"

I shook my head. "I did this when Mike tried to run me down with his car."

"That was after she knocked out Joey," William added.

"Joey?" asked Mr. Whitsun, still trying to sort everything out.

"The murderer." I smiled. "It's confusing."

"But it won't be when you finish writing the story," Mac said. "I can see it now. Another Keystone Press Award for Merry Kramer!"

"That's right," Jolene said, throwing herself back into the conversation with renewed enthusiasm. "Mr. Montgomery, did you know that Merry Kramer, *your* reporter, just won a Keystone Press Award for the outstanding series she did last winter? Isn't the *News* fortunate to have a reporter like her on its staff?" She beamed at me. I beamed back.

Congratulations swirled around my head, and I basked in them. It took some time before I became aware of Mac clearing his throat and looking pointedly at me.

"Oh!" I turned to Mr. Montgomery. "I couldn't have won the award without Mac. The story idea was his, and he's such a great editor, and he's done such a fantastic job at the *News* and—"

"What she's trying to say," cut in Jolene, "is that the *News* has a wonderful staff starting right at the top with Mac. He's a terrific editor. And Edie with the family page and features is great. And so's Larry, the sports guy. And of course there our award-winning Merry Kramer, Amhearst's own Lois Lane. And then there's me. I'm the best administrative assistant or whatever you want to call it that the paper's ever had. We're a unit, Mr. Montgomery, and together we'll give you the best newspaper in Chester County, maybe Pennsylvania."

Sometimes Jolene really got it right.

NINETEEN

Easter Sunday was a beautiful day, warm and sunshiny, just the way it's supposed to be. Curt and I walked hand in hand beside Chambers Lake at Hibernia Park, enjoying being together after the chaos of the past week. Our companionable silence was rich with satisfaction and tenderness. Any man and woman could make conversation. Only a special few were able to keep silence.

We rounded a bend and came upon a pair of Canada geese nesting in the high grass at the water's edge. As we approached, the male began hissing at us while the female continued to sit on her eggs.

"We won't hurt her, Papa," I said softly. "Don't worry."

He didn't believe us, but he did settle down after we were past them.

A big boulder by the water beckoned, and we sat side by side, shoulders touching. Curt had on his dress slacks and shirt, collar open and sleeves rolled back. I still wore my church clothes but had changed to walking shoes. I'd done enough fancy footwork in dress shoes to last for years.

I lay my head on Curt's shoulder, content just to be sitting next to him. He slid his arm around my shoulders and gave a gentle hug.

"Imagine," I said. "Randy and Edie both came to church this morning."

"I think they were impressed too," Curt said. "I watched them while Sherrie sang and the bell choir played. They were sitting at attention the whole time."

"Yeah?" With my minimal musical abilities, I had to concentrate so hard on my chimes that the whole congregation could have risen and walked out, and I wouldn't have noticed. "Especially Randy, I bet."

Curt laughed. "You should have seen his face. The boy has it bad."

"Poor kid. I think he's doomed to failure with Sherrie. But it's probably a good thing. Fifteen is too young to be that involved with someone."

"If he had any ideas about trying to talk with Sherrie after the service, Jess and Lacey cut him off at the pass. They were climbing all over him."

"It's good for him to be loved like that by the little ones. And it's good for their mother to be loved by Edie."

"Tina was pretty brave coming today with her face still so damaged. She's one courageous lady."

"I hope they all come again. I hope they come all the time."

"I wouldn't be surprised, especially if you ask them." He smiled down at me. "They owe you big-time."

I frowned. "I don't want them to come because they owe me. I want them to come because of the Lord Jesus."

"Maybe eventually that's why they'll come." Curt reached for my hand. "In the meantime, who cares why they come? Just so they're there to hear the Gospel."

"You're right." I laced my fingers through his. "I mean, Mac comes strictly because of Dawn, but maybe someday he'll fall in love with the Lord too. At least that's what I keep praying."

A pair of mallards floated by, the male's deep green head iridescent in the bright sun.

Apparently Curt was looking at those marvelously tinted feathers too. "God makes colors that I'll never be able to reproduce, no matter how hard I try." His voice had a fatalistic ring to it.

"But that's what keeps it interesting," I said. "The trying. If you could automatically do it perfectly, where would the challenge be?"

"And I need challenge?"

"Sure. We all do."

"Speaking of challenge, is Mac going to accept Mr. Montgomery's offer to remain as editor at the *News*?"

"He already has." I grinned. "It was all he could do not to shout, 'Yes! Yes! Yes!' when the man called, but he acted very maturely, just like a responsible editor should. 'I'll give you my answer within a week,' he said, all quiet and controlled. Like the answer was ever in doubt!"

"So the whole staff stays intact."

"Every last one of us, right down to Jolene, who probably saved us all with her impassioned speech the other night."

Curt ran his thumb across my healing palm. It tickled in a wonderful way. "She'd make a great politician. She could sell anyone on anything."

The thought of Jolene running even our town, let alone the county, state or country, was daunting, especially since she could probably organize us better than anyone had in years. I wondered what party she was registered under, assuming she'd ever gotten around to registering, which was doubtful.

"I saw her and Reilly talking with Stephanie Bauer this morning," Curt said. "They were very intent. What's going on there?"

"Jolene's going to give Freedom House some much-needed funding." I tried not to sound too smug.

"And who planted that little seed in Jolene's mind, I wonder?"

"I wonder." I giggled.

We fell silent, and I watched a glorious billowing cloud sail across the sky, entranced as wisps spun off to trail behind, then slowly disappear completely.

"What color is the sky?" I asked. "Azure? Indigo? Sapphire? Lapis? Delft? Cobalt? Ultramarine?"

Curt looked up and studied it with his artist's eye. "Blue," he said emphatically. "Very definitely blue."

I laughed. "I love you."

"Mmm. Me too." He bent down and kissed the top of my head. "Did I thank you yet for coming to my show the other night?" His voice was surprisingly serious.

I straightened and looked at him. "Well, of course I came. It was a very important night for you."

"But you'd just been through a terrible ordeal, and if that weren't enough, you had one of the biggest stories of your career to write. And still you cared enough to come. That meant a lot to me."

I was at a loss for words, a rare occurrence. I finally managed, "I'm glad it pleased you."

"I also want you to know that I'm very proud of you."

I probably glowed. "You are?"

He nodded. "Winning your award, helping Edie and Tina, taking in Randy, finding Tom, getting Mike and Joey. You had a pretty full week."

"I'm proud of you too," I said. "Your show went wonderfully well, you sold several paintings and Mr. Whitsun is taking your pictures. And of course Delia will continue to hang you in Intimations here as well as in Philadelphia."

"You're not worried about her anymore, are you?" He eyed me curiously.

I shook my head. "Not anymore. I believe you when you say you made your choice."

"You shouldn't sound so amazed."

"It's just hard to believe. Delia's absolutely beautiful."

"But you're real. And you're just what I need and want."

I hugged his arm. "I'm just glad you weren't embarrassed by how I looked when I showed up at the gallery. I was afraid that you would make believe you didn't know me."

"Never, love. You're mine, and I want the world to know it."

My smile was so broad, I felt like it would crack my face.

Curt reached into his pants pocket and pulled out a purple plastic egg with a pink ribbon tied around it. He put it in my hand. "Happy Easter, sweetheart."

I held it for a minute, then shook it. Something inside thunked.

"A miniature chocolate bunny? Or maybe a Hershey's Hug and Kiss?" I raised an eyebrow at him. "Personally I'd prefer one of yours."

Next thing I knew he had his arms about me and was very thoroughly kissing me. When we broke for breath, I rested my head on his chest.

"Mmm. I knew yours would be better. Sweeter too."

I felt the rumble of his laugh against my cheek. "Open the egg, Merry."

I sat up and made a big production out of untying the ribbon. Then I pretended the two halves of the egg were stuck and I couldn't pull them apart.

"Open it," Curt hissed in my ear.

I grinned unrepentantly at him, but I opened it. My curiosity couldn't stand the suspense any longer.

The facets of the diamond reflected sunlight in a myriad of sparkling rainbows as the ring fell into my lap.

"Oh, Curt!" I could barely breathe.

He picked up the ring and took my left hand in his large hand. "Marry me, Merry?"

"Oh, yes!" It came out in a whisper, but inside I was shouting. "Oh, yes!"

* * * * *

Dear Reader,

The other day in a mega office supply store, I overheard an older woman and a young clerk talking.

"I can't remember the number of the cartridge refill I need for my printer," she said.

"Why don't you call someone and ask?" he suggested.

"Call someone," she said, apparently amazed at the idea. "I can use my cell phone. I always forget I have it because I only carry it for emergencies."

She pulled one out, made a call and got the cartridge number she needed. Happy ending to her quandary.

I got thinking about the differences between the generations. It used to be old-lady lace-up shoes, blue hair and full-body girdles that marked old women, but not anymore. I don't know one older woman who even owns a girdle, let alone the armor they used to wear, and any lace-ups worn are stylish ones. Blue hair has given way to natural, though probably lighter, color.

Today it's lack of ease with things electronic, such as cell phones and iPods, that mark them off.

But one thing has always bridged the generations, and that's love of story. For those smart enough to know that there's nothing better than a good read, age means nothing. Age of heroes and heroines means nothing. It's the story, the excitement, the inspiration, the learning that come from reading good books that bind us together, regardless of whether we're seniors or teens.

And, of course, the Story that binds us closest is the Greatest One ever told. May that Story and the Man it's about drive themselves deep into your heart.

Gayle

QUESTIONS FOR DISCUSSION

1. Tom Whatley is dead. Tom Whatley lives in Amhearst. What are the difficulties of becoming someone else? Read Psalms 139 and 2 Corinthians 5:17. Can we ever become someone else?

2. Merry steps up to help both Randy and Tina and, through Jolene, Stephanie. Read Matthew 25:35–40. How are you practically following Merry's example and obeying these verses? What about personal safety issues?

3. Randy and Sherrie seem to be polar opposites, though their backgrounds are remarkably similar. What has made the difference in the two teens' lives?

4. Randy learns the hard way about the consequences of actions. There are also eternal consequences to our actions and choices. What do you think is the correlation between the consequences of actions and forgiveness, especially God's forgiveness?

5. Why does Curt choose Merry over the beautiful, sophisticated Delia? Read Proverbs 31:30. What does "fears the Lord" mean? How does Merry exemplify this notion?

6. Delia's presence awakes insecurities in Merry. How can we use such insecurities to grow stronger, and to recognize and help those weaknesses in others?

7. In most novels, especially ones with a comic feel like this one, the hero and heroine always escape at the end while the bad guys are caught. Such isn't always the case in real life. Read Habakkuk 3:17–19. What is the "yet" principle?

8. The risks Merry takes in her work cause Curt distress. What does it mean for him to trust she knows what she's doing? In what way has your ability to trust others been taxed? What advice would you give Curt in this situation?

9. Randy is unexpectedly tender with Whiskers. How can pets give comfort to those in need?

10. Out of the pain of an abusive relationship, Stephanie was inspired to create Freedom House. In what way can our difficulties and sorrows give us inspiration to help others? What examples can you cite in your community?

REQUEST YOUR FREE BOOKS!

2 FREE RIVETING INSPIRATIONAL NOVELS
PLUS 2 FREE MYSTERY GIFTS

Love Inspired®
SUSPENSE

YES! Please send me 2 FREE Love Inspired® Suspense novels and my 2 FREE mystery gifts. After receiving them, if I don't wish to receive any more books, I can return the shipping statement marked "cancel." If I don't cancel, I will receive 4 brand-new novels every month and be billed just $3.99 per book in the U.S. or $4.74 per book in Canada, plus 25¢ shipping and handling per book and applicable taxes, if any*. That's a savings of 20% off the cover price! I understand that accepting the 2 free books and gifts places me under no obligation to buy anything. I can always return a shipment and cancel at any time. Even if I never buy another book from Steeple Hill, the two free books and gifts are mine to keep forever.

123 IDN EL5H 323 IDN ELQH

Name	(PLEASE PRINT)

Address	Apt. #

City	State/Prov.	Zip/Postal Code

Signature (if under 18, a parent or guardian must sign)

Order online at www.LoveInspiredSuspense.com

Or mail to Steeple Hill Reader Service™:

IN U.S.A.: P.O. Box 1867, Buffalo, NY 14240-1867
IN CANADA: P.O. Box 609, Fort Erie, Ontario L2A 5X3

Not valid to current Love Inspired Suspense subscribers.

Want to try two free books from another series?
Call 1-800-873-8635 or visit www.morefreebooks.com

* Terms and prices subject to change without notice. NY residents add applicable sales tax. Canadian residents will be charged applicable provincial taxes and GST. This offer is limited to one order per household. All orders subject to approval. Credit or debit balances in a customer's account(s) may be offset by any other outstanding balance owed by or to the customer. Please allow 4 to 6 weeks for delivery.

Your Privacy: Steeple Hill is committed to protecting your privacy. Our Privacy Policy is available online at www.eHarlequin.com or upon request from the Reader Service. From time to time we make our lists of customers available to reputable firms who may have a product or service of interest to you. If you would prefer we not share your name and address, please check here. ☐

LISUS07

Love Inspired®
SUSPENSE

TITLES AVAILABLE NEXT MONTH
Don't miss these four stories in July

NO LOVE LOST by Lynn Bulock
Cozy mystery

She married a murderer? Gracie Lee Harris was sure Hal, her ex-husband, didn't have *that* dark a side. But with her ex as the prime suspect in his fiancée's death and her boyfriend, Ray Fernandez, as the lead investigator, Gracie could only pray that Hal's secrets wouldn't get *her* killed!

DEATH BENEFITS by Hannah Alexander
A HIDEAWAY novel

Attending a wedding in Hawaii seemed the perfect tropical dream to Ginger Carpenter...until an escaped convict began stalking her young foster nieces. To protect them, she would have to rely on Dr. Ray Clyde—the one man she never wanted to see again.

VALLEY OF SHADOWS by Shirlee McCoy
A LAKEVIEW novel

Heartbroken following the death of her nephew, the last thing Miranda Shelton expected was to become involved in a DEA investigation. Yet now she and Agent Hawke Morran were running for their lives, desperate to uncover the truth behind the betrayal that brought them together.

DANGEROUS SECRETS by Lyn Cote
Harbor Intrigue

The town of Winfield's peacefulness was shattered by the bizarre death of Sylvie Patterson's cousin. And as the last person to see him alive, Sylvie was square in the sights of investigator Ridge Matthews. But as another family member died and Ridge got closer to the truth, they must learn to trust in each other—and God—to uncover the deadly secrets lurking in her once quiet town.

LISCNM0607